s *Shanghai Girl*

"*Shanghai Girl* is superb literature ... one of the best of contemporary novels written by Chinese authors ... (Yang is a) Shanghai success ... We eagerly await Yang's next literary feat."

-- *EVE Magazine*

"*Shanghai Girl* – a feat in itself ... Yang puts a new, often lighthearted spin on frequently covered topics like Chinese identity, the U.S. immigrant experience and reverberations of the Cultural Revolution."

"A novel that is hard ... masterfully transports ... make any writer jealous and any reader sit up and take notice.

-- *Blogcritics.org*

"Yang brings with her an expanded array of journeys and experiences, reflective of not only a changing America, but also of a world in transition."

"Compelling story ... Inherently fascinat... language ... A pleasu...

"Another 'Tale of '... Dickens' famous n... Shanghai and New ...

"A new voice from S...

2|12
|5 95

Memoirs of a Eurasian

A Novel

Vivian Yang

ISBN-13: 978-1461013419

ISBN-10: 1461013410

Also available as a Kindle e-book

Designed by Katherine Wong

Vivian Yang

Vivian Yang is the author of the novels *Memoirs of a Eurasian* (2011), *Shanghai Girl* (2011 and 2001), *S.G. Shan Hai Gaaru* (2011 and 2002), and the nonfiction *Status, Society, and Sino-Singaporeans.*

Born and raised in Shanghai's former European quarters -- often the setting of her fiction, Vivian holds an M.A. in intercultural communication from Arizona State University and taught English and journalism at Shanghai International Studies University. She was a Literature Fellow in Prose of the New Jersey State Council on the Arts, a Publishing Project grantee from the Hong Kong Arts Development Council, a Tuition Scholar at the Bread Loaf Writers' Conference, a Woolrich Writing Fund Scholar and a Writing Program Scholar at Columbia University, and a top winner of The *WNYC* Leonard Lopate Essay Contest, the entry of which is a chapter of *Memoirs of a Eurasian.*

Vivian has written for *Business Weekly, China Daily, Far Eastern Economic Review, South China Morning Post,* and *The Wall Street Journal Asia,* and has published fiction in literary journals in the United States and in Asia. Her work has also appeared in the Opinion page of *HK Magazine, The National Law Journal,* and *The New York Times.*

Visit *www.VivianYang.net*, start a discussion on Amazon's Vivian Yang Page (*http://www.amazon.com/Vivian-Yang/e/B001S03LZM/ref=ntt dp epwbk o*), join the *Shanghai Girl* Page on Facebook, and follow Vivian on Twitter @ *ShanghaiGirlUsa.*

ALSO BY VIVIAN YANG

Shanghai Girl *
S. G. Shan Hai Gaaru
Status, Society, and Sino-Singaporeans

*An excerpt of Vivian Yang's novel *Shanghai Girl*
appears after *Memoirs of a Eurasian*

Contents

1 Beautiful Adulterated Chinese   3

2 Down with the Chief Dog   13

3 At the Pushkin Graveyard   19

4 Like Borscht for Discontent   28

5 Don't Know Much Biology   32

6 Love and the Troika Teens   49

7 Dreaming Stanislavsky   59

8 Seeing Red   67

9 Girls at Play   74

10 The Renaissance Shanghainese   82

11 A Revolutionary Étude   96

12 Heart on Top, Friend at the Bottom   114

13 Whether My Race Is Black White Brown Yellow or Red   122

14 Like Sleeping in Heaven   130

15 Until Daybreak It Sheds Its Tears   137

16 From Pravda to Prada   143

17 The Long Long Life Bar and The Pen Ball   155

18 A Query from Tokyo   163

19 Fortune Alley Revisited   174

20 And Quiet Flows the Huanpu   179

Appendix A: A conversation with *Vivian Yang*, author of *Memoirs of a Eurasian* and *Shanghai Girl*   194

Appendix B: A Brief Timeline for *Memoirs of a Eurasian*   197

An Excerpt of *Shanghai Girl* by Vivian Yang   201

Vivian Yang

The novel is the private history of nations.
Honore de Balzac (1799 -- 1850), French novelist

History is the development and discord of human race.
Liang Qichao (1873 -- 1929), Chinese statesman

1 *Beautiful Adulterated Chinese*

"Call me Mo Mo," I tell you, the first Westerner to interview me at Maison Jasmine.

You nod and admire the original mosaic window panels. "You must feel like living in a dream, Mo Mo."

"Chekhov said something to the effect that the perception of reality is a dream itself, and vice versa. In a way all of my life's experiences have led up to this moment."

You stop examining the dragon chopsticks rest and gaze at me. I am used to such a savoring manner. I belong to a rare breed: three quarters Shanghainese, one quarter Russian. Drops of my Chinese blood mix and blend with fewer drops of Russian, albeit in different shades of red. The Red Square's interpretation of Marxism-Leninism was badly tainted in the Chinese Communists' view. My racial amalgamation was deemed degenerate in the first decades of the People's Republic.

At a time when any scrap of jewelry was condemned, I was the latchkey kid known as "the bourgeois lackey on a necklace leash." The concept of a single parent had not yet reached China. Little if anything from the West had managed to infiltrate the ideological Great Wall of my socialist motherland. Whenever I asked about my father, my mother would say, as if spitting, "You don't have one. Just be grateful that you have me."

Mother herself was an orphan. And yes, I had at least her high nose bridge and cheekbones. Little cared about by the one parent, I made up a loving one I didn't have. I always wished that my father were an elite Chinese fluent in English. After all, I was born in British Hong Kong in 1962.

But English was banned when I was growing up in Communist Shanghai. In my versatile mother tongue, there existed a catchy phrase for that language of the U.S. and British imperialists. Revolutionary Shanghai denizens deliberately pronounced the word *En-g-li-sh* to make it sound like *yin-gou-li-chee*: belonging to the gutters. By contrast, I taught myself what was condemned to the sewers out of a desire to someday share my incredulous life with a Westerner like you.

In my mind's eye I can always visualize what I saw as a four-year-old the day I left Hong Kong: a red taxi with a white top, a dark train powered with coal, and a black chauffeured sedan. A passenger in each within two days, I was not to be on either for a long time to come. You see, in 1966, few automobiles could be spotted in Shanghai. Bicycles and buses for the masses, yes; but the few cars were for the exclusive use of the Communist Party cadres.

This day, Mami and I were leaving my birthplace Hong Kong for hers, Shanghai.

Ah Bu, our landlady and my nanny, was hailing a cab while Mami lugged our belongings to the curbside. To see us off, Ah Bu put on her new mandarin jacket that was meant to be worn during the upcoming lunar New Year. After helping the driver load Mami's music score boxes onto the back seat, Ah Bu stuffed a small packet tied with a string into Mami's hand, her jade bangle reflecting sun rays into my eyes.

"For Mo Mo during the train ride," she said and dabbed her tears with the sleeve of her jacket.

I knew it must be a Shanghai-style cucumber and dried shrimp omelet sandwich. It dawned on me that I would not be helping her beat the eggs and wash the cucumbers anymore, nor would I hear and the thump of her bangle hitting the edge of the kitchen table. I hugged her thigh and looked up at her. "Ah Bu ... Ah Bu ...!"

"She really wants to be with you," Mami said. "And I only bought one ticket for myself, as I told you. You can still change your mind. Maybe the church can ..."

I sensed Ah Bu's body trembling. She said, "I'm s-sorry I can't ... Nor can I let Mo Mo stay ..."

Mami came to pull me but I wouldn't budge. "You stay, then, I'm going."

I let go of Ah Bu and followed Mami to the taxi. Tears came rolling down my cheeks.

"Don't cry, my child. Don't ruin that beautiful face your Mami gave you," Ah Bu said.

Mami thrust me onto the back seat without a word and slammed the door shut. "Train station," she ordered.

I turned backwards onto my knees and waved through the window.

"Goodbye to you two. May God bless you!" Ah Bu called out as we pulled away from King's Road where the double-decker trams ran.

We had to ourselves the whole compartment: four berths, two upper and lower each facing one another.

"You're supposed to pay half fare, but I took a chance because nowadays there aren't many people going from Hong Kong to China. Listen, Mo Mo, you'll call me Mother from now on and don't ever talk back when people stare at us or say something about our looks. Just look away and stay quiet."

"But why, Mami?"

"Didn't I say no more Mami? Everybody would know we came from Hong Kong if you do, understand?"

"But, Ma- mm-mother, we *are* from Hong Kong."

"No, we're not! We're from Shanghai. You'd better remember that! And shut up and go to sleep."

Seeing my eyes brimming with tears, she shook her head and said, "Fine, I'll teach you to fold a special origami and you stay quiet for the rest of the time." She took out a stack of plain paper. "Here, use these."

"Oh! These are so much nicer than the newspaper I usually fold origami with."

"Forget about the newspaper, too. You've never seen one. Forget about everything from Hong Kong. You're a Shanghai girl who's spoken Shanghainese all your life anyway."

I nodded dubiously and caressed the soft texture of the paper that must have been from the family she gave piano lessons. At the top of the first sheet, I wrote in my still shapeless Chinese: "Dear Ah Bu, when I grow up I will make you proud. Goodbye from your Mo Mo."

The first stop after entering China was Guangzhou. Two men wearing the kind of gray tunics rarely seen in Hong Kong entered our compartment and settled on the seats facing us. They must be someone important as most other people on board were in mandarin jackets.

I avoided eye contact.

"Female Soviet expert," the one with a blue cap said to the younger man with thick glasses. He took out a pack of Tiananmen Gate cigarettes and placed it on the tiny table separating us.

"So fair and such big chestnut-colored eyes," the bespectacled one said as he fumbled for matches.

From the corner of my eye I saw Mother perched against the window, gazing outside. Our train continued to chug along this barren terrain, passing a landscape of sandy brown, sparse foliage, dusty rooftops, and peasants yoked like mules while dragging loads on their backs and plowing.

Tired of the sight, I tried to picture Shanghai. Mother said it was the most modern city in China. I began to wonder if it had the same double-decker trams like those outside our apartment or the red pillar letterboxes with the dome on top. Then I reminded myself not to think about Hong Kong.

"The little one is more Chinese. She may well grow up to be prettier than the half-breed."

Mother shifted her weight and crossed her legs, still staring at the yellow earth and occasional leafless trees outside.

"Yes, her father must be one lucky fellow," the young man said, lighting the cigarette for the other.

A laugh in unison followed.

I was always regarded as beautiful. Almost every grownup in our North Point tenement had complimented me and Mother on our good looks. I'd never given it a second thought until that moment: we're not pure Chinese, unlike the rest of the people in China. Maybe that was why Mother asked me not to look at them. I couldn't help but to sneak a peek at the men; their skin was beige and their eyes were narrow with no lid-folds and lashes so short they were hardly visible.

Before long, cigarette smoke began to fill our compartment. Mother coughed and moved her sitting position again.

"But Comrade Secretary, haven't all the Soviet experts been sent home following our ideological rift with The Kremlin?"

"In theory yes, but this one seems to have settled down here with a Chinese."

Mother uncrossed her legs and faced them. "Comrades," she said in Mandarin Chinese, "there should be many compartments on this train that aren't fully occupied."

The men exchanged surprised looks. "Do you happen to be an actress with the Shanghai Film Studio, Comrade Beautiful?" asked the younger man with a grin.

Mother did not answer. She just pointed her finger to the door.

We had the whole space to ourselves for the rest of the journey. After Mother opened the window to let out the smoke, she said, "Thank goodness. Now let's eat something from Ah Bu."

Between bites, I asked in a low voice, "Mother, you told me not to look back at people. Is it because we are not pure Chinese and come from Hong Kong?"

She replied in a whisper. "Yes. Even though most people in Hong Kong are pure Chinese, they're under the British rule. But few white people live in mainland China after Liberation, so people will stare at us involuntarily and think we are beautiful and different. Pretend you don't notice."

The monotonous but gentle rocking of the train lulled me into a semi-conscious state. Facts and fancies merged. Ah Bu's delicious omelet sandwich bought me back to the time she and I spent together in the tenement flat on King's Road ...

Mami was rarely in. Ah Bu watched me in the kitchen. "Ai-ya! So many of us Shanghainese refugees fleeing the Communists to settle here in Hong Kong!" The small-framed lady would repeat this while stir-frying with a pair of long bamboo chopsticks, the jade bangle moving up and down on her bird thin wrist. "Sorry I can't cook anything Russian the way she likes."

The smell of the signature Shanghai dish of hairy-peas with pickled vegetables permeated the kitchen air. I became the little apprentice in Ah Bu's domain. My tasks varied from removing pods to washing cucumbers to dicing carrots.

Mami shut herself up in the room to practice on a cardboard piano keyboard she glued to a small desk, our only piece of furniture besides the bed. Ever since I got slapped for smudging a black key that Mami outlined with a sketch pencil, I was forbidden to touch her "piano".

I felt most secure when Mami was out. "A rich Hong Kong family hires your Mami because they can impress their friends by employing a Western-looking teacher. But she's paid less because she doesn't have a Hong Kong diploma," Ah Bu once told me. "They don't particularly like her type but she's cheaper but makes them look good to outsiders. The real British won't have anything to do with her especially since she can't speak English."

The day Ah Bu came down with a cold I stayed in our room. Mami was practicing on the cardboard. With her stool inches away from the bed where I was, I kept as quiet as a little pilgrim in a Buddhist temple. I watched her from the back as her curly, smoky brown hair bounced like loose springs, holding my breath as she moved her torso so vigorously that the legs of the stool squeaked. Even though I never heard an actual melody except for the tapping sound of her fingers, I clapped when she finished and exhaled.

Mami turned to look at me; her large eyes glossy. "Would you like to live with Ah Bu?" she asked.

Unsure of what she meant, I said, "Don't we already live with her?"

She stared blankly at me and shook her head. Then, unprovoked, she yelled, "Don't stand in front of me!"

I burst out crying and ran to the kitchen where a sniffing and sneezing Ah Bu was making some comfort congee. She dried my tears with a face towel and said, "Don't cry like this again or you'll ruin that beautiful face."

A few days later in the afternoon, I was folding origami dolls at the kitchen table from a dated Chinese newspaper. Ah Bu was napping with her head resting against the wall. There was a knock at the door. "Miss Mo Na-di?"

I nudged Ah Bu, who was jerked awake. She rubbed her eyes and wiped her hands on her apron. "I'll get the door," she said.

A Royal Mail uniformed man was holding a telegram. I stood on tiptoes to appear taller. "Mami's not home. You can give it to me."

"You're pretty and clever but still too young."

"But I'll be four after the Chinese New Year."

"Tell your mummy to pick it up tomorrow at the post office," the postman said.

Ah Bu asked who it was from.

"The Affiliated Middle School of the Shanghai Conservatory of Music."

This was the first time I heard the name of my mother's employer.

As soon as Mami returned from the post office the next day she pushed me in the direction of our room.

"You go inside and close the door, Mami has to talk to Ah Bu." She was so serious that I didn't dare to linger. I placed my ear on the door but their voices were too low to be made out.

When Mami came in, she placed me on the edge of the bed, squatted down before me, and gazed into my eyes as though she had never seen me before.

"What is it, Ma-mi?" I attempted.

Rising, she scooped me up and said, "I'm taking you to Shanghai where we will have a better life. Are you happy about it?"

I pressed my lips together and asked, "Is Ah Bu coming with us?"

"She has to stay to help in the church ... sorry, forget about that word I just said. She can't come." Mami abruptly turned towards the desk, her slender but strong fingers starting to tear off the cardboard keyboard, bending the strip into two, then four, and then eight. Like a *kung fu* master breaking a stack of bricks into half with a bare hand, Mami chopped her makeshift piano repeatedly.

When she was done, the edge of her palm was crimson. I saw a glitter of tears in her eyes. She thrust the cardboard to me and said, "Go give this to Ah Bu. That wobbly dining table of hers could use a prop."

"Thank your Mami for me, my little treasure," Ah Bu said, blotting an eye with her sleeve.

"Why can't you come with us? Don't you miss Shanghai like Mami does?"

She held my hands and said, "I cannot return because I'm a Christian. The church's been banned in China. Hopefully one day I'll be like a fallen leaf that returns to its roots."

Ah Bu hugged me and choked back a sob. "Your Mami is smart and capable and Shanghai is her home after all. I really cannot do

9

what she's asked or I would. I'm in God's hands ... you're so clever and beautiful, you'll be fine in the end." She raised the lower hem of her apron to cover her face and nudged me towards our room.

Mami was putting her musical scores in piles. She didn't raise her eyes.

"Ah Bu said thank you but she's very sad. What did you ask her to do?"

She sat me down on the edge of the bed and said, "You're too young to understand my circumstances. Just do as I say and no more questions."

When I opened my eyes, a chunk of the sandwich was solid in my fist. Our train was pulling into Shanghai Station. Firecrackers celebrating the Year of the Horse were going off nearby as we exited. I had expected to see something similar to Hong Kong's Central District but was overwhelmed by the ocean of people dressed in blue or gray clothes.

Mother sat me down on one of her boxes and craned her neck as other passengers dispersed. I noticed her eyes misting up and thought she must be moved to see her native city. Then I saw what she saw: parked across the street, amidst an ocean of pedestrians, was a singular black sedan.

Mother waved.

A middle-aged man in a navy tunic and matching cap rolled down the backseat window and nodded in our direction. His youngish, wizened chauffeur got out and ran towards us. His clothes were in faded blue and had patches all over. Flashing his crooked teeth with a smile, he called out, "Welcome back, Teacher Mo! Oh, what beautiful little girl you have! Come. Let me get your luggage. Bureau Chief Chen has been waiting."

"Thank you, Old Wang."

As Mother and I approached the car, the back door was flung open. The man came forth, lifted me up at the waist and exclaimed, "Ah! This must be our beautiful little Mo Mo!"

Mother cast a fleeting look at the beaming man and said, "Call your Uncle Chief."

"Un-uncle Ch-chief ..." I muttered.

"Yes, my beautiful clever Mo Mo!" He held me against him, inadvertently squashing the pack of cigarettes in his chest pocket. It was the same Tiananmen Gate brand that the men on the train smoked.

As Old Wang loaded Mother's things in the trunk and the front seat, we sat down in the back. Uncle Chief put me on his lap and reached over to hold Mother's hand.

"Comrade Mo, on behalf of the Municipal Cultural Bureau, welcome! You made the right choice to return."

Mother withdrew her hand and stared at Old Wang's back. Raising her voice, she replied, "Thank you, Bureau Chief Chen. I'll work hard and serve the people well to deserve the Party's trust and to repay your generosity."

After some time we arrived in a neighborhood with many trees. Old Wang carried our belongings up to a European-style house. We remained in the car.

"So when can she start boarding school as you promised?" Mother asked flatly.

Uncle Chief moved me in between them and sighed. "Look, it's not as easy as you think –she's too young for the music program. Anyway, aren't you happy that I managed to get you this flat?"

She didn't reply but continued to ask, "What about as a child actor at the Studio?"

He shook his head. "Things have changed -- yes the Bureau still heads the Conservatory and the Studio, they're sending someone to run the Studio as we speak. Why don't you settle down first. Try out the 'turtle's head' I went into great lengths to get you."

"Oh, you managed to get one?"

"What's a 'turtle's head'?" I asked.

He burst out laughing.

"Not funny," Mother said sternly. "It's a gas-cooker that resembles a turtle Mo Mo will use to cook meals for us from now on if Uncle Chief doesn't enroll you in boarding school."

"Enough, Comrade Mo! This is not Hong Kong."

Scared seeing Mother biting her lip white, I said, "I don't mind cooking, Ma-um-Mother. I'll learn to cook Russian food for you, too."

Uncle Chief gave Mother a harsh look. Neither spoke.

A moment later, Mother looked at the rear view mirror with a sulking face. "Old Wang is back."

Uncle Chief smiled at me and said, "So little Mo Mo, this is goodbye for now. Listen to your mother and be a good girl!"

With an exaggerated nod, Old Wang opened the car door for Mother and me. He then turned to look again at the house we were about to enter, his eyes full of envy.

Seeing this, I could not wait to check it out myself.

2 Down with the Chief Dog

Our second floor two-room flat had white casement windows, wooden venetian blinds, and whitewashed indoor fluted columns. Mother moved all her "important things" to the bedroom and told me never to enter it. She stationed me in the outside room where a twin bed separated me from the area where the "turtle's head" was. A flush toilet sat in a small space near the entrance.

"Before they partitioned the house into faculty living quarters, this used to be the powder room," Mother explained.

"To store baby powder?" I asked, recalling the after-shower astringent Ah Bu applied on me in humid Hong Kong. "We want to protect your silky fair skin, don't we?" she used to say.

Mother seemed to realize something. "No. I don't think baby powder is sold here anymore. Anyway, a powder room is a bathroom without a bathtub."

"I like it here because I have my own bed. This is so much better than in Hong Kong," I said, bouncing on the springy mattress.

"I forbid you to mention that place again, you understand? Now, you're right this is a wonderful place. You are lucky because I work for the Conservatory and the faculty housing is right here in the former French Concession."

"French Concession?"

"People sometimes still call the European neighborhoods by their old names like the British or the French Concession although few Westerners can be found in Shanghai since Liberation."

"Except for us now."

"Correct. And you know, a thing is valued in proportion to its rarity, so I want to get the most out of this asset."

"What asset?"

"Never mind. For you, just remember to ignore the stares from others."

On the first Monday morning after our arrival, Mother went to work. She balanced me on the bare middle bar of her bicycle before mounting it herself.

"Don't talk or you'll distract me," she ordered.

Later, at the side door of an imposing European-style building, I was handed over to Old Wang. "Uncle Wang will have a playmate for you. I'm going to the office."

Old Wang led me up some marble stairs and hallway to a broom closet. Inside was a chubby girl with dirt-caked cheeks. She gawked at me first then announced, "Hello, foreign princess!"

"How do you do? My name is Mo Mo -- the Chinese characters for *jasmine* and the fragrant white flowers with evergreens."

Her mouth was opened when I described the written words of my name but she quickly followed suit. "And my name is Wang Hong, *Hong* as in revolutionary *red*. Now we can play."

"Good. I am returning to work."

"Bye-bye, Uncle Wang, and thank you."

"Why did you say 'thank you'?"

"Why? Because I should be polite to people."

"You really are smart and fancy! No wonder my dad said your mom is the most beautiful person in the whole school."

"Thank you," I said, relieved that she didn't seem to know that we'd just come from Hong Kong.

"You're nice. Nobody's ever thanked me before. Can I be your friend?" she asked, moving her hand tentatively in my direction. Ah Bu would be appalled by her nails as they had dirt caught in them.

I hesitated, asking, "What should we play?"

"Hopscotch," she said, withdrawing her hand. "If I win, you'll let me hold your hand?"

"What if you lose?"

"I won't. I play alone in the marble corridor here everyday."

"Just in case."

She considered for a moment. "I'll take you to the Piano Building and find an empty practice room to roll on the carpet."

"The Piano Building? And it's carpeted?"

"Of course. You don't know? Well, I can show you everything. Deal!" She grabbed my hand, catching me off-guard.

"But you're not playing fair," I said, shaking her hand nonetheless.

"You agree to be my friend?"

"Sure, as long as you don't call me a 'foreign princess'. I'm just Mo Mo."

"Hello, Mo Mo!"

Since then, Wang Hong and I met at the broom closet every morning. I taught her to fold origami animals and little people. She told me about the nooks and crannies of the campus. Old Wang would fetch us at noon and drop us off at the faculty canteen. Mother had offered to pay for Wang Hong's lunch.

"Mo Mo, you are my best friend. I'd never dreamed of dining here before. My mom used to pack us steamed bread sandwiches with pickled mustard plant for lunch: two for dad and one each for me and herself. I now make her mouth water when I tell her what I eat here."

"I'm glad you enjoy the food here," I said, thinking instead of the dishes Ah Bu used to make and how I could cook tastier food than what the canteen offered.

Since early summer of 1966, the PA system had been broadcasting news about a nationwide political campaign known as the Great Proletarian Cultural Revolution, launched by Chairman Mao. As a kid, I had no idea that the disarray on campus harbingered a decade-long social upheaval and economic chaos. All Wang Hong and I knew was that the students had stopped making the pleasantly repetitive deedle deedle dee sounds of music practice. Instead, they were "making revolution" by "defeating the counter-revolutionary academic authorities."

Then one mid-morning, Old Wang whisked us out of the broom closet to the school lawn. "Did you not hear the PA broadcast? Everybody on campus must gather immediately for the denunciation rally."

When we arrived, the lawn area was all but taken over by a fist-waving crowd. To allow me to see, Old Wang mounted me on top of a cardboard box by a tree. I tiptoed and craned my neck: in the center of the stage was someone whose dunce hat identified him as "Counter Revolutionary Cultural Bureau Chief Dog Chen", his mouth gagged and arms pinioned by two male students with Red Guards armbands. The words on the placard hanging from his neck read: "Down with the Capitalist-Roader within the Communist Party!"

My heart lurched into my throat.

Just then, Old Wang lifted Wang Hong up next to me. She squealed, "It's Bureau Chief Chen!"

The box under our feet gave and we fell into each other, sending off a scream.

Numerous heads turned in our direction, with some asking, "What happened?"

As we helped ourselves up, I saw Old Wang staring at someone in the front of the crowd, his mouth half open. The next thing I knew, I heard Mother's cracking voice barking from the microphone on the stage:

"Comrades-in-arms, don't look towards the back! Look at me here! I am a direct victim of the Chief Dog and I'll expose his imperialist-worshipping true colors right now! Chief Dog Chen personally forced me to perform in the British imperialist Hong Kong because he said it was the best way to continue our school's European tradition since it was modeled after the Leipzig Conservatory of Music. But I couldn't stand the British capitalist decadence there and returned to our great socialist motherland to make revolution. Comrades-in-arms, Chief Dog Chen is an out-and-out counter revolutionary capitalist-roader! Down with Chief Dog Chen!"

The crowd shouted: "Down with Chief Dog Chen!"

Wang Hong had let the clasped box lean against the tree and begun to climb on it. Old Wang held me up onto his shoulders just in time for me to see Mother charging at Uncle Chief. Her body shaking, Mother slapped across his face and kicked him in the groin. Uncle Chief collapsed on his knees, face down. The Red Guards dragged him off the stage as the audience roared:

"Down with the Capitalist-Roader within the Party!"
"Death to the Counter Revolutionary Chief Dog Chen!"

Confused and frightened, I said, "I want to get down!" Old Wang put me down and scooped up Wang Hong. "This is not something little girls should see. We'd better get you to the canteen before everybody shows up."

Wang Hong clapped her hands and said, "Good idea. Let's go!"

But when we got there, we found it closed. As we returned to the Administration Building, now as quiet as a morgue, we could still hear the shouting of slogans from the other end of the campus.

Back in the broom closet, Old Wang said, "Teacher Mo is not only beautiful but also brave and revolutionary. She always knew the right thing to do."

"What's going to happen to …?" I attempted.

"My boss? Well, nobody knows at this point. One thing is clear. You girls won't be able to play here anymore."

"And no more faculty canteen lunches?" asked Wang Hong.

"No. Everything is going to change – big, or they wouldn't call this the Great Cultural Revolution."

Wang Hong let out a sigh. "I'm hungry." Since starting lunch in the canteen, she was not given breakfast. Old Wang decided to take her home.

After they left, I waited for Mother while reliving the scene of her slapping and kicking Uncle Chief. Chills ran through me. The snug feeling of me sitting on the lap of the suddenly disgraced man returned. The odor of his Tiananmen Gate cigarettes, still very much drifting in the air of the building's hallways, hit my senses. I wondered about my future now that I couldn't play with Wang Hong anymore.

Then I dozed off.

Mother came to fetch me some time later, her cheeks flushed with excitement as she pointed at the Red Guard armband she was wearing. I wolfed down the streamed bread she brought and asked, "The Red Guards let you join them?"

"Yes! I'm one of the first faculty members to be admitted and the only one today! I've given up the bourgeois piano and taken up the revolutionary accordion for the Red Guard Revolutionary Propaganda Team."

She then exhaled deeply and took both of my hands in hers. "We'll be fine now, Mo Mo – thanks to my smarts and quick-headedness!"

"You mean ... Uncle Chief?"

She glared at me. "You saw? Were you also there earlier?" I nodded.

"Now Mo Mo, listen to me, don't ever call the capitalist-roader that anymore. Remember, you've never met him before and you only saw him being denounced at the mass rally today."

"But I did meet him."

A slap landed across my cheek, stunning me.

"Why on earth did I have such a stupid child?" she yelled. "Didn't I just say you'd never heard of him? Do you want to associate your young self with the most vicious bourgeois running dog in Shanghai?"

So that was the end of him for me.

It was not until Wang Hong and I started primary school together several years later that she would tell me boastfully, "He hanged himself with the very piece of rope the Red Guards tied him up with, and I know that exact place where he died."

It was a corner room in the Piano Building that the radical students had turned into a makeshift cell. But Wang Hong and I had never rolled on the carpet there.

I would nod absent-mindedly, remembering the slap Mother inflicted on me that same day she had condemned him.

He died.

I survived.

3 At the Pushkin Graveyard

I became what I am today at age ten, when domestic and international events first made me aware of my own peculiar position in this world. I also saw a masked man with engaging eyes sweeping the streets. Our communication was nonverbal, but everything seemed to have begun for me from that encounter.

Kids my age would have been in school already had it not because China's political circumstances then at home and abroad. The Sino-Soviet border conflict and the death of Chairman Mao's protégé and designated successor Lin Biao meant that the beginning of our schooling was postponed. I taught myself to read *The Liberation Daily* and to write as many Chinese characters as possible. *The Liberation Daily* was the only official paper in Shanghai and every business entity had to subscribe to it even though it was not always read. I got my copies for free at the nearby wet market where I shopped daily for groceries. A stack of them was always there to be used to wrap food in.

Nineteen seventy-two itself was an eventful year.

Three weeks into it, in the Micronesian U.S. Territory of Guam, Japanese soldier Shoichi Yokoi was discovered in the jungle where he had been hiding for twenty-eight years, pledging daily allegiance to Emperor Hirohito in the hope that the Empire of the Sun would win its Holy War and dominate the entire "Greater East Asia Co-Prosperity Sphere".

I heard this news from the transistor radio in the shop that sold bean paste and other condiments. The owner, whose salt and pepper hair never seemed to have been washed, would always flash a grin at me with his crooked brown teeth. "Pretty girl's shopping for her pretty mother again – she's certainly one *baijiu* drinker, that Russian lady," he would say with a chuckle. *Baijiu* was a fiery sorghum liquor.

The owner's only treasure was his son, also ten, like me. Whenever I shopped there, he would be gaping at me from a dim corner, the expression in his eyes alternating between fascination and resentment.

To conserve the battery, the owner's transistor was on at noon for ten minutes only. Neighborhood men would gather to hear the news. That day, after the radio was switched off, one man said, "The Japanese can be really obsessive."

"That's why they're known as the 'Eastern foreigners' and not 'Western foreigners' like some people," chimed in another, giving me a glance.

"The Western foreigners are good-looking and smart -- right, pretty girl?" the owner said.

I blushed and looked away, my eyes meeting those of the boy. He flashed me a grin. I snatched the refilled soy sauce bottle I had already paid for and ran out.

The Japanese are known as the Eastern foreigners as opposed to Western foreigners like ... me, I noted to myself. People automatically put me in a separate category.

A few weeks later, I was introduced through the front page of the paper to a real Western foreigner. On February 21st, U.S. President and career Communist-prosecutor Richard Nixon landed in China to shake hands with careerist Communist leader Chairman Mao and to be seen photographed atop the Great Wall. This was no Nixon-Khrushchev Kitchen Debate on the merits of capitalism versus communism reenacted, I half-comprehendingly read from *The Liberation Daily*. Holding its breath, the West watched as "Tricky Dick" Nixon posed toothily with a drooling Great Proletariat Leader, Great Teacher, Great Commander-in-Chief, and Great Helmsman. The panda-faced, German-accented mastermind Henry Kissinger and the Europe-trained Chinese Machiavellian Zhou Enlai, whom the West deemed charismatic despite his rusty English, "agreed to disagree" about the sovereignty of the island of Taiwan. A Sino-U.S. Communiqué was executed by the Secretary of State and the Premier. The setting for such an epoch-making event was, by no accident, Shanghai, the former "whore of Asia", the then boar of socialist Utopia. Make no mistake. Shanghai was credited for being the glorious birthplace of the Great Proletarian Cultural Revolution just six years earlier. But it was still the most international city within China and retained much of the pre-Liberation European hardware.

In May, in the vast Eurasian landmass collectively known as the Union of the Soviet Socialist Republics where part of my heritage could be traced, Secretary-General Leonid Brezhnev was determined not to be out staged by his Chinese archrival and signed with Nixon the Strategic Arms Limitation Treaty, SALT for short.

"You learned about SALT from the radio or the wrapping paper?" you, my interviewer, interjected.

Actually, neither.

I had not yet come across any English word, nor would a Chinese broadcaster use an English acronym. The only salt I knew then was for cooking, an activity I was destined to be associated with.

While SALT brought about an easing of relations between Washington and Moscow -- the paper said, I was aware that the Sino-Soviet relationships remained icy cold.

No salt to thaw.

In the fall of 1972, I finally started school. Wang Hong and the condiments store boy were in my class. They both were Little Red Guards, the name for the Communist Young Pioneer since the Cultural Revolution. Deemed unfit for the fêted ranks of the juvenile defenders of Chairman Mao, there was no school-issued red scarf for me. In my heart I prayed that my fellow pupils would not know the reason for my exclusion: I, the bourgeois adulterated versus them, the proletariat purebred.

I knew from the men at the condiments store that our school was formerly The St. Emanuel Grammar School founded by the Jesuits in the French Concession and admitted children of both middleclass locals and Western expatriates. After Liberation, it was renamed The Shanghai Young Revolutionary School.

China was run like the military, with Mao as our "Great Commander-in-Chief". Kids gathered in designated spots and marched through a rabbit warren of neighborhood alleys in "Mao Zedong Thought Revolutionary Propaganda Processions" to reach school. From Monday through Saturday, six Little Red Guards took turns carrying a Mao portrait at the front of the line. That kid was the day's procession-leader, followed by the one immediately behind who led inspirational slogan-shouting:

"Carry the cause started by our revolutionary martyrs to the end!"

"Down with the U.S. imperialists and the Soviet revisionists!"

"Heighten our vigilance and defend our motherland against the two superpower hegemonists!"

"Curb the Soviet revisionists' ambitions to invade our motherland!"

The last slogan originated in 1969, when China and the Soviet Union fought over the island known to them as Damansky but to us as Zhenbaodou (Treasure Island), the newscasters had emphasized. Naturally, we kids had never heard of Robert Louis Stevenson's namesake adventure story about some boy mingling with pirates. The young of Shanghai were never told fables such as Peter Pan and Neverland. Instead we were indoctrinated with tales like "The Foolish Old Man Who Removed the Mountains" in our first days of school. The old man, foolish only in the eyes of the unenlightened, removed three mountains blocking his front door by digging daily with a spade.

As hard as it might be for you to picture Chairman Mao playing Dr. Seuss, our Great Teacher himself authored that story. This shouldn't come as a complete surprise given that Mao was a librarian at Peking University where he devoured the writings by Hegel and Marx with the same enthusiasm he consumed the spicy cuisine of his native Hunan. Always filled with a fiery revolutionary pungency, Mao's works were required to be read, recited, and even memorized by all Chinese. Mao taught us that we could overthrow the figurative three mountains of the imperialist, feudalist, and bureaucratic-capitalist oppressors by fighting persistently. I took it to mean that as long as I was persistent enough, I could survive in a hostile environment, overcome the difficulties, and triumph personally in the end.

In any case, the anti-Soviet slogan got passed down to us. And believe me, you wouldn't want to be associated with the Soviets, or by analogy, the Russians. Our procession passed the site where a bronze bust statue of Alexander Pushkin once stood. In 1937, the White Russian émigrés built the memorial on the centenary of Pushkin's death. The engraved text read: *AU POETE RUSSE ALEXANDRE PUSHKIN (1799 – 1837)*, fittingly in French, the lingua franca of the then French Concession administration.

The monument was smashed in 1966, an incident Wang Hong told me she had eye-witnessed. The Red Guards regarded anything with a Caucasian face and European lettering as unsuitable for the cityscape of the heroic city of Shanghai, the birthplace of both the Chinese Communist Party and the Cultural Revolution. They prided themselves in daring to "go up mountains of knives and down into oceans of flames" in defense of the proletariat cause.

Guilty by association, the once manicured garden for the statue ceased to be maintained by the city's sanitation workforce and became an open-air garbage dump reeking of ammoniac odors of human urine, stray cat excrement and other offensive olfactory stimulants. As we passed the "Pushkin graveyard", my fellow pupils would cover their noses and stare at me in disgust as if I had personally defecated my twenty-five percent Russian feces on this otherwise holy soil. There was no doubt that my mixed-race status was now an open secret.

Not everyone was involved in such folly. Wang Hong remained my friend even though her belonging to the celebrated class could have made her a Little Red Guard leader had she tried. But she told me that she was not interested in carrying a Mao portrait three quarters her size, nor in being tied down to a title with little tangible benefits. Paraphrasing a popular metaphor, she announced with a pouting mouth that "I'd rather be a petit bourgeois weed than a proletariat seed."

When our Little Red Guard brigade leader offered to promote her to the front of the line, Wang Hong replied, "I am perfectly fine staying where I am. And by the way, when will you give me that aluminum marching whistle of yours to play? Tell them you lost it and they'll issue you a new one."

Unlike me, who was uncertain of my personal identity, Wang Hong, at age ten, had already mastered the essence of Shanghai pragmatism.

A bright spot in my life during this difficult time was the blue-capped and gauze-masked street sweeper with his empathetic eyes. The awkward way his hands applied the broom, the still visible creases on his khakis despite not having been ironed recently, and his high quality if unpolished shoes suggested that he must be a "bourgeois element" condemned to this job. Although keenly aware of this tall man's presence just several feet away, I only occasionally exchanged glances with him for fear of bringing on additional punishment to either of us. His intelligent eyes, however, always stayed with me.

I was grateful to the man and to Wang Hong because let's face it, anyone possessing even a sliver of Caucasian flesh might just as well have been a leper. Relegated to the very end of the procession, I dragged my feet along without confronting anybody's stares and sneers, without covering my own nose, yet simultaneously trying not to inhale. Mechanically, one foot after the other, I went through the motions, lost in daydreams.

I wondered about Pushkin's looks. Did he resemble my grandfather? Would I in any way look like Pushkin? It was simply not in my consciousness that three-dimensional beings with fair skin were capable of walking and talking, in English at that, a language I had never even heard spoken.

White people like you, my Western friend, were conceptual and not perceptual to me then.

Ironically, the only ones whose likeliness I'd seen were perpetually saluted and kowtowed to. Papier-mâché effigies these were not. They were in fact two-dimensional figures mounted on thick cardboards in the center of our school's assembly hall, a collective four known as our "Great Proletarian Revolutionary Teachers": Karl **Ma**rx, Fredrick **En**gels, Vladimir **Le**nin, and Josef **S**talin.

To facilitate our becoming their disciples, we were to pronounce their names by using the first syllables of their respective Chinese translation, or *Ma, En, Lie,* and *Si.* Their huge faces were on display in gilded wooden frames in the most eye-catching places, their virtual presence dominating our consciousness.

The cardboard *Ma* had a large beard which would have made him the perfect candidate for Santa Claus had he been a Christian and not an atheist. A bright red outfit would have matched his ideology perfectly as well. I, for one, would have chosen him out of all four dead white men to be my Santa Claus had I known the concept of Christmas presents for good children, not having received a single present in my life.

The cardboard *En* came across as a scholar or a deep thinker of sorts, the type that would be condemned as a "counterrevolutionary academic authority" had he been on the Conservatory faculty – another fanciful private thought of mine I was dying to share with Wang Hong but didn't dare to.

The cardboard *Lie*'s bald head appeared to be a shiny light bulb perhaps because of what our Chinese language teacher taught us that the revolutionary leaders were "like beacons lighting up our revolutionary paths". She also said that "Marxism, Leninism, and Mao Zedong Thought were truths universally acknowledged and applicable," adding that "a truth universally acknowledged" part was from an authoress of her favorite translated novel but she was forbidden to name which. Not until years later did I realize that she was referring to the opening aphorism of *Pride and Prejudice* that "It is a truth universally acknowledged that a single man in possession of a good fortune must be in want of a wife." You see, works from Jane Austin to Émile Zola alike were banned when we started school. *Lady Chatterley's Lover* and *Mother Goose Rhymes* were considered equally degenerate.

The cardboard *Si* was an army-uniformed man with handlebar moustache and gleaming starred epaulets, a marshal whose 2.5 million soldiers miraculously conquered Berlin in 1945 despite being mostly famished and inebriated. I read about it an old issue of the "Shanghai Film Studio Pictorial" Wang Hong had dug out from under a stack of scores inside a piano bench compartment. Like most other magazines after the Cultural Revolution, this one was discontinued and the Conservatoire's library had been sealed, but Wang Hong still spent time on campus. *The Russians beat up the Germans!* The captions of a photograph attached to the article so read. The same photograph of Stalin as the school's *Si* cardboard was in that magazine. Never had I seen as many honorary decorations on one individual's chest as there were on *Si*'s. Sometimes I thought that his sparkling sets of orders could have tilted a magnetic scale in his favor over a Mao tunic-clad, stick-thin Chinese man on a bicycle.

Marx and Engels were German and Lenin and Stalin were Russian. Fifty-fifty. Strange, I thought that *The Russians beat up the Germans!* So I lucked out, having in me some Russian rather than German blood. My weirdest sense of ambiguity manifested itself when I realized that despite possessing the blood of the victors of the Second World War, I was treated with contempt when we traversed the site of the now smashed Pushkin statue, the burial ground of my supposed countryman.

That morning, while immersed in such musings, I failed to join in shouting "*Curb the Soviet revisionists' ambitions to invade our motherland!*" This did not go unnoticed by the condiments boy who constantly cast fleeting looks at me and Wang Hong from the front of the line.

"How dare you not shout that revolutionary slogan?" he demanded. "Repeat after me: 'I am a Soviet revisionist mutt with hair like the color of straws!'"

I said nothing.

All the others chanted in unison, "Soviet mutt! Soviet mutt! Down with the Soviet revisionist mutt!"

Quick wits came in an emergency. "I'm sorry I didn't repeat the revolutionary slogan, but I'm not a Soviet revisionist. My Russian grandfather was a follower of the proletariat cause pioneered by our Great Teachers *Lie* and *Si*! And their hair color was not completely black, either."

Stumped, the condiments boy looked at Wang Hong as if for help. Wang Hong stuck out her tongue at him in return. The group began to laugh.

A rush of pride propelled me to search for the street sweeper. I was greeted with scorching eyes and a subtle but unmistakable nod.

"What are you looking at, you stinky bourgeois bad element?" Having lost face and fuming with rage, the boy suddenly screamed in the man's direction. "I'll have your bourgeois eyes poked out!"

The man resumed sweeping in a clumsy fashion, never to look up from the ground again.

The procession went on. It was a few more minutes before the leader started the next slogan. From then on, student leaders would avoid shouting the slogan regarding the Soviets.

Initially surprised by the courage I exhibited in front of my peers and its unexpected consequence, I grew to enjoy the surge of my self-confidence. I now no longer drag my feet, but put one foot in front of another with purpose and pride. I wished that the street sweeper could see me marching like this. I wanted him to know that he was responsible for changing me and I owed him all my gratitude.

But the street sweeper was since replaced by a middle aged woman wearing a wide-brimmed straw hat, blue uniform and mask, and black cloth shoes. Each time I saw her agile movements I was reminded of the affirming nod her predecessor had given me. The thought of him also left the sensation of a dagger churning in my underbelly. After all, he was the only adult besides Ah Bu who seemed to truly care about me.

"Do you think Condiments could have turned him in?" I couldn't help but ask Wang Hong a week later.

"I'm not sure about that. Condiments did this because he wanted your attention."

"Or perhaps he wanted yours."

"Perhaps, so stop worrying about a bourgeois element like him anymore. He's probably well taken care of at home in ways unimaginable to us -- to me at least."

Suddenly I had the strange thought that *a bourgeois element like him* would empathize with me as a Chinese with imagined European sentiments, that the man with the encouraging eyes could understand the private thoughts I had and appreciate the Russian meals I cooked.

I prayed that he was not suffering somewhere as a result of his encouragement to me, that I would one day meet him, and that he would love me the way Ah Bu in Hong Kong had loved and nurtured me.

4 Like Borscht for Discontent

"So a butter stick really tastes like soap?" Wang Hong asked.

Condiments had told her about my Sunday morning shopping trip to The Shanghai Food Provisions Store on Huaihai Road, formerly Avenue Joffre in the French Concession. His father dealt with the Store's supplies department. They knew that Mother and I were issued special food coupons thanks to our "overseas Chinese returnees" status.

"Sorry I can't answer that. I've never tasted soap."

She pretended to hit me. "You can be so cruel, you know. You're just a wet-market shopper most days, so don't be like this to me."

Wang Hong was right. I was responsible for buying perishables and cooking during weekdays. A refrigerator was a luxury few had. Neighborhood open-air grocery stalls compensated for that. Meats were dear and sources of proteins scarce. Rationing was in place so all had bits to share. Vegetables were abundant and easy to prepare. Mother warned me about the manure so I cleaned them with care.

The Sunday Russian dinner was an affirmation of our heritage discretely carried out. We painstakingly acquired the ingredients for its set menu. Cucumber salad for appetizer, *khleb* for bread, *borscht* for soup, and the fiery sorghum liquor *baijiu* for Mother's faux vodka.

To prepare the salad I used red bell pepper, green gourd, rice vinegar, and the prized brown "Cuban sugar." The rations allowed 50 grams per month for an ordinary Shanghainese. Our special status qualified us for double that amount. The Bay of Pigs-triggered U.S. trade embargo was well into its second decade, but China would pay no heed to the U.S. Paper Tiger's decree, our Politics teacher told us. We did business with Castro's Communist regime and shared with it the same sense of international justice. "*Guba bi sheng, meidi bi bai!* -- Cuba will win undeniably and the U.S. imperialists will lose for sure!" and "Cuba *Sí*! Yankee No!" We used to chant this in school.

I also bought at the store *khleb*, crisply baked on the premises the way the long-departed First Russian Bakery would have made it, genuine from the dough mix to the crumbs.

"Ten percent off for our prettiest regular!" the chef-capped master baker called out to the centralized cashiers, triggering envious looks at me that I would rather have avoided.

With our special dairy coupons I got half a pint of fresh cream and a stick of butter. At home, I poured the cream into an empty tin, tied up three pairs of chopsticks and beat it in one circular direction until a thick pile of white substance was formed. It was to be put on the *borscht*.

Water was being boiled in one of our two aluminum pots, both with a crooked lid. I had dropped them on the floor. When the second one became dented, Mother could not contain her anger. "Why did you have to smash them like this one after another? I can't exactly afford a new cooking pot, can I?"

I had bowed my head each time to apologize, thinking in self-defense that I was practically an Ah Bu to her here in Shanghai: cooking, shopping, and cleaning in addition to school. Besides, despite being only twelve years old, I qualified as a full "overseas returnee", effectively doubling our special coupons allocation.

But Mother emphasized that she played fair even though she always had two servings of *borscht* and *khleb* versus my one. She always said, "To raise you I gave up my own professional dream. I derive little enjoyment from dealing with talentless students who are here because of their parents' standing and connections."

Every Sunday we opened one can of tomato puree. The socialist planned economy meant that supplies rarely met demand. The cans were export rejects shipped to the store in bulk and Mother stockpiled them. Often they were not seen again for months on end. I used butter sticks for oil to stir-fry tomato puree with diced pork -- never beef as it was rationed to the Chinese Muslims only. "At least butter is made of cow's milk so there is a connection to beef," Mother once said.

I cut a head of cabbage, diced two potatoes, and sliced an onion. The last task often reduced me to tears. Seeing this, Mother would occasionally laugh. In rare moments like these, she appeared content and I felt less unwanted.

Everything would go into the water. We let it simmer. How fortunate we were to own a gas-powered "turtle's head"! A bright orange rubber tube connected to the meter was all it took, although it had to go through Mother's bedroom to reach the outside room cooking area next to my bed. Most people used coal briquettes for cooking.

Turtle's head was the affectionate nickname Shanghainese gave to this type of single-range due to its round body and neck-shaped stem. The phallic symbolism was utterly lost on me when I had first heard it mentioned by the now deceased "Chief Dog Chen". Despite the visual resemblance of the turtle's head in relation to its shell – now tucked in and now sticking out –actual male genitalia were nowhere for me to see at that time. Mother had refused to disclose my father's identity and there were no men under our roof.

No Little League. No trick or treat. No cooking show on TV. No TV, period. But the routine fortified my interest in cuisine.

In the winter of 1974, we had an accident while cooking. What started out as a casual remark on Mother's part had an indelible impact on my psyche.

"Beetroots are rarely on sale and sour cream is simply nonexistent," Mother said with a sigh when we were cooking that day. "But the *sup*-making efforts must go on! After all, our *borscht* is really good enough for *Luosong biesan*."

"You mean you and me – Russian beggars?"

"Well yes, hierarchy-minded old Shanghainese used to call stateless refugees loitering in the French Concession that name. The true masters of this city were Western expatriates known as the Shanghailanders, the Yanks, the Brits, the French and the Germans, you see."

"How insulting! I'll never submit to this kind of thing."

"We have no choice. You learn to be flexible to get ahead."

"But I got ahead by fighting back tactfully. A schoolmate of mine called me a Soviet revisionist and I said I'm a revolutionary descendant of Lenin and Stalin. Now everybody has stopped taunting me with that." I related my confrontation with Condiments but didn't mention the street sweeper.

Mother grabbed a glass, filled the *baijiu* to its rim, and took a gulp. "So you demonstrated your smart-ass racial pride in front of them all? Did it ever occur to you that he could be a cadre's son and his reporting on you could jeopardize my career?"

"But he isn't. He provoked me because he wanted attention."

"So you were right in endangering me further as if walking around with that face isn't enough!"

"But I got that face from you!"

Enraged, Mother charged in my direction. Her drink spilled onto the lit stove. The tongues of flame spread along the greasy rubber tube into the bedroom. She dropped her glass on the floor and dashed into her room. I followed her in.

Mother threw her burning bed sheets in my direction and set my clothes on fire. Still, she pulled a cardboard box from under her bed and smothered the flame with her body. Only then did she call out at me, "Roll over! Roll over quick, Mo Mo!"

I did so in reflex. Luckily only my outer clothes got burnt a little. I was unscathed.

"Thank goodness everything's fine," Mother said. "I'll get a replacement rubber tube from Old Wang so you can resume cooking."

After the former Bureau Chief Chen's suicide, Old Wang was assigned to the Conservatory's sister institution the Film Studio as a stage set attendant. Mother periodically recorded for revolutionary film soundtracks there.

With no apologies to me, Mother went on to examine the box she had rescued. Part of what appeared to be newspaper clippings was burnt. I reached over to get a closer look but she immediately thrust the paper back into the box.

"Get out of my room, now!"

Upon returning from school the following afternoon, I noticed that a different, newer rubber hose was connected to the turtle's head.

On the door to Mother's bedroom, a black iron padlock had also been installed. The brand name cast in its middle read: FOREVER.

5 Don't Know Much Biology

Fifteen years since China's 1949 Liberation, remnants of Shanghai's days as the Paris of the East still lived on in the prevalence of *pidgin* words in our city's patois. *La ss ka* for "the last", *jiu ss wun* for "deuce #1", and so on. *La san*, derived from the English word "lassie", referred to an adolescent girl with a burgeoning curiosity for the mystery of human procreation.

"Do you know where we come from?" Wang Hong asked me once after school.

"Nn-no," I stuttered, fearing that a question about my birth would follow.

A smug but hesitant smile appeared on her chubby face. "If I tell you the truth, would you let me go see your home?"

The embarrassing image of a padlock on a door within a flat came to my mind. "I'm afraid my mother wouldn't allow it."

Wang Hong stared down at the ground, her foot making a pattern on the cobblestone street to conceal her disappointment. Her big toes were poking out of her aluminum-buckled black cloth shoes. Come to think of it, other than her plastic sandals, I had never seen her in a different pair of footwear.

Presently, she looked up at me and said, "I'll tell you anyway. Come to my place and I'll show you."

"But I have to go to the wet market."

"*Ai-ya*, Mo Mo, it'll take only a minute!" Without giving me a chance to object further, she started to drag me.

She lived with her parents in a room on the ground floor of a house. "Our home used to be the garage of a bourgeois family. We moved into this house with four other proletarian families after they were 'swept out like dust'," she said.

I recognized the familiar term from the height of the Cultural Revolution when the homes of many former European concessions residents were divided and reallocated to working-class families. Suddenly, I thought about the street sweeper. He could very well have been "swept out like dust" from a house like this and ordered to literally sweep the dust on the street to reform himself.

As Wang Hong opened the door, I realized that it was the first time I had been invited to someone's home. I stood by the entrance, as there seemed to be little room to move about. It was even smaller than the room Mother and I had rented from Ah Bu, although my memory of Hong Kong was extremely vague now.

Four wooden planks atop three benches formed the bed that took up a third of the Wangs' living space. A tiny square table sat in one corner of the room with two stools tucked underneath it. Reading my mind, Wang Hong explained, "I sit on the edge of the bed to eat. Come in. We can sit on the stools now." I nodded, noting with my nose first that the only space left in her home was occupied by a wooden chamber pot for human waste. This household of three had to perform Taoist rites in a snail shell.

Wang Hong touched the uneven surface of the bed we sat on. "This is what caused my birth, because our parents slept together. It's called 'sex' and it's a lot of fun!" she announced knowingly, her butt moving about on the squeaking bed.

Ah, sex. I had heard that topic discussed amongst the men in Condiments' dad's stop. Sex was a decadent bourgeois act that our over 800 million people nonetheless never ceased to engage in.

"Too much sex and too many Chinese," one man had complained.

"That's why the government allows us one child per couple," said another.

"But you cannot always resist the temptations from those *la san*," a third admitted.

Wang Hong was not a *la san* but she was interested in sex. Wang Hong wanted to play hard and live well. She was envious of older *la san* who dared to give tantalizing smiles to peach-fuzzed boys, boys who would whistle or compliment the girls' swaying bodies as they passed by. Most of all, Wang Hong wanted to be asked out on a date even if just to share with the boy a bottle of *yanqishui*, the salty, carbonated soft drink whose pre-Communist day sultry formula was as well guarded as that of Coca-Cola.

Not that *yanqishui* should be considered the Shanghainese cousin of the ubiquitous beverage elsewhere in the world. To my generation of youngsters, Coca-Cola was not only unavailable, but also unthinkably undrinkable. Most would associate its dark brown color with a common cough syrup extracted from herbs. We had not yet encountered a Coke in any form, medium or state -- not the can, the bottle, or the sizzling bubbles floating atop the liquid. Nor had we seen Chairman Mao headshots à la Jackie O ones, or for that matter the Campbell's Soup Cans, be they Chicken Gumbo or Tomato Rice. The canned tomato puree rejects Mother and I made our Sunday borscht out of, yes. But those weren't the ones that would get you wall space at the MoMA or the Guggenheim. Red on top, white at the bottom, like the flag of Monaco, or the flag of Poland upside down, those red and white Andy Warhol prints we had never come across. We young successors of the Chinese revolution simply did not share the rest of the contemporary world's collective retinas.

Never heard of Woodstock, nor a bar of the music played there. Never knew about the Pill. Never realized pot was a recreational drug and not a container for collecting human feces where indoor plumbing was nonexistent. Never been told our city's bygone glories. Never watched "Shanghai Express." Never known Marlene Dietrich as Shanghai Lily. No Greta Garbo. No Joe DiMaggio. No Marilyn Monroe. No McDonald's Happy Meal. No Madonna soundtracks from "Papa Don't Preach". Nothing. Nowhere. China the country sealed off as good old Middle Kingdom ought to be. All imperialists and revisionist poisons were banned: English, Finnish, French, Spanish, Swedish, and Yiddish – all rubbish, except in the case of the aforementioned resilient *pidgin*.

Yanqishui was available for sale in the condiments store but Condiments himself would never be allowed to get a sip. Only couples who were dating bought the drink and they had to take turns imbibing it as one free straw only came with each bottle. Just as well, since it was the closest thing to a French kiss. For the pairs walking up and down the French plane tree-lined boulevards, capturing the right mixture of adventure and gratification was the key. The European atmosphere had an effect on Shanghai's adolescents especially then. When deprived, every little bit goes a longer way.

The motive behind sharing a drink was not always romantic. For ten *fen* (five cents), a stove-wheeling street vendor would sell you a hard-boiled egg in five spices, one of our city's favorite snacks. At a time when Chairman Mao declared the property-less the leading class, few could afford to indulge in a whole bowl of soup alone. A *la san* perching on an open-air stall could slurp down her half of a noodle soup without a second thought if only it were available to her.

She was thus looked down upon by the politically-proper plebeians. Perhaps the most contemptible thing about a *la san* was her ability to discern the anatomic differences between the genders in a human ocean of navy blue Mao-style tunics and use the observance to her advantage.

Endowed with a *la san*-ready body, I was quietly fighting my pubescent embarrassment when Mother asked me a question in the tone of an accusation. "You're not a little girl anymore. What are your plans for the future?"

"Nothing specific yet, but ..."

"But what?"

"You see, Mother ... I've never felt completely comfortable with ... looking different and ..." I paused, exhaling.

She looked at me askance. "I'm sorry my precious darling – that you'll have come to this world to put up with all this."

"That's not what I mean, Mother. I've always strived to better myself and to become someone who is not judged by the way I look. I don't yet know how but I'm determined to make that happen someday."

The expression in her deep chestnut-colored eyes softened a bit. "You should learn to create opportunities for yourself using what you do have. When I was your age, I could already read the notes, so when the Conservatory –"

"You seized the opportunity and enrolled in it at age 12," I completed her sentence, knowing that she had learned to read the notes from her early Catholic school education.

"Let me finish!" she snapped. "All I can see is a growing blob with no brains to match it."

"That's not true! In fact I've already signed up for the tryout for the School District Sports Authority's junior swim team."

"Really?" Mother frowned. "I would prefer that you audition at the Studio. I hear they're planning to reinstate the acting program. Why didn't you tell me you were interested in swimming?"

"I didn't know if I'd be selected, knowing our classification. I don't want to disappoint you if I were ruled out from the outset."

She nodded pensively. "At least you took the initiative. We'll see how this will turn out, then."

Mother announced on Sunday that I was allowed two servings of everything during dinner.

"You're in."

"The swim team? But they didn't even ask me to go to the tryout?"

"That won't be necessary. They know what you look like."

"What does that have to do with anything?"

"You tell me, you idiot! Now train hard and try to make the boarding program eventually. Don't you dare blow it!"

I started swimming the following month. Like the Soviet Union and the Eastern Bloc, China had a state-sponsored system to cultivate future Olympic medalists. We received after school free training three times a week. During the day we were taught little. *Don't know much about history* except for the communism over capitalism victory, *Don't know much biology* except for my own developing breasts, *Don't know much about a science book, Don't know much about the French* or English *I* never *took.*

But our goals were clear: to excel on the team and to advance to the next level. Competition was fierce and the attrition rate high. Only the crème-de-la crème could join the district, municipal, provincial, and eventually, the National Team. The ones making it to the municipal team would automatically turn pro and become boarding athletes, a status that, if obtained, would make both Mother and me very happy.

Most girls like me had not yet heard of menstruation. On the team, boys wore navy blue trunks with a white string as their uniform. Girls wore red suits with elastic bands sewn from inside such that they became virtual blobs of cloth bubbles. This design was intended to conceal the female body curves lest the boys should be distracted. The girls had a nickname for what was tucked inside a boy's shorts -- little sparrow which would mature into turtle's head complete with a thicker, extendable neck.

All were made to line up at the beginning of each training session. In a dramatic reversal of my position in the school procession, I became the person everyone looked to in forming a straight line since I was the tallest of both genders.

My breasts, sporadically sore and itchy, were protruding against the swimsuit bubbles. To conceal my nervousness, I kept my vision steady and straight. Eyes front.

My mental picture suggested that Coach Long liked my focused attention. Thanks to the ingenious design of the swimsuit, he wouldn't notice my bosom. Or so I thought.

"One, two, three!" Coach Long clapped his oar-like hands toughened by years of pushing water and pumping iron. "Jump now!"

I was always the first to be dropped into the swimming pool. Coach Long would call out: "Mo Mo! Ready? Go!" He would push me into the water before going for the tallest boy who was half a head shorter than me.

We moved our hands outwards and downwards, pushing, pedaling, doing a horizontal breaststroke.

Soon I learned to scull, to stay afloat: an important skill now in water and for later in life.

The coach held out a fishing rod-like bamboo stick with a plastic lasso attached to its end and extended it to a sinking child to grab on to. Standing firm like a pagoda with legs apart and chest bare, Coach Long emphasized structure and discipline.

"Train hard!"

"Aim high!"

"Swim well!"

"Honor our motherland!"

We recited these in unison throughout the session. My top spot on the team more than compensated for my apathy for slogan shouting on the way to school. I was by far the most audible, aware of the coach's eyes on me.

Coach Long often rested his broad hand on my shoulder and said, "You first, Mo Mo! Set a good example." While coaches generally did not raise an eyebrow when they heard kids sneeze, Coach Long would occasionally hand me a beach towel after training and say curtly, "Don't catch cold!"

Only coaches were allowed to use these beach towels left on the poolside bench by the cleaning lady. They had the same blue-and-white stripes as the mental hospital patients' overalls and bore the name of the swimming pool in bold, red characters. This labeling was essential to prevent theft. Most people wouldn't buy large towels because precious ration coupons for textile products had to be used in addition to *Renminbi* (Currency of the People), neither easy to come by. The coupons were generally reserved for buying material that could be made into clothes. Besides, bath towels would do us people little good when the majority of the households had no bathtub, shower stall, or indoor plumbing.

One day, when Coach Long put a towel in my hand, I met his gaze. It seemed to be penetrating my swimsuit like x-rays. Feeling as if my hand that held the towel was on fire, I blushed and ran into the changing room. Once inside, I was greeted by a chorus of rhythmic chanting:

"Mo Mo is big, Mo Mo is white.
Big white Mo Mo is the coach's pet!"

Usually I would be upset with such taunting but not this time. I enjoyed being called the coach's pet. Like every other girl on the team, I was secretly in love with Coach Long, whose last name *Long* was the same character for *dragon*. I adored the power and the grace he exhibited when he whipped and chopped the water like a real dragon with flippers on, butt undulating, his timing perfect, rhythm ideal, never missing a beat or a breath.

Coach Long seldom spoke to us on a personal level. Most of his words came out in the form of commands such as "Don't keep your head too high -- your hip will drop!" or "Watch your leg drive. Whip to full extension!" But the majority of the instructions were given in hand gestures, since he was mostly on land. I would close my eyes and relive the montages of him signaling us to enter or get out of the water. *Straight! Keep pace!* and *Ready, set, go!*

Long before I taught myself the English expression "tall, dark, and handsome", before I saw Da Vinci's anatomical dissection sketches of the human male and Auguste Rodin's *The Thinker*, with his flexed muscles, pursed lips and gripping toes, there had been this man eight years my senior who epitomized male authority, power, and dominance.

Despite my size, I wasn't the fastest on our team. But I didn't worry. Coach Long once patted me through the towel he had placed on me and said, "There's no need for you to feel awkward, Mo Mo. A good swimmer needs a well-rounded physique." His reassurance convinced me that I had a fighting chance. This endeared me to him all the more.

"*Yi, er, san, si. Wu, liu, qi, ba.*

Er, er, san, si. Wu, liu, qi, ba.

One, two three, four. Five, six, seven, eight.
Two, two three, four. Five, six, seven, eight!"

Coach Long would command in his booming baritone, occasionally letting his whistle do the work. Most of the time, though, the aluminum whistle on a red silk string just rested on his bulging chest like a pendant. I envisioned that to be a silver medal, a gold one if I were the person looping it over his neck.

The coach wore a crew cut so closely cropped that the contour of his skull in between the dark and spiky hairs was visible. In a sport where maximum propulsion and minimum resistance were critical, the completely shaved "Buddhist monk haircut" was not uncommon among male athletes.

The 1970's witnessed the arrival of the form fitting, "skin" swimsuit showcased by the East German Women's Olympic Team. Although deemed scandalous at the outset even by the Western media, the record speeds the body-hugging design had helped to generate silenced all critics. Naturally, nobody living in China could have heard about such decadent things. As far as our authorities were concerned, the East Germans were ideological lackeys for the Soviet revisionists, hence their practices were totally dismissible.

Coach Long's "skin" suit was his torso itself. With his bronze skin tone and gleaming teeth, he looked especially handsome when he smiled, something he rarely did. People spoke of him as being serious. I regarded him as focused. It was his routine to swim a 10,000-meter medley after he finished training us.

For the segment of our training devoted to "political consciousness-raising", the coach used the topics stipulated in the authority's handouts, often with some personal elaboration. Japan being one of the first developed countries to have reestablished diplomatic relations with China, there was talk of "Sino-Japanese friendship generation after generation" after our governments exchanged giant pandas and *sakura*-cherry trees as gifts. Because of the similar Northern Asian facial features, cultural customs and the common usage of Chinese written characters, the Japanese were the most acceptable type of foreigners.

"However, we should never forget the war crimes the 'Eastern foreign devils' had committed to the people of China and other Asian countries," the coach said.

He, too, referred to the Japanese as the Eastern foreigners, I noted.

"Remember the Japanese soldier who hid in the jungle for twenty-eight years and fed on leaves and animal meats?" I asked.

Not wanting to play favoritism in front of the group, Coach Long said, "You heard about this unusual story, but do you know what ordinary Japanese eat?"

"What do they eat?"

"Japan is an island nation so fish is abundant. The Japanese enjoy raw seafood known as *sashimi*, which is written with the Chinese characters *stabbing with a bayonet* and *body*."

We were all surprised. "Really? They like to eat '*stabbing with a bayonet*' into a '*body*'? How do you know this?"

So the coach told us about his old training buddies' experiences in Japan. "At a banquet welcoming the Chinese National Team, the athletes were served *sashimi*. Just like you now, our delegation found it unthinkable that the Japanese would find such a concept appetizing. The head coach warned that this could be their host's way of making our athletes come down with stomach problems, thus thwarting them from being in top competitive form. However, not only did nobody get sick, they all enjoyed the fresh raw fish themselves. I would try *sashimi* too if given the chance – to think that food is not rationed in capitalist countries!"

I was fascinated by his story as well as by him. From a teammate who had joined the team before my batch, we knew that he was a native of Qingtian in coastal Zhejiang Province who practically grew up swimming. Fast. So fast that, at the suggestion of his middle school PE teacher, he hopped on a Shanghai-bound freight train as a stowaway and got himself recruited by the Shanghai Municipal Team. However, his professional athletic career ended prematurely when he was reassigned as a team coach to us. This downgrade was a punishment for a "political mistake" he had made during the 1974 nationwide "Campaign to Criticize Lin Biao, Confucius, and Song Jiang". Here's what caused Coach's downfall:

Song Jiang was a 12th century personality immortalized as the bandit-leader protagonist of the historical novel *Water Margin*. Since the Cultural Revolution, all literature, be it Chinese, Western, historical or contemporary, had been banned. *Water Margin*, one of the four greatest Chinese classical novels, was no exception ("It glorified gangster heroism"). Coach Long had read the story about the Song Dynasty gang leader from a copy that was only meant to be used as the "negative teaching material" for group criticism meetings during the Campaign and told some of his teammates about its contents. Hence his expulsion from the team.

His personal misfortune aside, the girls on our team were just happy that he had become our coach. Coach Long was my hero, from head to toe.

I turned thirteen on May 15th, 1975. A child's birthday was rarely marked and an adult's, hardly remembered. The birthday party as a practice was condemned as bourgeois. The few determined to go against the tide would have been thwarted by the challenge of baking a cake due to the rationing of flour, eggs, and sugar and the absence of an oven. December 26th was the only exception as Chairman Mao was born on that day in 1893. All of China was legislated to eat "noodles of eternity" to wish him "ten-thousand lifetimes of longevity without limits".

At the beginning of our training on my birthday, I noticed Coach Long's eyebrows were knotted like two forceful Chinese calligraphy strokes. There was a tug in me when his eyes failed to sweep across me as they always did.

"Today, we'll streamline to make our team leaner and stronger. Same heat ordering, now!"

"Streamline" was a code word for team member elimination. I feared for my fate.

The splattering upheavals now over, Coach Long pronounced the death sentences for some. I could feel my heart filling with joy when I realized I had been spared.

"The verdict was reached collectively by all coaches. Today's results support our decision." So the list was pre-determined. The heat competition was just a formality.

Coach Long frowned when a girl began to sob. "Tears won't get you back on the team. Even though you don't have the talent for competitive swimming you can still achieve by focusing on your academic studies. Keep in mind Chairman Mao's teachings: 'Study well, and make progress every day.' There are many ways one can succeed in life."

The common phrase describing athletes as "possessing well-developed limbs but a simplistic mind" reinforced the perception that one could be a good student or star athlete but not both. I was always interested in Chinese composition although little was available for us to read to improve our writing. I dreaded being regarded as overly intellectual. My physical appearance was enough of a problem. I had been jotting down my thoughts in private and hid my notebooks under my mattress. Bold lines like "I admire him to death but don't know why," in which I confessed my nascent feelings towards Coach Long, would definitely brand me a *la san* if discovered and be classified as "bourgeois poisonous weeds".

Of course there were entries about the street sweeper who had vanished from the Pushkin graveyard area. During the past three years since I last saw him I had often imagined bumping into him again, with him unmasked and handsome. I had even written down what I'd say to him if I saw him again: *Please allow me to thank you for giving me the confidence to overcome difficulties in life.* I still remembered clearly the faint but visible creases on his khakis and the high quality but unpolished leather shoes he wore. I could always see his encouraging eyes. The appeal the street sweeper had on me was persistent, and my secret diaries attested to my largely make-believe attraction to him.

Well, that day, I was already drafting my birthday diary entry in my head while the "streamlining" was taking place. It should definitely be recorded, I decided. After the session, as I dragged my feet to the changing room, Coach Long strode over in my direction. I stopped to wait. Next, he snapped a towel at me as though to startle me. I was shocked at his open flirtation. Red to the root of my long bare neck, I thanked Buddha *Guan Yin* that none of the other girls had seen this. Coach Long draped the beach towel over me and whispered, "Wait for me outside where I parked my bicycle."

My heart jolted as my cheeks burned. A giddy feeling hit me. "Mo Mo, you have become a *la san* and Coach Long is your man," I told myself.

When I walked out, he was standing like a bronze statue next to his bicycle.

"Hop on!"

As soon as I side-saddled onto the metal rack on the back wheel, it began to roll. "Hold on to my waist!" he commanded without turning his head.

Steadying myself with my arms around him, I could feel my heart beat as if I had just competed in a swimming race. Then, without warning, he sped up and took his hands off the handlebars as the bicycle swished along. "Look, no hands!" he called out, revealing an adventurous side of him I had not previously seen.

I held tightly onto him, my cheek pressed against his broad back. "Where are we going?"

"You'll find out soon enough. I've got something for your birthday."

"How ... ? and what is it?" I'd never received anything for my birthday.

"The team's personal dossiers were reviewed for the streamlining so I know," he turned his head to tell me. "Now don't make me look back again."

He pedaled on. I clutched onto him, anticipation building inside of me.

Half an hour later, we arrived at an old building in Hongkou District. Coach Long parked his vehicle against the front wall and chained both wheels. Bicycles being the sole means of transportation aside from public buses, they were a highly prized commodity whose purchase required coupons, a long waiting list, and months' worth of salary. More so than towels, they were the most desired targets for thieves. The exterior of the house had many exposed bricks and moss had grown in the cracks.

"Who else lives here?"

"Other unmarried male colleagues."

So this was the Sports Authority staff residence. "You share?" I asked nervously, never having been to this part of town that was the de facto Japanese concession during the WWII.

"The facilities, yes, but I've got my own space with a coffin."

"A coff...?"

Before I could finish, Coach Long entered the front door and pulled me in. I bumped into a wooden shelf filled with mud stained rubber rain boots, umbrellas with bent spines, and nylon string-knitted net bags with used brown wrapping papers.

"Watch out!"

I looked down and saw a mousetrap with a darkened piece of fried dough on its hook. Hairy stuff from a rat's rear end graced the baseboard. I let out a cry.

"Don't scream," he said curtly, offering a hand, which I took.

"Why is the shelf right by the door?"

"Can't move it, it's fixed to the wall -- Japanese style. The Eastern foreigners stored their shoes here before entering the house."

Coach Long's dim room was even smaller than Wang Hong's home, about the size of two shower stalls. The first thing I noticed was another fixed wooden shelf heaped with piles of gym clothes and a pillow without its case.

"So this is the ...?"

"Yeah. The Japanese used to tuck away their comforters during the day and sleep on the *tatami* at night. We all jokingly call it the coffin, and I use it as a bed."

I gaped at the tiny straw-matted floor space and nodded absent-mindedly. A faded blue plastic sheet served as the curtain to a wood-framed window, which wouldn't fully close. A mound of envelope-sized papers sat in a corner. A wooden stool and a child-size bamboo chair constituted all the furniture.

Coach Long switched on the 15-watt bulb hanging down from the ceiling by pulling the attached rope. I was astounded to see that the rope was connected to a replica of the plastic lasso used in our training.

"Why do you use this here?"

"Oh, I took it from the pool because it's easy to be grabbed from the coffin in darkness. Now don't just stand there like a candle. Sit."

I fidgeted on the bamboo chair and wrung my hands.

Coach Long came squatting before me, one knee on the *tatami*. "I've got something very important to tell you, but first promise me you won't cry."

"I promise," I said, my hands clasped tighter.

"Good. Now, I didn't announce this in front of everybody, but today was your last training session as well ..."

"I knew it! I knew it!" I shouted, tears misting my eyes.

Coach Long put his hands on my shoulders and said, "You promised not to cry, Mo Mo."

Biting my lip hard, I struggled to hold back tears. "Sorry, Coach," I murmured, sniffing.

"Good. I told you I had something to show you, didn't I?"

He fumbled around in his trousers pockets. I caught a glimpse of something green. He tucked it down under one of his thumbs, stretched out all eight other fingers, palms down.

"If you guess correctly which thumb I've got it under, I'll show it to you."

I stared at his hands, transfixed. They belonged to a man in his prime: big, firm, blue veins popping, and very much in use. The nails were so closely clipped that their white tip sections were nonexistent. In yet another effort at water resistance reduction, swimmers often wore their fingernails short. No dirt could accumulate under those nails buried inside the flesh.

"Right one."

"You're right!" he chuckled, un-clutching to reveal a rectangular packet of five thin sticks with white paper sleeves, two of them empty. "See? These are the only three left -- American *kouxiang tang* that a former teammate of mine brought back from abroad!"

Ah, genuine American "mouth fragrance candy"! What an extremely precious commodity!

"This ... for my birthday?"

"You bet! Would you like to share one with me?"

I bounced up on my tiptoes. "Of course! Thank you!"

He took out a slice and let me hold one end of it. My hand shaking slightly, I stared at the wrapper bearing the letters "WRIGLEY'S *SPEARMINT* CHEWING GUM". The word "*SPEARMINT*" was italicized and distinctively printed across a forest green arrow pointing towards a little tree with three branches.

So on that day, my thirteenth birthday, I had the privilege for the first time of touching something made in the U.S. This was the time before Wrigley's "Double Mint, Double Pleasure" came into being, before the green-on-white wrapper was changed to mint green, before I knew that three quarters of the population of Singapore were ethnic Chinese and that chewing gum would be banned there. This was before I had a clue as to what life was like outside of China, before I could picture white people walking down the street chewing gum or drinking a whole can of Coke.

"Happy birthday to you, and let's *haafoo haafoo* this," he said, using *pidgin*.

He gave the stick a little tug and I let go of my end of it. I watched intently as his flesh-tipped index finger edged the foil-covered stick out of the wrapper and opened the saw-toothed silver paper. He broke the human flesh-colored piece into two halves, handed me one and put the other in his mouth. He then folded the foil along its creases and slid it back into the wrapper, inching along in the direction of the arrow, deliberately, precisely, one millimeter at a time until it was all the way, and snugly, in.

Seeing that I still had my half in hand, he said, "Let me feed it to you."

"This is delicious. Thank you!"

He chewed and chewed and studied me. I sensed the rhythm of his breathing in and out and visualized that pair of arms spearheading in water, his body defying its resistance. I broke the awkwardness and said, "Now I know why your teeth are so white. It's the American *kouxiang tang*."

He shook his head. "Nothing to do with it. This is the only packet I was given. My teeth are white because I don't smoke like most of the others do."

"And what made you not pick it up, then?"

"Revolutionary self-discipline. I don't believe an athlete should smoke. One has to exercise self control if he wants to accomplish something big in the long run."

Just as I savored the deep meanings of his words, he stooped down and switched to a playful tone. "Let's see whose teeth are whiter, yours or mine."

I displayed an exaggerated grin. He loomed closer, his sweet breath blowing on me. The pair of hands he used to slide the gum stick in and out of the wrapper was now burning on my cheeks. "*Nong zen piaoliang ah!*" – You are gorgeous!

I nearly bit his lip in instinctive resistance. But the next second saw us intertwined like a dragon and a phoenix, engaged in an effort to knead the two halves of the gum back into one. He cupped my breasts as if grasping on to a kickboard, admiring them uncontrollably.

"Mo Mo you are beautiful, beautiful, beautiful!"

He was breathing the way he normally did immediately after a few thousand meters of non-stop swimming. Then he lifted me onto the 'coffin', bellowing "*Ngo yao nong!*" – I want you!

Kneeling on a lump of clothes, he peeled off my pants and parted my legs. His hands felt familiar, for this was not the first time they were on my thighs. Showing me the angles of a precisely executed breaststroke with a frog-like kick during "on-land simulation" had required Coach Long to thus direct me by the poolside, with my stomach on a bench. But this time he separated me at the crotch, his hand massaged my peach fuzz, and chanted "Relax, relax … it's alright." Then, without warning, he thrust his index and middle fingers inside of me and started to churn.

As I cried out in a confused excitement, he pulled them out and dropped off his pants. His appendage, forever covered by his swim trunks, was now a fully extended "turtle's head". Spitting the piece of gum into his hand and flattening it with his palms, Coach Long capped it on his turtle's head, lubricated me with his saliva, and inched into me the way he had just pushed the piece of foil paper into its wrapper. I shut my eyes, sensing his manhood reaching every cell of me. This must be the fun sensation of "sex" that Wang Hong told me about …

Afterwards, the Coach's same fingers retrieved the piece of the gum which by now was coated with a paste the texture of egg whites with streaks of blood swirling around it. As I stared at him in a daze, he propped me up next to him and put his arm around me like a coach often would after a race.

"I've fantasized about you without a swim suit for who knows how long, Mo Mo. How can you be so perfectly developed without even starting your period yet?"

"Period?" I repeated, turning scarlet to the tips of my ears.

He gave my cheek a quick pinch and said teasingly, "Don't be shy, my beautiful Mo Mo. I know yours hasn't started as I don't have your Menstruation Record Card. I was just extra careful." He glanced at our piece of gum, now discarded on the *tatami*.

My head began to reel. "What record card?"

"No girls on your batch have had their onset yet, so you don't know about it. It's a card system to track and monitor our female athletes' monthly cycles so that their potential can be maximized. I'll show you one."

From the pile of papers on the floor he pulled out a card with pre-printed grids. Crosses were marked on various spots indicating the duration and blood flow quantity as well as physical reactions and training schedule.

I looked away and covered my face. "Oh, it's terrible of me to do this with you ...," I began, almost sobbing. "You're my coach, and in my heart you're like a hero to me – honest. But now we've done this together, you'll think of me as nothing but a *la san*."

Coach Long pulled me into his bosom. In an unprecedented soft voice, he said, "Don't be silly, Mo Mo. You're the woman of my dreams and no *la san* can ever come close to that. Do you understand?"

I jerked my head up and down nodding. Meeting his gaze, I gathered all my courage and said, "Yes, I do, but I'm not a woman yet ... maybe I developed faster because I'm not a hundred percent Chinese?"

He displayed the most charming smile I had ever seen. "Which is why I went out of my way to get you on my team."

"You did? ... and you've been good to me only because of this?"

"No ... of course not ... "

But I was not going to let him finish. My beating fists were fast landing on his chest. He stood stationary, letting me hit him like a punching bag.

When I finally stopped, Coach Long put his hands on my shoulders and said, "Now that you've done beating me up, you won't think of me as your custodian anymore, and I'm no longer your coach. You'll always be my beautiful idol, and I hope you will always regard me as your hero."

One arm encircling me by the waist, he lifted my chin with his free hand and kissed me gently on the lips. His facial muscles twitching, Coach Long held me up by my buttocks and carried me to a bare wall, pulling the noose switch off as we passed.

"What do you say to some serious celebration of your birthday?" he whispered in my ear.

With my arms wrapped around his neck and legs around his waist, he pinned me onto that Japanese construction which did not wobble as much as pulsate.

There, we celebrated and celebrated.

6 *Love and the Troika Teens*

I, the pianist's daughter, was now concerned about having to face the music at home. Initially, telling Mother about Coach Long felt like mission insurmountable especially in the context of my swim team elimination. Then I remembered that Mother had me when she was only eighteen and that her mother gave birth to her as a teenager as well. They apparently experienced "sex" as teenage girls, too, so there were the three of us.

Realizing this, I became less anxious. Besides, Mother hardly ever asked me about my life now that she assumed I was fine in the swim program. She never seemed to be interested in me much anyway. So if she did not ask, I would not tell, I decided.

Fueled by the exhilaration of first love, I was dying to know about my maternal grandmother Nga Bu's romance with my Russian grandfather. If I were lucky, Mother might even tell me who my father was. Our Russian meal generally put Mother in a better mood. I offered to wash her hair that Sunday afternoon and planned to bring up the subject of her parents.

I pondered all this as I combed my tangled hair with my fingers. The chlorine in the swimming pool was the culprit. As you might have guessed by now, the strictly rationed soap was not available in the shower stalls where we trained. I usually washed my own hair but Mother said she would wash mine this time in exchange for my offer.

Shampoo, or "fragrant waves" in transliterated *pidgin*, was not rationed but unaffordable. We used instead a solid black chunk of camellia exact. With boiling water I dissolved it an enamel washbasin that was resting on a wooden frame. I then added cold water to make the solution to the exact lukewarm degree Mother desired.

My hair was straight and almost all black except for occasional streaks of brunette. The plastic comb designated for me had embossed on it the words "Serve the People", a ubiquitous quote from Chairman Mao. I used to examine my brunette strands that were caught on it and flash the comb under the sun. Mother had a real brush that she must have had for years for it was molting and its wooden shaft crumbling. All the hairs on it were wavy and smoky brown.

When it was my turn to be washed, I bent my head to face a liquid mirror and asked in a muffled voice, "Mother, can you tell me how your parents first met?"

Her nails dug into my scalp. I clenched onto the washbasin to endure the pain much like someone with a stomach flu gripping onto the toilet bowl rim. The turbid water was getting into my mouth as I waited for her answer.

"After I finish with you, now don't move."

Her ivory-like fingers tapped my crown as though it were a drum. Presently she began humming "Red Is the East", her hands separating my hair into sections to let the camellia solution soak through. During one of her numerous delirious outbursts, she said that her parents had endowed her with those fingers to play Chopin, but now they only touched keys on the accordion. I knew that it was fortunate for her that she was allowed to play any instrument at all, as all things Western were considered "spiritual opium" to our revolutionary will power. Mother's survival instincts were attributable to her orphaned childhood. Just as Old Wang once said, she was the smartest in knowing how to adapt to the ever-changing political climates. While some of her colleagues had held on to their "commitment to art", Mother had volunteered to give up piano and take up the professionally despised accordion, the Red Guards' instrument of choice popularized, ironically, by the Soviet revisionists.

As the lead accordionist to the School's "Mao Zedong Thought Propaganda Team", Mother played tunes like "Red Is the East" and "Sailing in the Sea Depends on the Helmsman". The Red Sun in the East and the Helmsman both referred to Chairman Mao on whose leadership our nation of 800 million depended.

> Red is the East,
> Rises the Sun,
> China has brought forth a Mao Tse-tung.
> For the people's happiness He works,
> *Hu-er-hei-yo* –
> He is our great savior!
>
> The Communist Party is like the Sun,
> Illuminates every corner where it shines.
> Wherever exists the Communist Party,
> *Hu-er-hei-yo* –
> People there'll be liberated!

And:

> *Dahai hangxing kao duoshuo,*
> *Wanwu shengzhang kao taiyang …*

> Sailing in the seas depends on the Helmsman,
>   life and growth depend on the Sun.
> Rain and dewdrops nourish the crops,
> making revolution depends on Mao Zedong Thought.

> Fish can't leave the water, nor do melons the vine.
> The revolutionary masses can't do without the Communist Party.
> Mao Zedong Thought is the sun that shines forever.

Mother broke off in the middle of the song as abruptly as she began. I kept my eyes and mouth shut, listening to the sound of water dripping into the basin. I could sense that she had again entered a different world, a place where time had stopped like the hands of an unwound clock.

The washing over, I combed my hair with "Serve the People" as Mother began, "I never knew my parents so what I'm telling you may not be all factual. The orphanage record only had one photo of your grandfather but not your Nga Bu. Most Chinese women who had died in the 1940's couldn't have had a picture taken of them, you know."

"Can I see it?"

Mother patted her hands dry and went to unlock her room, closing the door behind her. I could hear boxes being shuffled inside as I twirled my hair, waiting for the privilege of seeing my Russian ancestor's visage for the first time.

She returned with a 2" x 1.5" snapshot, product of an amateur's lens judging from the overexposure mark left by the magnesium flash power. Once black and white, it was now yellow on the edges. I leaned over and stared: a young Caucasian man in a V-neck sweater was leaning against one of the Grecian pillars, hands on an accordion that read *HOHNER*.

"Hohner is a German brand for musical instruments, excellent sound quality. The photo was obviously taken on the Bund, the most valuable stretch of embanked riverfront in Shanghai. This edifice with a *fin-de-siècle* European look used to be the Hongkong & Shanghai Bank and now …"

"The seat of the Shanghai Municipal Revolutionary Committee," I finished it for her. "Was he a clerk at the Bank?"

"One would wish but no. Kirill Molotov," Mother uttered her father's name deliberately, "was a native of St. Petersburg and a musically-talented Russian barber by profession. His father had died in the conflict between the White Armies and the Bolshevik revolutionaries following the fall of Tsar Nicholas II."

"Which side was he on?"

"I have no way of knowing, but I've always insisted that he'd been a revolutionary soldier under Comrade Lenin, and therefore a martyr of the Soviet Union. Your grandfather was still a teenager when he fled with an uncle, trekking across Central Asia as stowaways on the Trans-Siberian trains. They arrived first in the Northeastern Chinese city of Harbin before getting south on freight trains to Shanghai."

This mixture of facts and fiction must have repeatedly gone around in Mother's head for she told them so engagingly as though she was reciting from a verse novel. The initial oddity of her referring to him as Kirill -- rather than Father as we Chinese always are required to show "filial respect" -- soon became unnoticeable. I was sucked into the whirlpool of her narrative.

"Like many of their compatriots, they reached 'St. Petersburg of the Orient', destitute."

Mother said "St. Petersburg" in a whisper for she knew well that I belonged to the generation that knew no St. Petersburg but Leningrad, no John Lennon but Vladimir Lenin, and no Marx Brothers but Karl Marx.

Uncle and Nephew settled down in the émigrés community around Avenue Joffre in the French Concession, an area dubbed "Neva Street" after the river back home. Signs here were in Cyrillic and English, with occasional French added for flair. There were the Baranovsky Department Store and the Sonola Music House. The First Russian Bakery was in heated competition with the Café & Bakery I. P. Tkachenko. The pharmacies Foch and Sine, Siberian Fur Store, Koneff Shirts Maker, Femina Silks, and Europa Shoes. By the time the tombstone maker Tomashvsky Architectural & Monumental Granite set up shop here, it was clear that the river in the old country was one of no return.

Never again Neva.

Kirill apprenticed at the Figaro Coiffure while the uncle stuffed fatty meats at the Vienna Sausage Works. Our folks had worked, Mother reassured me. Unlike some who hung around on street corners trying to catch lice for one another, Kirill had risen above the local stereotypes.

On one sultry summer night in 1944, about a year before Mother was born, my maternal grandparents had a fateful encounter under the ceiling fans of the Sonola Music House's accordion section. He, in an open collar white calico shirt, was fingering the keys. She, clad in a midnight blue three-quarter sleeves uniform *cheongsam* with a St. Emanuel Grammar School badge, watched him doing octaves. He had spoken first, in her patois, laboriously learned from the streets. Dimples showing and eyes gleaming with surprise, her pale face turned pink. Characteristically Chinese, she apologized in her first utterance that she knew not his tongue.

"You mean Nga Bu went to the same primary school as I do?" I asked incredulously.

Mother nodded. "Same physical location but St. Emanuel and your Young Revolutionary School belong to two opposite realms."

A clerk rang a bell. The shop was closing. The teens strolled into to the breezy evening heat, his arm coming to encircle the narrowest part of her. Shanghai's French Concession born and bred, my mother's mother was unabashed.

My heart began to race from hearing Mother's narration. Nga Bu must have experienced a similar sensation. He was three years older than her, Mother believed, with muscles three times firmer than hers. My own coach was eight years my senior, and oh, that much stronger than me!

Bound for the Bund, Kirill and Nga Bu walked and talked, thoughts boundless.

En route they approached the double-spanned Garden Bridge where Nga Bu stopped to brace herself for the body search by the occupying Japanese. As a Chinese she was expected to bow to the sentinels or risk being beaten up for "demonstrating disrespect for the Heavenly Emperor Hirohito". Many had died at the sentries' bayonet points for "attempting to smuggle rice" to the other side of the bridge or for simply being Chinese.

As Mother described this to me, I could visualize the characters *stabbing with a bayonet* and *body*, Japanese for *sashimi*, as Coach Long had told our team.

"As you'd expect, the Japanese let Kirill and his Chinese girl pass without bowing or body search?"

"But why?"

"Because the Japanese are obsequious to Westerners, then and now. In a Far East city like Shanghai or Tokyo, a Caucasian face could always help matters."

"Was Kirill offended by the double standard?"

"To him, this was the other peoples' war, I suppose. Sweet rice, sticky rice, short grain, long grain, crops from the paddies are staples for the East Asians themselves. The excitement of romantic adventure had never before so stirred the man who lived in a borrowed land on borrowed time. He must not have wanted to spoil that."

Mother drew a breath and went on with her fantastic tale: in the heat of that night, my grandparents were intoxicated by our port city's sights and sounds. The sampans' sails sagged. The Shanghainese lassie sighed. The Petersburgian lad asked what was on her mind. She jerked her head in an attempt to suppress a bout of cough.

"*Xi-qian sa-le!*" – How deadly annoying, she had complained, her voice raspy.

Kirill soothed her by way of kissing, oblivious to the passing rickshaws, pedicabs, wheelbarrows, and the chauffeured Daimlers or Packards. Kirill, inhaling the exotic exhalations from herbal lozenges, wanted to seize every moment of it.

As for Nga Bu, this was the first time she felt a prickly chin and smelled vodka breath. Kirill unbuttoned his shirt to let the breeze in. Sweat had soaked her summer *cheongsam*, rendering it clingy. With each lungful of air her chest rose like a pair of the Chinese steamed buns, Kirill gasped at the sight. *Brassieres* were unfamiliar undergarments. Shanghainese women of Nga Bu's generation were lucky to have escaped foot-binding by a mere decade, having been born just after the 1911 emperor-deposing Revolution. She coughed and giggled as he gasped at the outlines of her childish frame.

They gazed at the ripples on the Whampoa and the silhouette of the Bund edifices in architectural styles from Baroque to Romanesque. Pointing out the Russian Consulate, Kirill waxed homesick and began to reminisce. Between coughs she tittered at his fractured Shanghainese lingo. He had grown up on the banks of the Neva, no junks, no sampans, "*Niet, niet,*" he gesticulated for emphasis. A drawbridge would rise on schedule to let the ferries pass. The magnificent Cathedral of St. Peter and St. Paul was in the background. The annual "White Nights" period when it is bright day and night would occur in just about now.

She tried to visualize the romantic atmosphere his deep-set eyes portrayed. Growing up in the tenements surrounding the Western concessions, she looked up to the privileged Europeans and hated the Japanese. Her father made his living peddling snacks across cobblestone lanes on a wheeled kitchen: hard-boiled eggs in five spices, noodles with sesame sauce, and wonton in soup. On Sunday he wore his Mandarin jacket with broad white cuffs to the cathedral. Despite sermons in Latin peppered with broken Shanghainese, he could make out the gist: Believe in Our Lady and help thy brethren. Send thy young to schools, be it boy or girl: they were children of our Risen Lord, first and foremost.

Rudyard Kipling was not taught in school yet Nga Bu had absorbed the concept of "the White Man's Burden". "The Western Christians want to help us poor in China," she thought, justifying to herself her attraction to this white knight from the land of the White Night.

No "White Night" over the Whampoa but there came a white morning. The sky above the water had taken on an orange and white hue, heralding the arrival of another dawn. Kirill began to croon *Utro* (Morning), a favorite native tune, which Mother now hummed to me with deep feelings:

> *"Ljublju tebja!"*
> *Shepnula dnju zarja*
> *I, nebo obkhvativ, zardelas' ot priznan'ja,*
> *I solnca luch, prirodu ozarja,*
> *Sulybkoj posylal jej zhguchije lobzan'ja.*

> "I love you!"
> Daybreak whispered to day
> and, while enfolding the skies, blushed from that confession,
> and a sunbeam, illuminating nature,
> with a smile sent her a burning kiss.

"Do you know what vision I had when I sang 'Red Is the East' just now? I saw that day's dawn in Shanghai and I heard the tune to *Utro*. Strange, uh?"

Nga Bu and Kirill dated for a few months before she abruptly vanished. Kirill must have been disappointed but not devastated. Shanghai was the type of place where one came and went. In his spare time he sang and made love to his accordion. A customer introduced him to a Filipina dancer named Coco. Over shots of vodka he joined her in polka.

In fact Nga Bu had left due to circumstances beyond her control. Her father had carted her to the Ziccawei Ward for the poor, next to the yellow Jesuit building. St. Ignatius Cathedral's 50-meter high Gothic spires had inspired their awe. "You're in God's hands and you'll be fine" were the parting words of this working-class convert to his ailing teenage daughter.

In time, the confessional felt tinier and tighter to her. After repeatedly failing to kneel fully on the prie-dieux, Nga Bu was taken to see the head of the facility Father Michel. It was there that she saw on his desk a black box under a dumbbell with a long tapeworm-like tail. A metal plaque was affixed under the clock face dial with the words: *Bell Telephone. MFG. Company. ANVERS. BELGIQUE.* Between bouts of coughs she confessed that there was more than tuberculosis growing inside her. Father Michel pointed to the device and offered her its use but Nga Bu knew neither the number nor the exact address of Figaro Coiffure.

During Mass several days later she was rushed away by a sister whose solemn face was framed by stiff coifs. At the clinic, a white-coated nurse in angular cap and soft-soled shoes gave instructions as the lassie wailed. There was blood from her mouth and down below. She exhaled her last breath when a Eurasian infant was pushed out of her small frame. One look at its features and the nurse cried: "Sinful, sinful! Holy Mary, Mother of God, we ask for your mercy and forgiveness!"

An envelope was safety-pinned to Nga Bu's clothes. Inside was a photo with the words "Kirill Molotov" in the back and a note in an origami knot.

Dear Father Michel:

If I die and the baby survives, a boy shall be named Dmitry De-ming (virtue and enlightenment) and a girl, Nadia Na-di (beauty and enlightenment). I came to this mortal world in darkness; I shall go having seen Light and Truth. The baby is innocent. I beg you to keep it here in our Lord's sanctuary.

"Remember the special origami pattern I taught you on the train?" Mother asked. "I learned that from carefully folding and unfolding the origami Nga Bu had left."

"Really? Thank you, Mother, for teaching me something so precious to you. Is it in your room with the other 'important things' and can I see it?"

Mother sighed and gave me a conflicted look. "I handed it in voluntarily shortly after starting music school to prove that I had drawn a clear-cut line of demarcation between the spiritual opium world that was Christianity and my young revolutionary stance. A conservatory leader burned the origami in front of my eyes and I didn't even flinch. As a result, I was included in the first batch to become a Communist Young Pioneer. Unbeknownst to them, I kept the photo, at great risk of course."

"You really are a brave survivor, Mother," I said admiringly.

She shook her head. "I may have survived but I've not thrived professionally ... but let me continue."

Nga Bu's last wish was granted. Baby Nadia Molotova was transferred to the Ziccawei Orphanage next door. Father Michel had a Chinese nun put her name down as Mo Na-di, acknowledging that it was always easier for the Chinese to read in Chinese, *bien sûr*.

Kirill Molotov never knew that there existed a Mo Na-di. The duet "Coco & Molo" was formed. It played in nightclubs until May of 1949, when the People's Liberation Army took over Shanghai. One of its last numbers was Rachmaninov's *Prokhodit vse*:

> *Prokhodit vse I net nemu vozvratal*
> *Zhizn' mchitsja vdal', mgnovenija bystrejl*
> *Gde zvuki slov, zvuchavshikh nam kogda-to?*
> *Gde svet zari nas ozarjavshikh dnej?*
> *Rascvel cvetok, a zavtra on uvjanet.*
> *Gorit ogon', chtob vskore otgoret'...*
> *Idet volna, nad nej drugaja vstanet...*
> *Jan e mogu veselykh pesen's pet'!*

> Everything is passing with no return.
> Life goes by in the blink of an eye.
> Where have the sounds of the words we once listened to gone?
> Where are the dawns of yesteryear?

A flower blossoms today but withers tomorrow ...
A blazing fire burns out in time ...
The next wave will rise over the current one ...
Happy songs I can sing no more!

Foreigners of any color or creed were declared *persona non grata.* Coco and Kirill shanghaied themselves to the Philippines' Tubabao Island, to seek new fortunes and to play new tunes, waving *Dasvedania!* forever to the "Paris of the East" and Street Neva ...

When Mother was finished, my hair was dry. "I never realized that you are somewhat of a brunette," she said. "Perhaps that was the color of my father's hair."

"I'm glad I have something of him in me. As to Nga Bu, I think of her in the image of Ah Bu, for she is a devout Shanghainese Christian, too."

"You still remember that Ah Bu?"

"I'll never forget her. She loved me."

A harsh expression flashed in Mother's eyes. "What are you trying to say?"

"Nothing. I suppose I just envy you for having something tangible relating to your father, unlike me."

"It's for your own good that you don't. He's dead so it won't make any difference to you. You'll just have to go on with your life. I did."

"Yes, I know. You were an orphan but I still have you, right? But do you realize that I may have the same desire to know about my father? Your mother died and your father disappeared. Why do I sometimes feel I'm in the same boat?"

Mother pulled me by the hair and jerked my head around. Inevitable slaps landed on my cheeks. "You ungrateful little bastard! I hope that nobody will ever love you!"

"I'll be more loved than you ever will be!" I shouted, unyielding and unapologetic.

7 Dreaming Stanislavsky

The very next day after school I asked Wang Hong, "Can you verify something for me from your dad as soon as possible?"

"Depends on what I get in return."

"How about some Russian bread?"

"The kind they sell at the Second Food Provisions Store bakery on Huaihai Road? Of course! Here, let's do a pinky swear." She hooked my pinkie and chanted, "Heaven has eyes, Earth has soul. Whoever breaks the promise will be doomed!"

I told her about my elimination and wanted to confirm that the Film Studio Young Actors Training Program would soon be reestablished. If so, I planned to apply to the people in charge without going through Mother.

Wang Hong soon returned with the news that Studio Party Secretary-General Ouyang had just received clearance from the "higher up" – commonly understood to be Madame Mao, a former actress in Shanghai herself – to reinstate the Young Actors Program in the fall.

It had been almost a decade since I was last in the Administration Building where Wang Hong and I played catch in its marbled hallways. A dreamy sense of familiarity propelled me up the winding stairs to the second floor where I was greeted by a cigarette odor. I peeked in from the half-closed office door marked "Secretary-General" and was taken aback. Sitting behind the mahogany desk was none other than the senior cadre who had boarded our train from Guangzhou to Shanghai in February of 1966!

Mo Mo, I told myself, *your opportunity is here. Take heart and go for it!*

After knocking gently on the door, I walked past a cluttered small table towards his desk.

"Secretary-General Ouyang, how do you do?" I announced, standing upright and looking directly at him.

Ouyang popped his head up in reflex and tried to place me. "You are ...?"

"My name is Mo Mo. I was the girl ..."

"Ah -- yes, of course. You're the daughter of Teacher Mo! How you have grown!" He cast a glance at the small table behind me and asked, "Did your mother send you here to tell me something?"

"No. I came here by myself."

"Is that right?" the Secretary-General said, lifting his eyebrows. "How can I help you, little comrade?"

"I'm here to apply to you directly for the Young Actors Training Program."

"Was this your mother's idea?"

"Not at all. It's my own decision, and she doesn't know I'm here."

The Secretary-General lit himself a cigarette and studied me. "You have a lot of guts to come and see me. I like that in a young girl. Tell me, little comrade, why do you want to join the program?"

I gave him my pre-rehearsed line. "Because I want to entertain the people by tapping into my artistic talent."

Ouyang clapped his hands twice and said, "Good." Rising from his leather upholstered armchair, he walked by me to close the door before heading back. "Impressive, very impressive, little comrade. Our revolutionary ranks need young actresses like you," the Secretary-General said as he placed his arm on my shoulder. "Would you like to perform a song and dance number for me now?"

Enveloped by a nameless sense of apprehension, I eased myself away from him and replied, "I'm sorry Secretary-General, but I didn't come prepared with one today. Please let me get prepared and show you next time. Of course I will schedule it through the Training Program's political instructor first."

No sooner did I finish than he turned his back on me as if to avoid letting me see the expression on his face. But I had already caught a glimpse of a surprised, perhaps even shocked look.

Ouyang returned to his desk, took a long drag of his cigarette, and extinguished a good half of it. "That won't be necessary. I was just testing you and I see you can certainly make a good actress," he declared, suddenly all smiles.

"Does that mean I'll be in the program?"

"I'm not the best judge to determine that professionally. Why don't you tell Teacher Mo to come to speak to me and we ..."

"Sorry to interrupt, Secretary-General, but I really don't want to get my mother involved. In fact, could you please promise me not to mention our meeting today? I'm determined to enter the program on my own strength. Should I contact the political instructor to schedule for a professional audition, then?"

Ouyang looked at me and considered for a second. "I don't think that'll be necessary. You're good enough to be in the program."

"So I'm in for September?" I asked excitedly.

He nodded deliberately and said, "Your mother won't know about this meeting and you'll have to promise me not to contact anybody else regarding the program, understand?"

"Yes, and thank you so much, Secretary-General! But how do I know for sure if ...?"

He waved his hand. "Admissions material will be sent to your school in due course and you can go from there. Now I'm very busy so you can just leave the door ajar on your way out."

"Yes, of course, Secretary-General. Thank you so much for your time, and of course for promising that I can join the program. You won't regret it!"

"Good bye, little comrade."

Hopping down the marble stairs, I came face to face with a bespectacled man on his way up. Uttering an instinctive "Excuse me," I rushed down, realizing with a thumping heart that he was Ouyang's assistant on the train.

My bubbly swimsuit, intentionally dampened, continued to be dried on the days I used to train. Since our confrontation following the hair-washing, neither Mother nor I talked much. I prayed daily for the Studio admission information to reach my school. It would be a great relief for both of us once I moved out in the fall.

Meanwhile, I had saved five *jiao* (a quarter) to cash in my promise to Wang Hong about the bread. We went to the Second Food Provisions Store in the early evening to take advantage of the bakery's forty-percent discount after six o'clock. I loved food and knew the counters there well, although Mother was the person who actually shopped there.

Hand in hand Wang Hong and I gallivanted about in the store before stopping under the big wall clock with Roman numerals. Our eyes darted between that and the bakery counter.

"What's the foreign name for that type of bread?" Wang Hong asked.

"It's called *khleb* in Russian. Hard crust with soft dough inside, kind of like a Chinese streamed bun that has sat in the air for a while and the skin breaks."

"I'm sure it's much better that a stale streamed bun. How much money do you have?"

"Five *jiao*."

"Enough for a loaf after six o'clock?"

"I hope so. If not, I can always buy five *jiao* worth of slices and you can have them all."

"Can I hold the five *jiao* note for you?"

I let her. Wang Hong smoothed the purple profile of Chairman Mao's head.

As it turned out, during the discounted period they only sold the bread by the loaf, which cost six *jiao*. Our disappointment was not unnoticed by a chef-capped baker. He said to the female cashier, "It's Teacher Mo's daughter -- just give her a few slices."

"For free?" Wang Hong asked.

"I can pay five *jiao*!"

"No need. Just for your pretty blushing face, I'll give them to you for free."

"Oh, you're really a kind kind man, Master Baker, and you too, auntie!" Wang Hong reached over the counter and received four thick slices.

"Thank you so much," I said to the baker and the cashier.

As I watched Wang Hong chewing the *khleb*, I noticed that dirt no longer accumulated under her nails.

"This is more delicious than I imagined," she said. "You're so lucky, Mo Mo. Everyone does special things for you."

"To tell you the truth, I'd rather be treated like an ordinary person."

"But you're not like the rest of us. Nobody would think twice about you shuffling from one Huaihai Road store to another because you belong in this classy place, unlike us."

Immediately, I thought about the masked street sweeper. In my imagination, he would be the type of person who truly belonged here. Although the establishments' names had been changed to either political or numerical, most of the storefronts from Avenue Joffre days still remained. I could almost picture him shopping here, wearing his well polished shoes and his crisply ironed trousers.

"But everybody is allowed on Huaihai Road," I said. "All you need to do is to come and window shop."

"From now on, I'll do just that," Wang Hong said.

In time, Wang Hong would learn to walk the walk and talk the talk of the Shanghai folks, sophisticated in commodities selection and quality assessment. She might not have had much "People's Money" *yuan* then, nor much Japanese *yen* later during she sojourn in Tokyo, but a yearning for social and commercial success would be with her forever.

On the Sunday of my departure for the Film Studio, Mother was away with her students in the "sending the educated down to help with the autumn harvest" campaign. Owning only one set of bed sheets, I brought one and kept the other at home until such time when we would have enough cloth ration coupons to acquire a new set.

From under my mattress I took out my notebooks. The sheet was folded in half to proximate a square spread. Swimsuit and underpants went in first to serve as a cushion. The secret diaries were tucked in the middle, buried between the changes of clothes.

I boarded a public bus with the bundle and my People's Liberation Army-green satchel, standing by the back windowpanes as it pulled away. In my heart I said goodbye to the little white house I had called home for over a decade. Only then was I struck by a strange sense of relief. I would not have to see the big black padlock on Mother's bedroom door everyday anymore.

There were sixteen of us, eight of each gender. The1975 recruits for the Young Actors and Actresses Training Program were juvenile employees of the Shanghai People's Film Studio. Although unpaid, we were thrilled with the benefits. Each of us would receive three pairs of black cotton pants, no cloth coupons required. Lantern-like knickerbockers with baggy design and wide elastic bands, they were intended for physical training yet we wore them exclusively since they could be replaced once worn out.

All were also issued a Municipal Bus monthly pass and meal tickets redeemable at the employee canteen. The menu was scratched out in chalk on a blackboard, often smudged but always discernable as selections were limited. Stir-fried chicken-feather vegetable and hairy-peas with pickles were the staple, the latter was a far cry from the way Ah Bu used to make them for us back in Hong Kong but I loved it still. The matchbox-sized 1/6-inch thin "big pork chop" was a rare treat.

We occupied two adjacent rooms with concrete floor and bunk beds. Wooden-framed windows were without curtains and didn't close well. Gauze bed nets, fending off mosquitoes in the summer and keeping the unheated room a tad less bone-chilling in the winter, provided an unintended screen of privacy – something hard to come by elsewhere in China. As in Coach Long's dorm, one bare bulb extended from the ceiling. An originally white but now gray nylon clothesline was tied to nails across the room. Conflicts often arose when the girls rubbed against each others' hand-washed laundry, accidentally or deliberately, while climbing up into or down from their bunks. Curfew was 10 p.m., when I often began writing my journal with the aid of a flashlight, mosquito net drawn.

Military music from the loudspeaker on the Chinese parasol tree served as the initial reveille at six o'clock, followed five minutes later by extended bugle calls from our 14-year-old boy class-monitor. By six-twenty we would have gotten dressed, finished with the communal washroom, and been ready for roll call in the compound. Between the callisthenics music, we shouted slogans like the following:

"Exercise our bodies, heighten our vigilance, and defend our motherland!"

"Let a hundred flowers bloom in artistic fields. Weed through the old to bring forth the new!"

Breakfast consisting of steamed buns, rice congee and soy sauce-pickled rutabaga slices was served between seven and seven-thirty. Classes began at eight. School pupils no longer, we were working boys and girls, future actors and actresses.

Math was dropped and Chinese became the core. "Revolutionary Performing Arts Techniques" was the sole techniques course. We studied theatrical theories developed by a Russian with the tongue twisting name of *Si-tan-ni-si-la-fu-si-ji*.

"As a partial possessor of the Russian dramatic genealogies," I wrote in my secret journal, "I may share something with the master on a minuscule level that can help me study the performance art. After all, my mother and grandfather were musically talented."

Better known to the world as Konstantin Stanislavsky, the great producer held that an actor's main responsibility was to be believed, rather than to be recognized or understood by the audience. His theatrical model known as "The Method" had been condemned in China following the Sino-Soviet ideological breakup in the late 1950's but reinstated to coincide with the resumption of the 1975 training program.

"Bear in mind that The Method should be studied with severe reservations," we were pre-warned by the teachers.

What was taught without restraints was the revolutionary artistry demonstrated in the 1974 People's Liberation Army Film Studio movie *The Brightly Shining Red Star*, in which the protagonist Winter Boy Pan keeps a red star badge from his father's Red Army cap as inspiration to stand up to the "despotic landowner" Hu Hanshan. For weeks, the theme song played in my head:

> *Hongxing shanshan, fang guangxcai,*
> *Hongxing cancan, nuan xionghuai.*
> *Hongxing shi zan gongnong de xing,*
> *Dang de guanghui zhao wandai!*
> *Hongxing shi zan gongnong de xing,*
> *Dang de guanghui zhao wandai!*

> The red, red star, shining bright,
> The red, red star, warming our hearts.
> 'Tis the star of our workers and peasants,
> The brilliance of the Party will shine 10,000 generations!
> 'Tis the star of our workers and peasants,
> The brilliance of the Party will shine 10,000 generations!

Thanks to my appearance, I was assigned the role of a Uighur girl in *Xinjiang Is a Wonderful Place*, a film to be released to coincide with a political campaign to promote the great unity of all nationalities of China.

The gist: an olive-skinned farmer with a Muslim skullcap and thick stubble steals watermelons from the People's Commune before they are completely ripened. The authority sees this as a vicious attempt to sabotage nationality unity. My role is to illustrate how well the Uighur minority are treated by the *Han* majority, here represented by the People's Liberation Army soldier.

I sat through photo shoots wearing various "babushka" head-scarves, prompting one Assistant Director of Photography to remark how similar I looked to Zoya Kosmodemyanskaya, the WWII Soviet teenage heroine Mother had portrayed on stage two decades ago.

Mo Mo, you should try your best to out-perform your mother and succeed in your career, I urged myself.

As part of the role preparation, I learned to eat like a native by nibbling on the boiled sheep's feet, chewing up sinews and soft bones off a carcass and washing it all down with "brick tea", a black exact dissolvable only in boiling water. Consuming "grabbed rice", a concoction of grain, raisins, nuts and grated carrots fried mutton lard, involved fingers instead of chopsticks commonly used by us *Han* people. A skilled diner's hand had no contact with the mouth; the thumb "shoots" in a marble-playing motion, a technique I mastered readily. Compared to what was being served in the employee canteen, this was a gastronomic heaven. Unaware at the time, what I was exposed to then would help me develop Maison Jasmine's fusion style menu several years later.

Like Winter Boy, my character was to demonstrate her strong gratitude for the People's Liberation Army. One of my key scenes involved me slipping from the river bank into the muddy waters and simulating drowning before a heroic People's Liberation Army soldier came to my rescue. In a dozen takes I managed not to swallow any water while still looking realistic. My swim training came in handy in the most unexpected way. I only wished that Coach Long, whom I now saw only on Sunday afternoons, could substitute the actor whom played the solider.

We trainees could leave the Studio late Saturday afternoon and be back by seven Sunday night. I told Mother that I had to return after lunch and took the bus to the Native City where Coach Long and I would amble down streets in search for inexpensive eateries. He had taken to calling me his "film starlet" and continued to refer to himself as my hero.

Someday, he vowed, looking steely-eyed, *someday, I will make it big and become a real hero.*

8 Seeing Red

The ninth day of the ninth month of 1976 was earth-shattering for China. The Great Teacher, the Great Leader, the Great Commander-in-Chief, and the Great Helmsman Chairman Mao passed away. By government decree, our nation of nine-hundred-million people went into synchronized mourning. Studio employees gathered for a mass ceremony in central Shanghai's People's Square, site of the pre-Liberation Race Course built to accommodate several thousand people. So many more congregated there that mid-September day that not a drop of water could have trickled through.

For hours while surrounded by the sounds of wailing, I waited with my colleagues for our turn to enter the Shanghai Municipal Grand Mourning Hall behind the Rostrum. A gigantic portrait of Mao framed by black ribbons and yellow cloth flowers was mounted in the front center of the Square, dwarfing thousands of black crowns below. The non-stop funeral music – a combination of revolutionary marches and Peking opera drum tunes -- filled the air. Slogan shouts came from various handheld speakers:

"Comrades, battle-companions, revolutionary masses, turn our grief into strength and carry Chairman Mao's great cause through to the end!"
"Chairman Mao is the red sun that will never set in our hearts!"
"Eternal glory to Chairman Mao!"

Having held back the urge to pee, I grew restless as I sensed tepid ooze creeping down my crotch. The sensation reminded me of Coach Long's probing fingers. Remembering the Menstruation Record Card he had shown me, I wondered if my first period, known colloquially as *jian hong*, or seeing red, had begun. Yet sandwiched like a sardine, I could not make it out to the public toilet and thread my way back. Fortunately, with my training lantern pants, nobody else would notice what was happening down there.

Back at the dorm hours later, "seeing red" was confirmed. This was good news as I now qualified for the monthly one *yuan* (50 cents) "hygiene subsidy" for female employees, twice the amount given to male employees for haircuts since men were forbidden from wearing hair below the earlobes. Actors reaching puberty and beyond were not issued condoms, however. Abstinence was expected although not always practiced, as Coach Long's ingenious utilization of the Wrigley's gum illustrated.

Subsidy notwithstanding, every *fen* (half a penny) counted when it came to actual supplies. Wang Hong would not tell me about the existence of tampons until much later. At a time when the tears of our nation were being shed on millions of faces, I needed something to contain my dripping vaginal blood flow. Sanitary napkins were sold in the pharmaceutical counter of the Shanghai Women's Products Store on Huaihai Road, but they were way beyond most teenagers' budget. Even Mother rarely bought a package.

My initial "hygiene subsidy" had to be applied for in writing and verified and approved by the Studio accounting office. As the idiom goes, "Water far away is of little use in putting out a fire." I had to turn to our political instructor for help. She happened to be the wife of Secretary-General Ouyang but used her maiden name professionally like all other female Party cadres. Few knew about her connection to the Secretary-General but Old Wang did and Wang Hong told me about it.

"You're so full of bourgeois thoughts, Mo Mo!" she scolded as soon as I stuttered out the words "sanitary napkins." "How many girls your age in China do you think are already having their period? Very few! Your kind develops earlier and you're already been given a movie role. You should set a good example for the rest and not fall into the trap of pursuing a luxurious lifestyle!"

Taking in an earful as I stood with my head low, I could feel a chunk of bloody tissue sliding down my thighs. The political instructor was making a dig at my "kind" as having earlier-than-most menstrual onset as though I had control over the timing of it. But Mrs. Ouyang was a responsible revolutionary cadre after all. Once her reprimand was over, she showed me what most menstruating women did at the time: using toilet papers wrapped around pieces of shredded cotton to hold the flow. The part of cotton not stained should be reused, she emphasized.

This self-assembled pad was fastened in chastity belt fashion on a "sanitary band," one of which she gave me for immediate application. She had personally sewn it using plastic strips and scrap cloth from worn out clothes. It would be insane to waste ration coupons to buy new material for this purpose. Once worn, the sanitary band looked not unlike the loincloth worn by a Japanese sumo wrestler.

"I keep a few newly made ones with me so our trainee girls can have them for the first time," she said.

I thanked her and turned to leave but not before she patted me on the shoulder. "Mo Mo, you're a woman now and you should work hard to be an actress deserving your good looks and body image. Be sure to tell me first if the Studio leadership sends for you to do anything."

It dawned on me that she was referring to her husband who, I realized with a chill, had also placed a hand on my shoulder – although not quite on the same way as she just had – during my self-initiated interview. His wife's potential wrath was the reason Ouyang had changed his mind about having me "perform a song and dance number" for him. I could suddenly hear him calling me "little comrade."

Another chunk of bloody tissue fell.

I was now a woman with good looks and good body image. Indeed.

It was a time of bewilderment; it was a time of enlightenment. Within a month of Chairman Mao's death, Madame Mao and her Gang of Four in the central government were incarcerated and held responsible for the disastrous, decade-long Cultural Revolution. Deng Xiaoping, who had been condemned as the "Second Biggest Capitalist-Roader in China" before, gained supreme power. Socialist planned economy was on the wane and market economy was taking hold. Our great motherland had entered a new era of Communist optimism.

"Much of Xinjiang is pastoral desert where the likelihood of a Uighur girl falling into a river is close to nil, and the only passerby is an Army soldier?" With these words, the script of *Xinjiang Is a Wonderful Place* was criticized as "divorced from reality" and the shooting was abandoned. Secretary-General Ouyang was ousted as a Gang of Four underling who had ingratiated himself with Madame Mao. Our political instructor was removed from her post by association. The one-year-old program was also disbanded and all sixteen of us were let go. My "film starlet" career was terminated before it ever took off.

When I next saw Coach Long, he greeted me with "Welcome back, my Little *Kemaneiqi!*"

"What little *kemaneiqi?*" I asked grudgingly.

"Did you not hear about the 1976 Montreal Summer Olympics in Canada? She is the biggest international sensation now, from Romania, and she looks just like you."

In shoddy, unformed Chinese handwriting, he penned *ke*: a division; *ma*: a mare; *nei*: the inside; and *qi*: the rare. "This is how it's written." Each character had a definable meaning, yet when they were conjoined, her name made no sense to me.

Coach Long took out a clipping from a foreign newspaper placed in two pieces of celluloid candy wrapper and taped around to form a frame. I read out its caption: *Another lighter than air spectacle of 14-year-old Romanian gymnast Nadia Comaneci*, faltering only on the words *spectacle* and *gymnast*.

"You see, here is *Kemaneiqi* flying on a balance beam doing a Perfect 10 split. She looks as graceful as a white dove, just like you."

"And Nadia is the same as my mother's Russian name," I blurted out, smoothing the used candy wrapper for a better look at the subject. My admirer was right: the pony-tailed Caucasian girl's features vaguely resembled my own. "She is my age, too, and already an Olympic champion, unlike me, not athletic enough to stay on a swim team and not lucky enough to finish starring in one film."

"Don't start again, Little *Kemaneiqi*. You've got something few Chinese have, beauty and intelligence. You are so smart you can even read French."

"No, I cannot. That was English."

"But my friend from the National Team who gave me this said they spoke French in Canada, so the newspaper must be in French, too."

"Believe me it's English," I insisted. "And I've learned many words myself, so I know."

His face reddening, Coach Long moved his index finger back and forth on the candy wrapper. My attention was drawn to the tip of his closely-cut nail, then to the wrapper. "Aren't those from the mixed fruit drops sold in the Second Food Provisions Store?" I asked, surprised that he would have had anything to do with a store on Huaihai Road.

"Oh ... um, someone gave me a few, just a sample," he said, his eyes shifting. "You'd be gone for weeks without seeing me ... and you'd be so immersed in all these foreign names and artsy things to care for candy ... and candies melt, you know ..."

I glared at him and said, "Right, they can melt and so can a relationship with too artsy a *Kemaneiqi* who's been kicked out of the film studio. Are you happy now?"

To my surprise, he disregarded my sarcasm and replied instead, "Reorganization is taking place everywhere these days including our sports field, so try not to feel too bad. You're so young but already so far ahead of me ..." He stopped short as though his chain of thought had been chopped off. He grinned at me, his gleaming white teeth showing. "Let's not say hurtful things to each other, my beautiful girl", he said. "Everything will be all right for you in the future, Little *Kemaneiqi*. Trust me!" he coaxed, putting his firm hands on my shoulders before making their way down to the rest of me.

While back at school but without swim training, seeing Coach Long became logistically difficult. The next time I had planned to visit him was three weeks later, on a weekday my former team wouldn't be there. Coach Long was not at work. A female coach pointed her finger at me and shouted, "Training is in session. Don't stand around here!"

I went into the female changing room where the cleaning auntie greeted me enthusiastically, "Ah, Coach Long's former trainee girl's here for his *Xi Tang*! Come over to my supplies locker. I still have a few packets to give out on his behalf."

Xi Tang, or Happiness Sweets, were customarily handed out by newly-weds to friends and colleagues to celebrate their union.

My heart stopped. "Coach Long got married?" I asked in disbelief.

"You didn't know? He sure has met his match. He showed me her photo before going to join her in Beijing. Took the train to the capital last week. Said to give these joyous candies out for old acquaintances who may stop by here. His former teammate just retired from the National Team and got her coaching position. Here, have a packet he left with me."

I felt a weakness in the knees as I took the packet. Throat tightening, I turned without thanking her and dashed out, tears rolling down my cheeks. It all made sense now: the Wrigley's chewing gum from abroad, the detailed account of the National Team's *sashimi* feast in Japan, the Comaneci clipping from Montreal!

"Trust me, Little *Kemaneiqi*!" -- Coach Long's last words to me resounded in my ears. My tongue had suddenly gone dry. A piece of Wrigley's chewing gum would have helped to alleviate the drought, but ...

As though my hands were no longer a part of my body, I tore open the red packet embossed with the golden Double Happiness character *Xi*. Eight pieces of fruit drops in clear cellophane wrappers scattered, the same type he had used to protect the newspaper clipping! There was no note, no contact information, nothing else.

One by one, I kicked the candies into the opening of a street gutter, aiming at the middle as if shooting a soccer goal, imaging the grates to be the gate leading to the realm of *Yin* – hell -- to hell with that so-called hero who had professed to love me the great beauty with brains!

Then, I simply stood and stared, transfixed.

Moments later I could hear myself sob, right there on the sidewalk in open view of passers-by. I was gripped by the fear that I could become a teenage mother myself just like my mother and her mother before her. The dreadful family history could repeat itself. I sniffed uncontrollably until my tears were drained and eyes swollen.

On the public bus ride back, an intellectual-looking man with a fountain pen weighing down on his chest pocket said, "Pretty girl, you need eye drops to prevent infection. Some swimmers urinate in that big pool, you know."

I nodded in appreciation: *Yes, I know.* I also knew that one swimmer had pissed from a once gum-wrapped dick into the core of my heart. Then came the magical moment of sudden ecstasy: I felt a warm gush between my legs. The time of the month was here.

During the rest of the ride, I bit my lip to collect myself, thinking that I would buy some onions at the market to bring home. I could start chopping them as soon as Mother returned so she wouldn't suspect that I had been crying. I certainly didn't want her to know about me and Coach Long, especially now, after I was dumped. When I caught sight of the cucumbers in the next stall, a deliciously vengeful idea came to me. Along with two onions I bought one cucumber with the prickliest pimples and the most protruding veins.

At home, I took out my notebook, torn off the page with my menstrual records and began breaking the ghastly gourd on it until it became a mash of seedy flesh. Heading to the bathroom with the disintegrated sheet and pulp, I dumped it all in the toilet bowl and proceeded to tend to my business. Feeling cleansed and refreshed with my sanitary band on, I flushed everything down in one cathartic go: "Goodbye and good riddance!"

Returning to the notebook, I wrote:

Dear diary,

This too, like being terminated from the swim team and the Studio, shall pass. His betrayal has shown me that he is not worthy of me. Sour grapes, I realize, as I still care a great deal about him and it'll take a long time, if ever, for me to get over my first love. But I've learned a hard lesson of life and I will move on.

I shall and I must move on!

9 *Girls at Play*

Entertainment as you Westerners know it was nonexistent in the late 1970's. Watching and re-watching one of the "Eight Revolutionary Modern Model Plays" personally sanctioned by Madame Mao was the only recreational activity. Such was the environment in which the open stall wet markets – so called because the ground was regularly hosed down -- thrived as the prime locale for socializing. The correlation between *xiao caichang* (the wet market) and *xiao shimin* (the petty urbanites) was demonstrated by the modifier *xiao*, which denoted the same trivial-minded nature of the place's ambience and the traits of its residents. Here, the Shanghainese swapped gossip, gave unsolicited advice, and rendezvoused.

Three "s"s characterized a typical market: smelly, swarming, and strident. Still we had to visit it daily for want of a refrigerator. The 1930's Shanghai songstress Zhou Xuan, the "golden throated", had summed up the way foodstuffs were sold:

> *Fen che shi wo men de bao xiao ji,*
> *Tian tian zao chen sui zhe ta qi.*
> *Qian men jiao mai cai,*
> *Hou men jiao mai mi ...*

> *The carts carrying our night soils are like chickens crowing in the dawn,*
> *We get up daily as we hear them pass.*
> *The sound of hawking vegetables in our front door,*
> *The sound of hawking rice in our back door ...*

Thankfully, human manure was no longer transported in wheelbarrows although indoor plumbing was still scarce. The end of the decade welcomed a gradual ease of meat and poultry rationing. Chickens, in particular, were becoming more abundant, although our residents' taste buds were increasingly challenged by farmed rather than free-range birds.

Mother now often returned home late, having already eaten, but she never notified me beforehand so I continued my weekday shopping routine. That afternoon, when I was at a chicken stall, I heard someone humming the Zhou Xuan tune. It was Wang Hong, leaning on a bamboo pole that supported the stall, her eyebrows happily arching at me.

"Oh, hello," I said, avoiding eye contact. This being our first encounter here since I purchased that symbolic cucumber. I was afraid that she could somehow detect that I was no longer a virgin and newly unceremoniously jilted.

"Hello yourself. Still depressed over having to leave the Studio?"

"Can't say I'm happy about it but there was nothing I could've done differently – I'm ... just fine."

"Glad to hear that," she said, pushing herself away from the pole in an exaggerated motion. "Let's go play, then."

I began walking slowly. She trailed me to a vegetable stall. "What else do you need to buy? Cucumbers? Let me pick these nice fresh ones for you and help you carry them ... home?" She said in a way that was more a plea than a suggestion.

Cucumber -- Coach Long, I thought in succession. Decision on the spot: "You can stop by if you want."

Eyes in one line from grinning, she exclaimed, "Really? Let's go!"

"But maybe not for long," I retracted a bit.

"Of course not, just curious about your place, I've only seen the windows from outside the house. You've been to our dump so it's my turn, right?"

I nodded weakly, remembering the predominant piece of furniture in her "dump", the bed made up of planks mounted on benches. I wonder what Wang Hong would say when she saw my twin bed with a spring mattress, known in *pidgin* as a *ximengss*.

A few years later, when my English became more proficient, I would develop an appreciation for the brilliant transliteration of the term. Not only was the pronunciation of *ximengss* close to that of Simmons, the American brand, but also its meaning: *xi*, a piece of hay-woven mat used for covering the bed; *meng,* dream sweet dreams; and *ss*: to think of, to miss someone dear. *Ximengss* was therefore sensual, romantic, and above all, utilitarian, much like the prosaic Shanghainese ourselves. In this city's fun-filled heyday of hitting the hay, the Westernized men and women had exposed themselves to the enduring pleasure that Simmons could provide. They had heartily rolled on a *ximengss* mattress or two.

Wang Hong's reaction upon entering our flat was expected. "A whole room all to yourself? And your own *ximengss* bed. How luxurious of you!"

I pointed out that it was my mother who had a room to herself. Yes, that's her place behind the big black padlock. I slept in the all-purpose room, amidst the turtle's head cooking range, wash basin and the door-less and tub-less bathroom. "I wouldn't call this luxurious."

"But look at this – you've got a pillar like they have on the Bund in your room!" Wang Hong dashed towards the fluted column, straightened an arm to hug it and started twirling around in a pole-dancing move.

"Whee—ee--!"

Finally she stopped; hand on forehead perhaps fighting a dizzy spell. Steadying herself, she walked over to bring back a cucumber I had just bought. Moving it up and down the column's fluted groove she giggled like mad.

"What are you doing? This is silly."

"Silly silly silly – I'm a silly girl," she chanted, imitating me as she headed towards my bed. "Can I sit on your fancy *ximengss* for a minute, puh-leez? I've never been on one."

"Just don't bounce too hard. My mother will kill me if I break anything. We're not well off as you think. Besides, *ximengss* are not sold anymore nowadays and nowhere to get them fixed."

She sprang up and down on it anyway, blissful. Suddenly she sat up straight and asked solemnly, "Do you believe that one day I'll have money and I'll have everything you have?"

"That won't surprise me. I wish you luck."

"You're so sweet, Mo Mo. Come join me. A mattress is supposed to have two people on it."

Sitting next to her, I thought about Coach Long's "coffin".

"Come. Let's be a pretend couple and enjoy your soft *ximengss*," she urged,

Her arm was around my waist, sending a current of tickling excitement. I did not want to tell her what I had already experienced. Quivering, I sensed my cheeks burning to my ears, ashamed at the thought of being with another girl.

Wang Hong drew me to her bosom. Her dexterity amazed me and her caresses fanned my desire. "You'll make a good lover," I gasped.

"I know that," she chirped. "Someone showed me a handwritten passage that described how to do it and I learned everything by heart already. But how do you know?"

I cupped my hand next to her ear. "I did it with someone ... only not on a *ximengss*."

"You did? With whom?"

I pressed my palm on her mouth and said, "It's all over now."

She seized both of my hands and demanded, "Already? So what was it like?"

The floodgate of my long-suppressed emotions was unexpectedly released. I told her my infatuations with the coach and how he simply took off without a word to get married in Beijing. In tears I vowed, "I don't miss him – I won't miss him ever again. He is uneducated and unscrupulous. He's just a wolf in sheep's skin."

Uncharacteristically Wang Hong listened without interjection. Then she embraced me and said, "Forget about that sleaze ball, forget about him. You have me. Show me you pretty smile, Mo Mo ... that's right," she cooed.

I began to giggle. "Stop! I'm ticklish."

She laughed, grabbing a cucumber and wielding it at me like a sword. I used my pillow as a shield and the cucumber bounced off and fell. Picking it up and tossing it into the air like a juggler, she broke it in half and squeezed, pointing and shooting like neighborhood urchins with water guns.

Girls at play.

Later, as Wang Hong knelt down to clean up the sappy mess, I began to cook. If only we had known then that the succulent trail of fruit acid on the floor could keep our faces tender and skin soft, she and I would have been bathing in a fountain of youth.

There was no sign that Mother would be back in time for dinner. I asked Wang Hong to stay. This was the first time I made a meal for someone other than Mother and I utterly enjoyed it.

"Your cooking is out of this world, Mo Mo!"

"You haven't seen anything yet."

Deng Xiaoping's reign bought gradual changes to our nation. "Socialism with Chinese characteristics", it was called. Mother's students were beginning to practice authority-approved etudes by Western composers. By the time Wang Hong, Condiments, and I were finishing high school in the early 1980's, I began to experience a kind of popularity I would have never dreamed of in the decade before. Looking Caucasian was fashionable and my schoolmates openly envied my natural double-fold eyelid. Selected hospitals in Shanghai even began to offer plastic surgeries to create an eyelid crease to form the double eyelid.

"Mo Mo is my best friend," Wang Hong announced to anyone who would listen. "Always has been and always will."

She and I walked side by side, holding hands as same-sex friends usually did and humming American folk rock tunes like "Rocky Mountain High". John Denver had performed the song for Deng Xiaoping during Deng's U.S. visit and the Conservatory was among the few places in China which had the cassette recording of it. Wang Hong and I learned to sing it. Underground copies of The Carpenters cassette tapes also became highly prized and our favorite song was Karen Carpenter singing "Sealed with a Kiss."

With Madame Mao now serving a life sentence, her revolutionary plays had ceased to be the exclusive form of entertainment. Still, classic literature published prior to 1966 -- banned, burned, buried in sealed libraries, the glue on their spines being eaten up by rats – had yet to all resurface. The vacuum gave rise to an underground, hand-copied pulp fiction market which was flourishing at a speed like that of bamboo shoots after a spring rain. It was from one of these that Wang Hong read about the description of foreplay, she told me during the dinner I cooked for her.

The Silver-gray Tie and *A Lock of Blond Hair* were among the most sought after titles. The passion for things Western was evident in such titles featuring non-indigenous Chinese clothes or hair. The heart of a Shanghai maiden like Wang Hong was undoubtedly attracted to men with ties and women who were blonds.

A recent afternoon brought me face to face with a dog-eared copy of *A Maiden's Heart*, "the most exciting novella circulating," according to Wang Hong. For the privilege of reading it later, I had to help her hand-copy it first. "Condiments let me have it for two days only. If we go copying it in your place now and you continue to do it alone whenever you can, we'll have our own copy to keep."

"Why don't we read it first to see if it's worth copying?"

"You don't get to read it unless you copy it. Once I have a copy, I can rent it out for money, so you have to help me, Mo Mo."

I understood that it was time for me to reciprocate.

Crouching over the small stand next to the turtle's head, a.k.a. our family "dining table", Wang Hong and I started copying, stroke by stroke. I suggested that she start from the beginning while I did from about one-third down. I found a bookmark with a red silk string and a Chairman Mao quote "Study well and make progress everyday" on it and put it at the beginning of my section. Wang Hong had to copy word for word as she had not committed to memory the strokes of many Chinese characters. I would read a couple of sentences at once then wrote them down without referring back again, progressing at a much faster pace than her.

After about an hour and a half, we took a break to stretch and yawn. Apprehension hit as I checked the time. "What if my mother comes home for dinner and sees us doing this?"

Wang Hong slouched back and began to twirl the ballpoint pen on her thumb. "Just say I forced you to do it. Since I'm from the leading class, she won't criticize or tell on us. Who knows? She might be reading one of these herself. Anyway, her students are back to playing romantic pieces written by foreigners so what's the difference?"

I continued copying the following day after school and finished in time for Wang Hong to pick up in the evening. I leafed through the end product as I massaged the sore writer's bump on my middle finger, disappointed at its content. My secret diaries recording my thoughts and feelings towards the street sweeper or Coach Long seemed to surpass the depictions of the maiden's heart.

When Wang Hong came, she snatched the opus from me and waved it joyously. "What time did you finish?"

"About fifteen minutes ago. I copied like crazy and my hand hurts."

"Oh, my poor foreign baby doll." She took my hand and gave it a peck. "And guess what? At your rate, we can do this again. Condiments is friends with guys who have accesses to all sorts of things. We can copy more and rent them all out."

"Who would pay to read this stuff?"

"You'd be surprised. You know I'm good with people and very persuasive." She sank on my *ximengss* and started reading an "adolescent enlightenment poem" from the book:

> *Yi ge wan shang,*
> *Liang ren tong chuan.*
> *San geng ban ye,*
> *Si jiao chao tian.*
> *Wu zhi mo fu,*
> *Liu shi jin gong.*
> *Qi shang ba xia,*
> *Jiu jin jiu chu,*
> *Shi feng guo ying.*

> One night,
> Two persons in bed.
> Three o'clock in the morning,
> Four limbs dancing.
> Five fingers exploring,
> Six postures charging.
> Seven times up, eight times down,
> Nine ins nine outs and
> Tenfold the pleasure!

I covered my ears. "Stop, would you? It's so infantile!"

"Infantile? No. It's real adult stuff. Can you figure out what the six postures are?"

"No, and I don't want to."

"Come here," she said, scooping me over. We both landed on the mattress. "Help! I'm having a heart attack!" she screamed as my chuckles turned into laughter. The bed jerked as I heard something fall. "Stop, please!" I called out, springing over to pick up my diary book.

"What is it? You've got a hand-copy you're not telling me?"

"No, it's not a novella. It's my own thing."

"Let me see. Ai-ya, my *Guanyin* Buddha, you can write in English? My *Guanyin* Buddha ai-ya-ya! What do those wiggly words say?"

"Nothing ... just some notes to myself over the years ... and some English words and phrases I've been teaching myself." I tried to play it down, knowing full well that this notebook bore witnesses to my innermost self: musings and vagaries recorded in my unbuttoned moods; tears and fears; joys and sorrows; facts and fancies; Chinglish grammar and *pidgin*-inspired Shanghainese diction.

"How amazing, Mo Mo. You're a true genius. I have an idea now. You keep writing and save it well. When the foreigners are here you can charge them to read it. Foreigners are all very rich."

"What are you talking about?"

"Oh, I forgot to tell you. My dad says there'll be foreigners coming to teach at the Conservatory next term. He's going to have his old job back, this time driving the School van, you see – shipping them around to the airport, the specialty Friendship Store, and fake antiques markets, etc., etc."

"Really?" I asked excitedly. Mother would not tell me things like that although I was sure she knew about it already. Perhaps that was why she had been so busy at work nowadays – to prepare for the arrival of the foreigners. Imagine that the former *Yin-gou-li-chee* language would soon be popping out of the sewers and floating in the air in Shanghai! "Make sure you tell me once they are on campus. By the way, you should never mention my notebook to anyone. Promise?"

Our pinkies became entwined. "Promise!"

10 The Renaissance Shanghainese

I recognized her to be the very housewife who had a confrontation with the wet market seafood vendor over "the deadly fish that caused my old man's loose poop." Like several weeks ago, her graying hair was in plastic curlers. Now, standing in line before me for tofu, she spoke to a fellow housewife in flannel pajamas topped by a hand-knit woolen vest. "Can you believe? She paid for that bicycle coupon with her virginal ass!"

Tucking her bamboo vegetable basket tighter on her arm, the woman in PJs responded with a chuckle. "Let me tell you, Ah Zheng, whether or not she'll get to ride on the new bicycle in the end remains to be seen. He's badly in need of a bike himself, you see."

"You're so right." Ah Zheng tapped the forearm of PJs and cupped her own mouth, edging an inch closer. "A slut like that. She may end up having a job done up there instead. He'd have to take her home on the back rack, he-he." Her carrot-like finger pointed at the "Professional Veterinarian Clinic" sign in the lane, her torso swayed in my direction. Our eyes met. I averted her gaze instinctively, aware that my features had brought about recognition. She nudged PJs and they became silent.

After buying dried tofu squares I walked in the direction of the cluster of stalls selling chickens. There, a score of blood-drenched crackling birds were flipping and flapping, with some shooting into the air from the wire baskets containing their fellow doomed mates, leaving pools of blood and trails of feathers. Vendors in knee-high mackintoshes and rubber aprons were picking up the dead ones by the leg and throwing them into a vat of water for plucking as small streams of pink water run down the gutter.

What I saw next was most peculiar: a white-pelted dog with a loose leash was chasing an injured, brown-feathered rooster. This man's best friend was turning the crowded marketplace into a circus. A swarm of people had formed a circle, some on tiptoes yet none making an attempt to separate the canine from the fowl.

"There's a bloody good cock!" cheered one man in a faded blue mandarin top with white brimmed sleeves. "Peck that bitch hard! Yes! You've got nothing to lose but your little head, ha-ha!"

A younger man with a crew cut and a cigarette dangling at a corner of his mouth egged the dog on. "That's right. Bite that chicken's head off! There you go!"

Still others lingered around from a short distance to avoid being splashed with blood or showered with feathers. They craned their necks nevertheless so as not to miss the free entertainment. A woman nudged me aside and squeezed herself into the crowd before me, crushing the tofu in my plastic bag into shreds in the process. I was about to protest when I saw the plastic curlers on her head and decided to swallow my frustration with Ah Zheng.

Then, overriding all the cacophony, I heard him! For a split second it sounded like Coach Long's masculine and operatic baritone. Yet this one was a touch more burnished, almost mellifluous.

"Daisy!" the voice called out in Shanghainese-accented English, its pitch urgent, its tone terse. "Daisy!" But I knew for a fact that my onetime hero Coach Long, whom I had been painstakingly purging out of my system, spoke not a word of English.

In the instant that followed, I located the man whence the voice came. Wearing a tweed jacket with a twilled silk foulard, the tall figure with a chiseled profile was at the outer edge of the crowd, either unable or unwilling to break through. The hustle and bustle surrounding the chicken stands all but drowned out his fretful yet restrained plea. Still, he had managed to attract curious stares around the fighting ring. For one thing, smartly dressed men like this were rare in open-stall markets. The flying birds' draining blood or their last remaining load of droppings could very well soil his outfit. Furthermore, a middle-aged man with such a bearing would not ordinarily go to the market himself. An older maidservant from the pre-Cultural Revolution days would suffice. Failing that, there would be someone in his family who took care of that task.

"Daisy! Please stop! No!" the man commanded, waving an arm in the air to no avail.

The wide-eyed canine kept toying with the rooster whose head was attached to the rest of its body, ever so tenuously, by a piece of skin.

"*Hao! Hao!* Well done!" The crowd released one round of laughter after another. A few spectators whistled, a non-indigenously Chinese act often associated with hooliganism.

I edged toward Daisy's master and got a closer look at him: cleanly shaven, his sharply angled cheekbones were prominently revealed, giving him a well-heeled if weathered appearance. My heart jolted when I saw his piercing eyes: they belonged to the masked and capped street sweeper near the "Pushkin graveyard"!

Ducking through the rubbernecking crowd to the middle of the action, I surprised myself by darting towards the dog, aware that my bag of tofu had gotten caught in the crowd. In one scoop I took Daisy up and away. The poor rooster's head, coated with feathers and redder throughout than its limp crest, landed by my feet.

"Ai ya-ya!" An exclamation erupted from the crowd. More whistles. Scattered laughter. Sighs of disappointment that the carnage was over. The crowd dispersed as quickly as it had gathered, clearing the way for the man to rush towards me, his eyes bright with gratitude. "It's you! Thank you so much! I always knew you would turn out to be a remarkable girl."

"Thank *you* for the encouraging nod that time. I never forgot that. I hope that incident didn't get you in trouble for you disappeared since ..."

He waved dismissively and said, "It could have been worse. I had the feeling that we would see each other again under better circumstances and here we are, thanks to Daisy."

I handed Daisy to him. Her cold nose had been rubbing my wrist as warm air came from her nostrils. Holding the dog like a baby while ruffling its hair, he mumbled something to the effect that God had answered his prayers. He then put the chicken-fighter into a metal basket mounted in the front of his parked bicycle. I noticed the terry towel inside and envied Daisy for her movable seat. Few Shanghai residents could afford such towels for their own use let alone for a dog bassinet. Daisy immediately began gnawing on a piece of wood there that appeared to be a three-inch heel from a ladies' shoe.

With a hand on the handlebar and a foot on a pedal to steady the bicycle, he asked with smiling eyes, "What is your name?"

"Mo Mo," I answered in monotone, thinking that he might have put the two together and guessed I was Teacher Mo's daughter.

"*Mo* as in *jasmine*?"

"Exactly," I replied, amazed that he had guessed the right *Mo* out of its many homonyms.

"The name suits you."

"Thanks. By the way, I like the name Daisy and she's lucky that you treat an animal so well."

"She's getting old and I need to take care of her ... although many regard keeping a pet to be too bourgeois for our revolutionary taste."

The man's own taste was by no means revolutionary. Despite his bicycle's black paint peeling off at different places, the spokes and the bell were shiny rather than rusty, and it had a heron bird head badge. Not made in China, I concluded. There existed few Chinese models, all having the same design and a beat up look to them. I guessed that this one could be the well-cherished English brand translated as *Lailin* in Shanghainese. As all imports from the West had stopped after the 1949 Liberation, I had yet to see a *Lailin* for real, unless this was one.

From under his pressed khaki pants, his raised leg on the bicycle pedal showed his sock to be an overlapping maroon-colored diamonds on a black background, a pattern similar to the tartan skirt displayed on a Huaihai Road window. Men usually wore socks with small, bumblebee-like designs on the ankle area. His sock pattern – Argyle, I was to be told later -- his mien, his gait, his tone of voice, his polished leather shoes, indeed everything about him led me to exclaim to myself:

How FLY he is!

Pronounced *fee* for "figure" in *pidgin*, the concept of being *fly* was singularly Shanghainese. It first came into our locution after the Second World War, when the victorious American GIs brought with them Coca-Cola, KLIM (the reversed spelling of "milk," as Condiments' dad told me once in passing) milk powder, popcorn, donuts, and indeed chewing gum. *Fly* carries the broad meaning of being classy and knowing. A *fly* man is an enviable character with superb taste.

"Can I call you Uncle Fly?" I asked spontaneously.

Visibly flattered, he replied with a quick grin, "If that's what you want to call me, by all means. Now, get on my bicycle and we'll drop Daisy off. Then I'll take you to dinner to thank you."

Not wanting to appear effusive, I played coy by changing the subject. "You have a very nice bicycle."

"Thanks. I have no pull in securing coupons for a new one. Luckily this old tank still rolls well. It's an English make, Raleigh."

"*Lailin*?"

"Exactly, now come up and try to keep your balance."

Daisy let out a bark as though in agreement.

With a little hesitation, I eased onto the Raleigh and was greeted by a faint musky scent. It hit me that I had not sat on a bicycle since Coach Long deserted me. Taking a deep breath, I snapped out of the thought of him and exclaimed to myself: pet-lover, cologne-wearer, and *Lailin*-owner – what a fly Uncle Fly!

Uncle Fly's home, a quaint gardened house, was a short ride away from my own, in the former International Settlement. I would later joke with him that I knew which one his house was the moment I saw its wire-fenced front yard as it was in a similar state of neglect as the "Pushkin graveyard". Scraggy patches of grass intermingled with weeds. Little shrubbery was left except for a banyan tree of parched bark and listless leaves. Bamboo poles loaded with the washings crisscrossed over a barren parcel, with blouses and underwear in light colors and jackets and slacks in navy or black.

Carrying Daisy out of the metal basket, Uncle Fly dusted off a few of her hairs and pressed one of the three doorbells. Three mailboxes with different surnames written on each crowded the door frame.

While the white house where Mother and I lived came across as French, his had English-style gables and red roof tiles. Unattended ivies adorned the outside walls like interweaving cobwebs. A branch hanging down scratched me, prompting this rhetorical comment from him: "They're just naturally fecund so they keep growing -- kind of like our population despite the 'one child policy', isn't it?"

Wanting to avoid the topic of birth, I rubbed my face with the back of my hand and said, "It doesn't matter," referring to the cut.

"Here." He took out a man's handkerchief, starched and folded into a square.

"This is so nice I'm afraid I'll soil it,"

"Don't be silly. That's what it's for – to be used. At least it's cleaner than your fine little paw."

A tingling sensation passed through me as he blotted my forehead. "Thank you," I said, feeling my cheeks warming up.

"Don't mention it. Ah Fang should be down momentarily."

"Is she your maidservant?"

"I'd stopped using that term long ago. My parents initially hired her as my wet nurse so she's like family. Since the Cultural Revolution we only had the top two floors. The first floor had been confiscated and allocated to two working-class families."

Just like the house Wang Hong lived in except he was the original bourgeois owner here, I thought.

"So exactly how many years has she been with you?"

"I'm not falling for that one," he said, laughing and steering clear of the bait.

I laughed, too.

Just then, a woman whose graying hair was in a neat bun held by a lacquer pin opened the door. She gave me a polite glance and took Daisy. "She got the shots?"

"Yes, she tolerated them well, but acted up later and got in a fight with a rooster. If it were not for this girl here leaping into the fray to save her, she'd be in trouble. We're going out to eat so no dinner tonight, Sis Fang. Thanks."

Ah Fang looked at me with squinting eyes and said, "Thank you, pretty girl."

Pushing the bicycle as I walked by his side, Uncle Fly asked, "Is Maison Rouge alright with you?"

Barely able to contain my excitement I replied, "Of course, thank you. I haven't been there yet, but I've heard that their borscht is really authentic."

With a faint smile Uncle Fly shook his head. "Nothing is authentic these days, I'm afraid. But borscht it is for your appetizer then."

I knew the exact location of Maison Rouge, formerly Chez Louis on Avenue du Roi Albert. Wang Hong and I had walked past it several times, peeking into its interior through the filmy white curtains. In the 1970's it was practically the only Shanghai restaurant serving Western food. Even Premier Zhou Enlai, who had been a young revolutionary in France, reportedly liked its food.

He motioned that I sit on the back of the bicycle and got on it himself. Minutes later we were at the restaurant. "This bicycle is so steady to sit on," I said, dismounting.

"Glad you found it so. Truth be told, a bicycle is nothing to take a girl on. If only my Harley still ran ... it's been sitting in the corridor ever since the import ban on parts."

"Your Harley?"

"That's an American motorcycle, the most coveted toy for Shanghai's big boys after the Second World War. They became available in China after FDR signed the Lend-Lease Bill. My late father got me one 'on reserve' as I was just a boy then."

Reminded of the half-piece Made-in-America gum I received for my turning thirteen and the vanished Coach Long, I nodded in silence.

The maître d' greeted Uncle Fly familiarly and led us to a table at the wainscoted French window. Just as I was puzzled by the many plates, forks, and knives in front of me, Uncle Fly praised me. "You're so well-composed, Mo Mo. Get anything you want. It's a 'Thank You' meal."

"I never expected this," I said, holding up the menu but not knowing what to order.

Uncle Fly sat back and folded his arms. "Borscht to start. You want me to pick a main for you?"

"Yes, please. Thanks."

He smiled and ordered the Grilled Steak with Mustard for me and Baked Clam comme à la maison for himself. Desserts were Baked Alaska "For the young lady" and the Soufflé Grand Marnier and "café noir" for himself.

I sat straight with clasped hands on my lap, savoring the gladness of being called a young lady and looking forward to finding out what "café noir" was.

Leaning a bit closer, Uncle Fly asked, "Your parents work at the Conservatoire?"

"My mother does ... she teaches piano."

A twitch passed his face. He took my fingers into his hand. "Let me see."

"I don't play," I murmured, withdrawing my hand.

"That's fine, Mo Mo, neither do I. What about ... "

Assuming he would ask about my father, I didn't let him finish. "My father ... is dead."

Briefly, he held my hand again. "I'm so sorry."

His tenderness melted me.

"I never met him ... but ..."

"You don't have to tell me anything if you ..."

I looked up from the two concentric plates before me and blurted out, "But I want to tell you. My mother ... she's half White Russian and I got my looks from her."

"I see," he said, nodding knowingly. "That's why you like borscht?"

"Yes. We make it at home."

"Do you have a Christian name, Mo Mo?"

"No, but my last name is the Chinese translation for Molotov, my maternal grandfather's name."

He cocked his head and asked, "So Miss Molotova, are you by any chance related to Comrade Molotov?"

"Who's that?"

Uncle Fly chuckled. "I forgot they don't teach you kids about the glories of the Bolshevik Revolution any more. Vyacheslav Molotov was the spokesman for the Soviet Union during and after the Second World War and believe it or not, the only man alive who has shaken hands with Winston Churchill, Adolf Hitler, Franklin Roosevelt and our very own Chairman Mao. The Molotov cocktail -- inflammable liquid in a bottle hurled at a target after being ignited -- was named after him."

"Never heard of such a thing, either."

"You have now. As a matter of fact, you remind me of one – a Molotov cocktail-strength Shanghai fireball."

It took me a moment to figure out what he was saying. Never before had I encountered a person like him, humorous, temperate, and cultured -- an embodiment of sophistication itself. I gazed at Uncle Fly, mesmerized.

"Can I see you again after this meal? I mean, in the future?"

"What do you think?" he asked for a reply.

Heartily we laughed.

As I approached Uncle Fly's house, I had a sudden appreciation of Wang Hong's frame of mind when she came to our home for the first time. Anticipation and apprehension combined made me feel like there was a bunny hopping inside my chest. I pressed the buzzer and waited for Ah Fang but it was Uncle Fly himself who came down, his long sleeved black polo shirt tucked into beige, cuffed trousers.

"Good afternoon," he greeted me with a smile. "Come with me to the pavilion room."

Typically located on the top floor of a Western-style house, the pavilion room was so named because of its gabled shape. Beams of afternoon sunlight via the Venetian window flooded one-third of this room, which was refracted to the rest of the space by the wax-polished teak floor. A vintage ceiling fan was circulating the odor from a citronella mosquito-repelling coil. Tucked under the tapering roof on one side of the room was a tan leather wing chair with a tall back, corded upholstery seams, and nail heads. A rosewood desk with brass-handled drawers was a couple of feet away. On the other side of the room I saw something familiar: a single gas range turtle's head. On it was a cylindrical aluminum pot with a spout and a clear glass top. I made a mental note of its unusual shape.

"Would you like join me for coffee?"

"Y-yes. Thank you. Do you use that kettle?"

A quick smile swept across his face. "It's a percolator. Come, I'll show you how it brews."

I watched him add the grinds to the filter basket inside and pour hot water from a thermos. "I'm afraid we don't have milk or sugar for you," he said, remembering.

"I don't need them. The 'café noir' you had at the restaurant didn't have them."

"You're an observant girl, aren't you? So you prefer black. Won't be too bitter?"

"A-actually, I have never had coffee yet, but if it's not bitter to you, it shouldn't to me."

"We'll make sure nothing is bitter for this sweet girl, then."

A smooth aroma accompanied by the rhythmic popping sound permeated the space. It occurred to me that this atmosphere could be a close approximation to the opium-wafting environment Uncle Fly's ancestors had lived in.

"The smell is intoxicating."

"That's because the beans were ground this morning. Ah Fang got them at the Second Food Provisions Store. Their Yunnan coffee is quite drinkable."

I nodded appreciatively. Moments later, as I poured coffee into two cups, I felt him studying me as if he were a casting director auditioning me for a specific role. I held my breath, brought the coffee to the teapoy, and sat down across from him, my back straight. As I took my first sips of coffee with a lifted pinky, he asked, "Does this all come naturally to you, your bearing and fine manners?"

"Oh … not really," I replied casually, thanking in my heart the Film Studio training. It was a personal quality of mine he was admiring, not just the way I looked. An urge to tell him about myself rushed forward. "It's so kind of you to say such nice things about me. Actually I've had some un … eh … unusual experiences and not all of them are pleasant ones."

He put down his cup and leaned a bit closer. "Would you like to tell me about them?"

I placed my cup next to his, making sure that only its handle and not its rim touched his. Swallowing a deep sigh, I gave Uncle Fly the condensed version of my life: Hong Kong-born, Shanghai-bred quarter-blood with disparaging nicknames; fatherless, mother careless; swim team éliminée; film school dropout (hence my posture he admired). But I left out Coach Long, Ouyang, and Wang Hong. "I feel that people judge me based on the way I look and not who I am, but I can't change my appearance, can I?" I concluded, surprised by my straightforwardness.

Uncle Fly listened intently. "Do you remember anything from Hong Kong?" he asked afterwards.

"Only vaguely. My mother had banned me from mentioning Hong Kong until after the downfall of the Gang of Four. I remember the Shanghainese ah bu who took care of me. She was the kindest person I'd ever met."

"I spent some time in Hong Kong when I was young, too."

"Really? Do tell me about it. In fact, tell me about your life, please. I've told you mine."

"You're the most intriguing young woman who has showed an interest in me for a long time. Hope I don't bore you."

When he was born in a British Concession hospital, Uncle Fly's merchant's family was already at a late stage of its "Chekhovian decline". His father, the family's "young master" was based in Hong Kong for business and decided to send for the wife and son as soon as the baby was weaned from the wet nurse. But Ah Fang did not follow them to Hong Kong because she knew no Cantonese.

They were put on board the HMS Princess Elizabeth accompanied by a butler who was Cantonese. The family took up

residence at The Peninsula Hotel and he went to a preschool in
Kowloon Tong where Scottish woolen knickers and English leather
shoes were part of the uniform. He recalled swimming and water gun
battles with the butler at the Repulse Bay and Tsing Yi Tam Shan
beaches and riding on the funicular railway to the Victoria Peak. The
day after Christmas, 1941, Hong Kong fell to the Japanese who
promptly turned The Pen into their headquarters, renaming it The
Toa Hotel.

Repatriating to Shanghai, he began kindergarten at St. Francis-
Xavier for Boys and later graduated secondary school from there as
well, enrolling at St. John's University, the "Harvard of Shanghai" at
sixteen. In 1952, his senior year, St. John's was permanently shut
down by the new Communist regime since the school, founded in
1879 by the Anglican Bishop of Shanghai, by definition "represented
an enemy of the Chinese people."

"Not until then did I regret having skipped classes in pursuit of
the more leisurely things in life."

"Such as?"

"Such as spending too much time listening to the wireless on
600KHz AM, the U.S. Armed Forces Radio, swirling on dance floors
to the music of Benny Goodman and Artie Shaw, or sauntering over to
Café Renaissance on rue Père Robert to read a Western book while
nursing an espresso. Uniformed McTyeire School girls would often
see me there and one of them, Helen, playfully dubbed me 'The
Renaissance Shanghainese' and the name stuck."

"That's a great nickname."

"Well, not during the Cultural Revolution when I was yelled at
by the head of the Neighbourhood Revolutionary Committee, 'What
Renaissance Shanghainese? The knowledge you have is nothing but
feudal, bourgeois, and revisionist!' I was classified as an 'unemployed
social youth' then so the Committee was my political authority."

"You were lucky they didn't classify you as a dandy *flâneur*."

"I suppose I was a well-read idle man-about-town, someone
they couldn't condone. They assigned me to sweep the streets to
'reform through labor' and that's when …"

"… I first saw you looking so awkward wielding a broom! But
seriously, what happened after the incident? Did that classmate of
mine report on you?"

Uncle Fly smiled faintly. "He did, but it wasn't that bad. The Committee decided to punish me by sending me off to a camp in the outskirts for 're-educating bourgeois intellectuals'. There, I became an apprentice to paddy field peasants. Believe it or not, I even acted as dance instructor for the production team's *LOYALTY*-Character Dance."

"That experience of being sent down to the countryside did you little good, it seems or you wouldn't have been so hesitant to retrieve Daisy from her fight with that rooster."

He gave me an embarrassed look but quipped, "Then my prayer that I would see you again wouldn't have been answered so soon. And honestly, I found it impossible to push my way through the crowd – it would be so impolite. Anyway, the camp experience was something out of the Arabian Nights for me, choreographing and leading female peasants wearing red arm bands and holding 'Loyalty to Chairman Mao' placards, scurrying around on a makeshift stage on the rice field."

"That's so sadly funny, I have to say. Reminds me of the type of dance I had to learn while preparing to shoot *Xinjiang Is a Wonderful Place*."

Uncle Fly rose and walked towards a recess of the room. A creaking sound echoed as his leather soles touched the loosening teak floor. He opened the door to a walk-in closet and switched on the light. I saw a floor-to-ceiling bookshelf next to a space where half a dozen *qipao* dresses hung. Underneath were ladies pumps: pointy toes, high heels, black, white, cream, and patent. He took out what appeared to be a small suitcase and a stack of square cardboards and placed them on the desk. He then removed a red ribbon from a rolled up sheet of paper and smoothed it. "Look."

It was a September 1973 concert program of the Philadelphia Symphony Orchestra, the first American ensemble ever to visit the People's Republic of China, with the great, septuagenarian Eugene Ormandy conducting.

"*Aomandi!*" I cried out as I saw the Chinese characters for Ormandy. "You went to see Maestro *Aomandi*?"

"Sh-uuu ...." Index finger on his lips. "Keep your voice down."

I apologized with a grimace. "Sorry I was so excited."

"Now there's a sweet little imp I can't bear to scold."

"Were you at his concert?"

"Yes, I was very lucky to get a ticket. I knew you might appreciate this. Not many in your age group will recognize his name or know of the Orchestra."

"Unless one's mother happened to have seen the Maestro in person giving rehearsals of Beethoven's Fifth Symphony - Fate! But of course that was three years before the Gang of Four was smashed, so direct communication with him was strictly prohibited."

"Yes," he agreed, wearing a thousand-yard stare, lost in memories. "I was moved to tears at the concert and later joined like-minded people who followed his motorcade up Huaihai Road, like a pilgrimage -- and I'm saying this as a Christian who could only worship in my heart. I had never done anything like this before -- it was an awesome experience."

"I'm sure it was. Thankfully you can now say you are a Christian, at least in private. My Nga Bu came from a devout Christian family in the former concessions."

"Did she? Shanghai certainly had her share of Christians in the concessions. In fact the friend who gave me the ticket works at the Conservatoire and he is a fellow Christian. He was at the rehearsals, too."

"*Da-Da-Da-DUH! Deh-Deh-Deh-DI!*" I sang the short-short-short-long opening motif of Beethoven's Fifth. "*Thus Fate knocks at the door!*"

"I used to have the Fifth, but it's all gone. Come." He opened the hard-shelled box to reveal a gramophone, and the stack of cardboards was vinyl album LPs -- 78s and 45s. He placed one record on the turntable. The yellowed sleeve featured a puppy looking into a large conical horn next to a Caucasian man. Running his finger across the words *RCA Victor Company, SHANGHAI*, he explained, "Here's a Nelson Eddy from the 1930's RCA released exclusively for the Chinese market."

"Cute dog."

"That's Nipper, RCA's trademark fox terrier. I grew up listening to many of the records from *His Master's Voice* label ... unfortunately, the Red Guards later smashed most of them."

Music, the kind I had never heard before, rose as he put the needle on the record, disseminating in this sun-drenched space. "I don't suppose they taught you any ballroom steps along with the Uighur ingénue's Xinjiang dance?"

"No, that would've been condemned as being too decadent, but I'm sure I can follow if you lead."

He drew me close and began to glide, our steps getting longer as we twirled. "You're a natural," he complimented, "You float."

Optical illusions generated by dust particles in the air made me feel like being in a mirage; a simultaneous sensation of familiarity and strangeness filled my heart as I was cradled and swirled in his arms, in sync with the turntable as it reached this 1930 Gershwin song:

> *Embrace me,*
> *My sweet embraceable you.*
> *Embrace me,*
> *You irreplaceable you.*
> *Just one look at you,*
> *My heart grew tipsy in me.*
> *You and you alone bring out the gypsy in me.*
> *I love all -- the many charms about you.*
> *Above all -- I want my arms about you.*

> ......

> *My sweet embraceable you!*

As the intermittently scratchy music died down, dusk had befallen outside. Uncle Fly pushed open two facing windows, letting in an aura of serenity.

"Enough of a taste of the West for today, young lady."

Daisy whined outside and rushed up to Uncle Fly as soon as he opened the door. She sniffed my ankles with her cold nose before being picked up by her master. "Let's go down together," he said to me. "It's time for her walk."

11 A Revolutionary Étude

It was a heady time for all. With the Communist Bamboo Curtain removed, the West rediscovered the Great Walled China. "Yellow fever" had hit. Still more Chinese caught the "going abroad fever". Not a few tried by hook or by crook to leave.

Wang Hong told me that a young man with long blond hair had arrived in the Keyboard Department. The following events happened at this juncture in my life but I would not become aware of the details until sometime later.

"Teacher Mo Na-di, the Conservatory leadership assigns you the important task of working with an American musician," said Secretary-General Zhao who, after years as personal assistant to former Studio head Ouyang, now sat at his old boss's mahogany desk. Zhao had cooperated exemplarily with investigators looking into Ouyang's alleged affiliation with the condemned Madame Mao.

"I'm honored, Secretary-General Zhao. Please rest assured that I'll try my best to fulfill this glorious task," Mother replied, the gaze from her large eyes penetrating Zhao's glass lenses soiled from sweat and dust. Substituting a missing nose pad on his clear plastic frame was an adhesive tape rolled into a cushion, its color now charcoal gray. Zhao's eyes distorted by lenses as thick as the bottom of Tsingtao beer bottles beamed at her.

"Very good. You know I could've chosen other suitable teachers but I trust that you'll do a good job."

"Thank you for your personal trust, Secretary-General. You know I'll fulfill this assignment beyond your expectation."

"Let me show you his profile here." With his nicotine-stained index finger underlining the top of a form, Zhao tapped the following emphatically: <u>Name</u>: *Mick Popov*. <u>Name formerly used or Alias (if applicable)</u>: *Михаил Попов (Mikhail Popov)*. "Take note. This man was born in the Soviet Union but is now an American, so his background is both U.S. imperialist and Soviet revisionist. In your role as his piano accompanist, you have to be extra vigilant in your daily observation of his behavior -- this, in addition to learning from his professional musical skills to benefit our students and eventually our revolutionary arts-loving masses."

"Yes, I understand. And I'll report anything suspicious to you," promised Mother while her eyes were fixated on the photo on the form. Aquiline nose, bedroom eyes, pale face, thin lips, and shoulder-length mane. This was the young Russian-American soon to be her co-teacher in the violin honors class at the Affiliated Middle School.

Born in 1952 in the Soviet republic of Ukraine, Mikhail Popov had a golden childhood. Around the collar of his white shirt he wore a red kerchief which symbolized a corner of the Hammer & Sickle flag dyed crimson with revolutionary martyrs' blood. He and his fellow Communist Young Pioneers would stand ramrod straight while delivering this daily salute: "For the struggle of the cause of the Communist Party, we are prepared at all times!"

For his class assignment "What I Want to be When I Grow Up" young Mikhail drew astronaut Yuri Gagarin and wrote "My hero" underneath. Nobody would dare to tell him about Rudolf Nureyev, the great ballet dancer who had defected to the West shortly after Major Gagarin's *Volstok 1* reached outer space. Later in life, Mick would reflect on the irony of his childhood hero worship and his own decision to defect.

Brought up in Kiev in an upscale apartment by Stalin-era standards, Mikhail and his sister Olga spent summers out in the country, practicing the violin and cello respectively in a *dacha* allocated to their father. Comrade Professor Popov had been a university music historian in the Republic's capital until a call of duty brought him to Moscow in the late 1950s. The siblings would forever remember their welcome present: attending a concert by the cellist Mstislav Rostropovich, winner of the Stalin Prize. Greatly inspired, they vowed to become "revolutionary music prodigies" and resumed their training with some of the USSR's best tutors.

The young musicians' fate changed for the better yet again in 1969 when their father was appointed cultural attaché to the Soviet Embassy in Warsaw. It was there, in the more liberal Poland, that Mikhail listened to the jammed shortwave broadcast of the U.S. Armed Forces Radio relayed from its military base in West Germany. As he would later tell his attractive Chinese colleague Teacher Mo, he had heard The Rolling Stones for the first time. Something within him stirred. Before long, Mikhail was calling himself Mick, after Jagger.

His transistor usually sounded like somebody pointing a hairdryer into a microphone while talking. However, Mick was a captivated listener and his antenna-ed device became as endearing to him as his instrument. His heart jumped like a bow hitting all four strings on one day in 1970 when he made out from the static the name of a compatriot: *Alexandr Solzhenitsyn*. The Swedish Academy had awarded a Nobel Prize to the dissident author. As inexplicable as it appeared even to himself, Mick secured an English phrase book in immediate response to hearing the news. He hid it inside his violin case in the middle of the music scorebooks and began to memorize words and phrases with the same enthusiasm he reserved for learning numerous etudes by heart.

On one gray Warsaw winter morning, Mick was sitting outside his father's office when he overheard a conversation about a Volga being dispatched to the U.S. Embassy in fifteen minutes. A surge of excitement ran through him as he experienced a moment of epiphany. The choice of his life was made on the spot: he would crawl into the trunk of that sedan and sneak into the U.S. territory in Warsaw. There was no time to fetch his violin, no time even to say "*Dasvedania*" to his father.

Not having any I.D. on him, Mick breathed out "My name eez Meek Popov." to the American who saw the trunk popping up. Realizing that "Meek" wanted to seek political asylum, the American whisked him into the building proper, where the youth gesticulated that a violin was needed to present his case. A junior's version of the apparatus borrowed from the daughter of the U.S. cultural attaché was brought in. The diplomat knew of his Soviet counterpart from cocktail functions but the two had rarely communicated during those Cold War days.

Mick Popov played Prokofiev's *Violin Concerto No. 1 in D Major* from memory. The instrument's limitations notwithstanding, his performance all but put the Embassy staff into a trance. One blurted out: "This kid could one day make it to Carnegie Hall!"

As the Americans applauded and cheered, Mick felt tears rolling down his cheeks. He could not speak. He would not speak. With the bow sticking out in the middle of the air, he took the longest and deepest bow of his life, holding back emotions, insisting, persuading, pleading, and waiting for the sentence of his life to be pronounced.

After a moment of eerie buzzing and phone calls with subdued "O.K.", "Fine." and "That's it.", Popov's wish was granted. A short while later, as the daughter looked on, the U.S. cultural attaché presented him with that junior's violin. "How I wish you could stay in Warsaw and be my violin teacher," the girl said, shaking his hand. "But I'm sure you'd rather go to America right away."

"*Da! Da!* Yy-es! I go New York!"

"Work hard there and make good use of the violin," a career visa-stamping officer urged. Other embassy staff had their host country-trained housemaids cum petty spies raid their drawers for some clothes for the teenager. Mick wore a pair of denim bell-bottom trousers the day he boarded a plane to New York, carrying nothing else but the violin.

Popov Sr. was recalled by Moscow, expelled from the Party and stripped of his "Comrade" and "Professor" prefixes. The three remaining Popovs were sent packing back to Kiev where Olga was debarred from the Communist Youth League and declared unfit for the cello. Although regarded as "an enemy of the people," Popov Sr. considered himself lucky that Secretary-General Brezhnev had spared him the fate of being exiled to a Siberian gulag on a cattle wagon wearing a soiled, sable trapper's hat inherited from some deceased prisoner.

In time, Mick Popov graduated from The Julliard School although he did not quite make it to Carnegie Hall. It was again the music of the Stones that gave him perspective:

> *And you can't always get what you want,*
> *Honey, you can't always get what you want*
> *You can't always get what you want*
> *But if you try sometime, yeah,*
> *You just might find you get what you need!*

Mick found what he needed in becoming "the Russian sub" – not a submarine but a substitute teacher at the Special Music School of America across from Lincoln Center, where musically-talented New York kids received a free education. This was the least he could do to repay the girl who had given him her violin. One young talent was an immigrant from Shanghai. "Did you happen to catch *From Mao to Mozart* on the PBS the other night?" she had asked her teacher one day.

"No. Was it any good?"

"It sure was. I'll loan you the tape my parents recorded. My parents told me that Shanghai used to have lots of Russians like you."

The fascinating Asian city and her music scene portrayed in the 1979 film greatly impressed Mick. After *From Mao To Mozart: Isaac Stern in China* won the 1981 Academy Award for Best Documentary, Mick became interested in the history of the White Russians' contributions to the Conservatory in the 1920s and the 1930s. He began sending out his CV for teaching opportunities in Shanghai. By August 1983, he was in the Affiliated Middle School on a 12-month work visa under the category of *Foreign Expert*.

Mick Popov was instantly smitten with his co-teacher who looked not a day over thirty and oh, so Chinese in the most complimentary sense. Knowing little English or Russian did not stop Mother from writing down everything Popov said in Chinese phonetics for later self-study. Wanting a common language should present no barrier, Expert Popov explained to Teacher Mo. *We share the same universal language of music.* He gesticulated this by mimicking the movements of a violinist and a pianist.

"Nadia!" Mother announced, her shapely index finger resting in between her cleavage, visible from her pink silk blouse. Not too long ago, this part of her anatomy would have been concealed under an army green tunic buttoned up to the throat.

"Nadia?" Mick repeated mechanically, his eyebrows arching.

Her finger flew away from her bosom to dance in front of his straight nose, fleetingly touching it like a dragonfly skimming through the surface of a pond. "You, Mee-ker, I, Nadia. You Papa *Luosong*! I Papa *Luosong*!"

"*Luosong*?" he repeated, gaping at her lips. "Do you mean that our fathers are both *Luosong*? You mean ... ah, do you mean Russian?!"

"Yes! Yes! I Papa *Luosong*. I Mama Shanghai. I haafu *Luosong*!"

Mick would never have dreamed of meeting a half kin in China, but he did and in what flesh and blood! Soon, Teacher Mo was his "Nadia, my dear" who played Liszt's *Dream of Love No. 3* and Chopin's *The Revolutionary Étude* just for him. Her dexterous fingers were in heated competition with his. Her expert hands – sensual, skilled, and strong – matched the equally well-trained pair of the foreign expert's own. Their fingers competed on piano keys and on violin strings, and off; they played with each other, unlocking and locking themselves tight, bringing their own music to crescendo after crescendo.

No other language was needed.

Mick knew the power of such non-verbal communication well. At the makeshift chamber music hall of the U.S. Embassy in Warsaw a decade earlier, he succeeded by playing a solo violin concerto, with not a word spoken. He just let his limbs and semi-closed eyes do the talking, his desire for freedom manifested through notes floating in the air.

Few could appreciate the efficacy of the School's Piano Building as much as Mother and Mick did. Rooms were situated row after row and stacked up on each floor, their size no larger than a king bed, the furniture nothing more than an upright piano, its seat which doubled as storage for scores, and a stand for solfeggio. The carpeting first laid by the White Russians may not have been cleaned in decades, yet it provided a cushion for the sinking floor. Once the bilingual *"Private Lesson in Progress. Do Not Disturb."* sign was up and the door locked from within, few tended to seek them out. Chances are, whatever music or love being made inside would be drowned out by the reprimands and interrupted etudes from adjoining rooms.

At the end of one passionate session, his still trembling hands helped her fasten her bra hooks from behind. Nadia, both hands free, pointed to the ears on the Beethoven bust sitting atop the piano and giggled like a bell. Another rush of excitement hit him and her brassier was unbuckled again.

"Yes," he agreed. "Beethoven's deaf." He hugged her from the back, polar bear-style. Mother and Mick resumed their intercepted composition under the watchful eyes of the hearing- but not sight-impaired Maestro, entering into and exiting from *largo, presto* or *allegro*, until it reached its final movement. Now one limp egg roll against a wall, they were oblivious that the metronome Nadia had set in the beginning was still ticking.

The tempo must go on.

In her broken English, Mother told Mick: "Your idol Yehudi Menuhin. My idol Van Cliburn. I dream U.S.A. from one-nine-five-eight. That year U.S.A. piano man win top prize in Moscow.

Tchaikovsky Competition. I give myself eight year to one-nine-six-six. I want go Moscow, make Mo Na-di name next Van Cliburn. But you know what happen China one-nine-six-six -- Cultural Revolution. Moscow dream to *Yin* world. My hope, my music all die! I not allow touch piano. They not trust I only *haafoo* Chinese. Now, you come inside me, inside my dream grow. I want live U.S.A. all people white like you. Oh, Mee-ker, my dear Mee-ker, take me, go U.S.A.!"

Caressing her head on his chest, he kissed her smoky brown hair. Mick understood Nadia's psychology. Shanghai to Nadia today was like Warsaw had been to him in his late teens. She must long to breathe the free air in the West. Yet she was naïve to assume that he couldn't see that she saw him nothing more than a ticket to the U.S., and unbeknownst to her, he wasn't leaving Asia anytime soon now that he had experienced this most fascinating part of the world.

"Nadia, my dear, in the West it's very hard to make a living as a musician, and race has little to do with it. In fact there're quite a few successful Asian-American classical musicians. The thing is that just about any form of support for the artistic community is difficult to come by."

"I know I know, I no want your support! I support me all my life! All self! I teach piano to Chinese childs. No need *Yin-gou-li-chee* (belonging to the sewers) in Flushing."

"Flushing in Queens?" he asked, surprised that she had heard of that New York City borough.

"Yes, Flushing like toilet. Many big moneys Taiwan peoples love to Flushing! I read Chinese article in school library."

Mother had done her research to map out her future. A magazine article had stated that many affluent new immigrants had populated the place, set up oriental grocery stores and weekend Mandarin schools. The nouveau riche's demand for quality Chinese-language instruction in ballet, piano, violin, or Western painting far exceeded the supply.

"'Flushing like toilet' – you are hilarious! And seriously, I can't be more impressed by your spirit of independence, but ..." Mick stopped short as if trying to swallow a well-contemplated thought, his neck turning scarlet.

Without speaking, Mother sat on the piano bench and swung her thin legs over to its other side. She reached to pull Mick over, pushing him down to the carpet at the same time. She let his head rest on her upper thighs, on top of her gray, ankle-length polyester pencil skirt; she ran her hands over his soft, flowing hair. She thought of her father, Kirill Molotov and the texture of the type of hair he must have dealt with at the Figaro Coiffure.

Tick tock. Tick tock. The metronome beat on.

Mother waited for him to continue; she waited the way he had waited in the Warsaw U.S. Embassy years earlier. She waited for the question that could change her life again – this time for the better:

"Will you marry me, Nadia Na-di Molotova?"

To which she would reply *Yes!* and *Da!*

Beethoven wouldn't hear this, but his knotted brows and intense gazes would have been there to bear witness to a holy moment orchestrated by Mother and matched to the very last bar of a romantic serenade.

But this was not to be. Mick Popov rose from the floor and combed his hair back with his fingers. "Let us focus first on making the concert a success, my dear."

"You say no go U.S.A., Mee-ker?"

"I'm saying nothing of the sort. Our priority at the moment is to ensure the success of the concert, don't you agree?"

"I do, Mee-ker, I do."

"Very well then. So long."

Mother would sit on the bench for a few more minutes, motionless. Have I misread him the whole time, she asked herself, or do I still have a chance? Either way, she would have to find out after the concert, and that was what she should go all out for right now. She had promised Secretary-General Zhao, and Mick, this much.

She closed the door to this piano room and went into another one on the ground floor. This used to be exclusively hers, twenty years ago, assigned to her by the School as a special reward for being its top student. It was there, not long before she got her spot on the delegation to perform in Hong Kong, that she had been deflowered. She sat down and played from memory *The Revolutionary Étude* that she had been practicing when her visitor interrupted the session.

She then went to the top floor corner room that once served as a temporary prison cell for the disgraced Municipal Cultural Bureau Chief Chen, and said Good-bye to all that.

I didn't remember ever seeing Mother in a floral dress but there she was, looking pretty and radiant. "This is the Russian platye I wore on stage in Hong Kong and it still fits perfectly."

"Hong Kong!" I repeated, completely missing her point.

"You see, Secretary-General Zhao has put me in charge of the American expert Mick Popov's farewell performance of the violin concerto *The Butterfly Lovers*, so I need to look my best."

"A concerto adapted from that legend about Liang Shanbo and Zhu Yingtai? What's the plot again?"

"Yes. It was composed in 1959 by two of my alums but has only recently been released from censorship. Liang was the male protagonist and Zhu was the daughter of a wealthy family sent to school disguised as a boy, as girls were not allowed to be educated during the Jin Dynasty."

"That was the third to fifth century, right?"

"Approximately, yes, anyway, Zhu secretly fell in love with her schoolmate Liang but was summoned home to marry another man. Realizing Zhu was female, Liang eventually died from lovesickness. Broken-hearted, Zhu ran away to mourn at Liang's grave which opened at the flashes of lightening whereupon she threw herself into it before it closed back shut. Liang and Zhu had since been turned into butterflies, flying happily ever after."

"How romantic!"

"Yes, but remember it's merely a fairytale. Here's something to keep in mind if you care: don't be blinded by the so-called 'Love conquers all' theory. In life, there is only pragmatism and self-interest."

Given that she rarely gave me advice, Mother's words struck me as reflective of her own state of mind at the moment. "Thanks for that. But I'm still interested in the concert. Do you have a pair of complimentary tickets that I can have?"

"So that you can come with the Renaissance Shanghainese?"

"How do you know I was going to …?"

She glanced at me. "Ours is a small but meddlesome community. I suppose I can get you the tickets. Come to think of it, you've never seen me in action, putting together a major event like this, have you?"

"No, I haven't. Nor have I met the American expert violinist. Can you introduce us to him in the green room afterwards?"

"I gave you an inch and you'd take a mile. He doesn't even know you exist."

"If I meet him, he will. He'll be the first American I ever meet and I can try a little English I've learned with him. Come on, Mother."

She considered and said, "Fine, then. But just come by yourself, and be brief and sensible."

"Thanks so much, Mother." Taking a deep breath, I asked, "By the way, do you have another *platye* that I can borrow?"

"I think it's best that you ask your date what to wear. We all know that his taste is beyond reproach."

My date. I hadn't exactly thought of Uncle Fly that way although I had been captivated by him ever since he was a street sweeper in the Pushkin graveyard.

"What do you say we go to the Shanghai Concert Hall?" I asked casually the following day while visiting him.

"You got tickets to the violin concerto?"

"What a know-it-all you are!"

"I'll be happy to go. Thank you. I hear that they've fixed up the place quite nicely. The last time I was there was 1978 when Herbert von Karajan conducted the Berliner Philharmoniker."

"Oh yes, that was another first in Shanghai in that era. Compliments of your Conservatoire friend as well?"

"Indeed it was."

Mustering up my courage, I suggested, "Can I borrow one of these *qipao* dresses you have hanging in the closet for the concerto?"

There was a twitch in his eyebrows. "I don't suppose you have a *cheongsam* somewhere yourself?"

"I don't even have a dress or I wouldn't ask you. And by the way, after Liberation, those are no longer called *cheongsam* but *qipao*, my Renaissance Shanghainese," I corrected him but cringed immediately at my disrespect. "I'm sorry, you were saying …"

He gave me a meaningful smile and said, "What modern young things like you don't realize is that *cheongsam* and *qipao* aren't one and the same. The *cheongsam*, the 'long dress', is reminiscent of Shanghai's past, always custom-made according to the lady's exact measurements, form-fitting like the Victorian bodice. By contrast, the hem of the *qipao* they make nowadays is often raised above the knee so that it's no longer a 'long dress', thus less elegant. You're welcome to pick out a couple to try on and you'll see what I mean. There's a wardrobe mirror in the back."

Unable to contain my excitement after putting on the first one, I came out and struck a pose with a *"Ta-Da!* I'm going in this one!"

He gazed at me with a subtle nod. "Clothes do make the man, as Mark Twain remarked. This will do for the concert. We'll make sure to get one of your own in the future, though. I know a master tailor who custom-cuts the patterns you by plucking a chalked string to draw lines in the fabric. The fit is always perfect."

"Were all the splendid *cheongsam* in there made by the same tailor for your mother?"

"They are not my mother's. They … belong …"

"… to?"

There was a long pause.

"Helen," he said at last.

"The same Helen who gave you the nickname?"

"Yes, Helen Jen. The *cheongsam* and shoes were left by her … I meant to tell you long …"

I didn't let him finish. "But why didn't you? I feel so stupid … I've always assumed that those were your late mother's. Who is she to you exactly that you're keeping her personal belongings …?"

"Listen to me, Mo Mo! I have been wanting to tell you but … she's just an old friend who left Shanghai a long time ago, lived in California for years and only recently moved to Hong Kong after she was widowed, so you see …"

"Widowed? Oh good, so she's lurking right outside the gateway to China and you still have all her things right here and …"

He waved his hand to stop me. "If you'll just calm down and listen to me from the beginning, will you please?"

"Fine."

"Well, Helen Jen is the daughter of a Nationalist diplomat and his concubine whose great beauty matched her Chinese name, *Hai-lun*."

"*Hai*, as in Shang*hai* and *lun*, as in *without peers*?"

"Precisely. Hence the peerless beauty of Shanghai, like Helen of Troy."

"Who's Helen of Troy?"

"Ever heard about the Trojan War? Helen of Troy's exceptional beauty was the cause of the decade long conflict."

"Was Helen Jen that beautiful?" I asked, my jealousy evident in my tone.

He paused, then admitted, "By the aesthetic standards in the mission schools at the time, yes. Her face was at once angular and possessing the exquisiteness characteristic of us southern Chinese. But ... but you are stunning in a different way, with your high cheekbones and Cupid's bow lips ... then you're composed but at the same time you ..." he stammered in search for the right words "... you flaunt your sensuality so effortlessly ..."

"Although not necessarily effectively."

"Oh yes," he objected, suddenly blushing like a choirboy. "Forgive me. I have no right to entertain such thoughts ... I was just saying that after Helen graduated from McTyeire Girls' School she entered St. John's also and instantly became the darling of the campus. I was among several young men who fell for her, but she managed to keep us all on a short leash. Just before the Communist takeover, her father went to Taiwan with his first family. Her mother had been an addict used to quality opium and the Liberation ended her access. After withdrawal episodes involving drooling, diarrhea, and delirium, she swallowed a gold bar and ended her misery. She was branded a 'class enemy' posthumously, rendering Helen an 'offspring of the class enemy'. She rang me up one morning and wanted to meet at the church at noon. I showed up in my usual suit to find her in a wedding gown. I was shocked beyond words when she said that the priest had been waiting inside to marry us, so I fled the scene without going in."

"You 'fled the scene'?" I asked, almost laughing.

"Yes, I did. Knowing her temper I thought she'd never forgive me for such a slight but to my great surprise, she phoned that very evening to say that I remained her favorite admirer. In the months that followed, she constantly complained to me about her financial distress so I offered ongoing help."

"You gave her money despite such crazy behavior on her part?"

"Now it appears incredulous even to myself but at the time I was naïve and thought that was what romance was all about. Then one day in 1966, right around the Chinese New Year, she asked me to pick up two suitcases to store in my pavilion room as she had 'run out of space'. Two days later when I called on her place, she had already moved out. I searched for her in agony for days before realizing that she had already left for Hong Kong. I found out later that a half brother of hers living abroad had sponsored her to marry a Chinese-Portuguese from Macao."

"She deserted her 'favorite admirer' just like that?" I asked, thinking of Coach Long. I was not the only one who had endured abandonment, I thought to myself. But his answer was surprisingly revelatory of him.

"Well, as a Christian, I've since forgiven her. It was best for her to go then, what with the Cultural Revolution beginning in just a few months. She had no other way to leave China and she feared that I would not let her go had I known."

"You're really a man with a golden heart, Uncle Fly. How did you later find out about all this?"

"A letter with a stamp bearing the Queen's silhouette arrived two weeks later. She apologized for taking French leave and said she didn't get married but instead paid the fellow to disappear using all the money she had managed to bring out with her."

"In other words, the money you had given her."

"A good portion of it, I suppose. Either way, to me it was spilled milk, and at least it was put to good use. The Cultural Revolution soon became full blown. Letters were intercepted and we lost touch. Apparently she worked as an airline hostess until she met her restaurateur husband from San Francisco and settled down there. "

"It was almost the same time that my mother took me from Hong Kong to Shanghai when she went to Hong Kong. What a coincidence!" I exclaimed, hoping that he would follow up with something like "Perhaps you're the present sent to me by God."

"The wheel of fortune is forever turning," he said instead. "Life has a strange way of manifesting itself, doesn't it?"

On the day of the concerto, I went to Uncle Fly's for an early dinner before getting changed. The black silk *cheongsam* with silver plum blossom embroidery and his suit hung side by side on the dry-cleaner's hangers. His brogues were newly shined as well.

"If a mosquito were to land on these shoes, I bet it would slide down," I teased. "But all kidding aside, you look terribly smart, not a trace of the street cleaner I first saw."

"You don't look bad yourself: dignified and ..." he drew in a breath.

"And what?"

"God have mercy on me but you are bewitching!" he exclaimed.

Blushing with joy, I said radiantly, "So you better watch out."

The Shanghai Concert Hall was the only Baroque structure designed by a Chinese architect during the 1930's heyday of European-style architecture, Uncle Fly told me as we entered its granite archway. Although I had watched movies here before, this was my first time I had dressed up for an evening event. I admired the vaulted ceiling as we ascended the curved marble staircase. At the entrance, a gray-uniformed usher handed us each a program. Taking a birds' eye view of the stage and the orchestra pit, Uncle Fly said, "It's nice to be here with you, Mo Mo. Thanks again."

I imagined him reminiscing about his prior visits with Helen Jen, but I maintained my cool. "It's nice to be with *you*, Uncle Fly. Can you tell me what to expect from a violin concerto?"

"I've not seen the score before." He consulted the program. "Let's see, one movement broken into sections. Pay attention to the melodies. They usually tell the story and advance the plot."

"Good thing I already know the storyline."

"Right, something of an ancient Chinese Romeo and Juliet. The violin represents the female protagonist and the cello represents the male, so listen for that. The violin and cello duet is the saddest part of the concerto. It says here that the flute is at the beginning of the concerto, and then the violinist comes in."

"Mother will let me meet him right after the show. Sorry I'm supposed to go alone."

He gave me a stern but fleeting look, the significance of which I was to realize only later.

After the show, Uncle Fly and I parted company at the exit. He held my hand briefly and said, "I really enjoyed it. Please thank your mother for me and good night."

"I certainly will. Good night!"

From the half drawn velvety curtain to the green room I saw Mother and the American expert sitting on stools facing each other, neither speaking. No celebratory mood could be detected after a successful concert.

Mother stood up after she saw me and beckoned me in. The violinist shot up as well and stared at me.

"This is the American expert Mee-ker Po-po-fuu, the star of tonight's concert. Mee-ker, this is my daughter Mo Mo," she introduced us in Chinese.

The American expert strode over and gave my hand an engaging shake. "*Ni hao*, Miss Mo Mo! So nice to meet you. Teacher Mo never mentioned she had such a beautiful Chinese daughter until tonight." Except for his How do you do in accented Chinese, he spoke English.

"*Ni hao*! So nice to meet you, too, Professor Popov," I replied in English.

"Call me Mick, please. Your English pronunciation is very good. Who is your teacher?"

"Thank you, Mick. Actually I followed the tongue position illustrations of the International Phonetic Alphabet chart in a textbook and practiced myself."

"Amazing. I wish I'd met you sooner – I could have been your teacher. What do you like to do when you ..."

"O.K., O.K.!" Mother interrupted. Speaking to me in Shanghainese, she said, "You go home now. He and I have things to discuss."

I turned to smile at Mick and said, "It was very nice meeting you, Mick, and congratulations on the success of the concert. Goodbye."

"*Zai jian*," he replied in another Chinese phrase he had learned.

My heart singing like a magpie after receiving praise for my English from an American, I smiled all the way home. Once there, I got changed and lay the *cheongsam* flat on my bed where it wouldn't get creased. While looking at it and trying to picture a *cheongsam* that Uncle Fly suggested would be custom-made for me, I had a strong urge to see all of Helen Jen's things in his possession destroyed. He's definitely downplaying his feeling for her before me, I thought. What else would make a man keep a woman's clothes and shoes in his own closet for so long?

Just then, Mother stormed in without a word, unlocked her bedroom and slammed the door behind her, sending the padlock rocking on the hinge.

"You little seductive skank, are you deaf or mute?" Mother suddenly emerged from her room and yelled this at me. I said nothing. The next moment saw her sitting herself down on the stool next to the fluted column, and she began to weep.

"What is it?" I asked.

"That Mee-ker, that American Mee-ker ... he is a mean pathetic little prick ... like all of them, that Mee-ker ..."

"What did he do?"

"He said no to me ... Mee-ker said he's not returning to America yet ..."

"But to continue teaching in Shanghai?"

"No, no! Mee-ker said Asian women behave differently in Asia than in America ... Mee-ker said he loves Asia ..."

"Mick, not Mee-ker," I couldn't help but to correct her pronunciation. "And what did he say no to you for?"

"Getting married and going to New York, of course!"

"You wanted him to marry you?"

Mother looked at me with her swollen red eyes. "Mee-ker was my only chance and he said no, right after such a successful concert. I went all out for him."

"What does that have to do with agreeing to marry you? He's obviously not meek, nor stupid. He can see through your true motives."

"Whose side are you on? Can't you see that my whole life has been ruined because of you and prickly male pigs like him? He saw you and began harping on how attractive Asiatic women in Asia are ... how stunning you look in a Chinese dress ... it's all little devilish seductresses like you that ruined my chances."

"So this is my fault now?"

"Are you laughing at me? Basking in the pleasure of your *schadenfreude* moments, are you, you ungrateful little temptress? He prefers these slit-eyed Japanese with chests as flat as a Hongqiao Airport runway and stout radish-like legs wrapped inside a kimono moving in little pigeon-toed steps ... and Tokyo, Taipei, Thailand, any freaking Asian place that will take him ..." Mother sounded like she was spitting. "And here you are, defending him!"

"You are rambling nonsensically and your jealousy is utterly misplaced! Get hold of yourself, Mother!"

She stopped talking and stared at me as though stunned. In a flash, she charged at my bed to snatch the *cheongsam* and started to pull it in an effort to rip it. I sprang over to rescue it and my cheek was scratched by her fingernails. "Get out! Get out of my house!" she screamed, flinging out her arms and shaking her pianist fingers about like two possessed octopuses.

I grabbed the *cheongsam* and dashed out to the street.

How I ended up in Uncle Fly's place late that night was all a blur to me now. I must have run all the way through the dimly lit streets and lanes, clutching onto the *cheongsam* as if it were something alive. As I approached his house, a ground floor neighbor returning from his factory night shift happened to be unlocking the communal door. I made a sprint and followed him in, panting my way up and breaking the door open.

The pavilion room was dark except for a pyramidal stream of light from the lamp next to the wing chair. Uncle Fly rose in a start, dropping a hard cover book he was reading.

"What happened?"

Staring at the blood-streaked *cheongsam* in amazement, I leaned on the door, gasping for air.

"What happened to your face?"

He took the *cheongsam* and began blotting my cheek. Only then did I experience a sharp sting.

Too ashamed to tell the truth, I told a white lie on the spur of the moment, "Nothing ... it's nothing serious ... it m-must be the ivy d-downstairs ..."

"Enough," he said, angry. "Did she do that?"

A sharp tingle rose up my nostril. The tears I had been holding back rolled down. I nodded emphatically. "She blamed me for everything when the American declined to marry her so that she could go to the U.S."

"She should not have pinned her hopes of going abroad on that bloke. She can't possibly serve two masters with opposing needs and expect to get away with both. As an early product of the Soviet Russia himself, the violinist may very well be aware that her role was more to spy on him than to be an accompanist but he just went along, playing a little seduction game on the side."

"Mother serving two masters?"

"I had the Venetian playwright Carlo Goldoni's *The Servant of Two Masters* in mind. Truffaldino, the servant, juggles between two masters to comic effect. What your mother attempted was not as funny, I'm afraid."

"Mother wanted to please the School authority and Mick Popov at the same time and it backfired. But she always blames me for everything ... everything! I wish I knew who my father was. I'm sure he wouldn't let me suffer from my mother's abuse like this ..." I choke up.

Uncle Fly stepped closer and let me rest my head on his chest. As I sobbed on his burgundy cardigan, he hugged me.

12 *Heart on Top, Friend at the Bottom*

The emotional gulf between Mother and me widened further after our latest confrontation. For months now, she had treated me with civil detachment, not that I had ever experienced a close bond with her. Uncle Fly's friend reported that Mother had received praises for her work with Mick Popov. During a Municipal Cultural Bureau conferring session Secretary-General Zhao cited her and was in turn commended for his own leadership. Like she had done before, Mother had reinvented herself and become a star of a different kind at age thirty-nine.

Alone in the all-purpose room of ours, I felt as if I were living in a void, the black FOREVER padlock an apparition. Mother was hardly around. The thought of Uncle Fly filled my mind.

Ai, Chinese for love, is a combination of two parts forming one character: *heart* on top; *friend* at the bottom. According to Uncle Fly, the American poet Ezra Pound was called "The Genius" for his interpretation of the Chinese ideogram as a vehicle for meaning, both linguistically and visually. Some Westerners regard Pound's theory to be an earth-shattering discovery, and rightly so. Occidentals like you whose languages are alphabet-based may find it inconceivable that strokes coming and going in all directions could be sandwiched into a tiny space the size of a Chinese character, and that any sense could be made out of it. Growing up comprehending concepts through images, I was always in search for signs of *the* man who would put his *heart* above the *friend* for me.

Would he be Uncle Fly?

"One rain and it's autumn," so states a Shanghainese saying about our weather. With each late summer rain the temperature dips down a notch on the thermometer. Autumn is the time when Shanghai recovers from its heat and humidity for the season of harvest. This would be the time, I had wished, that my association with Uncle Fly would bear fruit.

Together we walked the streets of this city, circling central parts of her, caressing her tar-paved surfaces with our rubbery soles. *My* rubbery soles, to be exact. They bore the trademark *Huili*, *pidgin* for jai-alai, a handball game played with a curved wicker basket.

Banned since Liberation, jai-alai's former stadium was converted to the Cultural Square where proletarian consciousness-raising entertainment was staged. But *Huili* tennis shoes' quality survived, as did the durability of Uncle Fly's hand-sewn footwear from Bob's, the originally British-owned shoemaker translated in our patois as *Bobu*: "plentiful" and "steps", another instance of a happy translation akin to that of *ximengss* for Simmons mattresses. Communism notwithstanding, Shanghai had so subtly retained bits and pieces of her "Paris of the East" reputation that only eyes like those of Uncle Fly could discern them. At his prodding, our soles together felt hints of this fantastic past.

Side by side we promenaded, his hands buried in the pockets of the beige trench coat, its collar turned up and tail flapping in the wind; this sight of elegance I breathed in. You could find us on Huaihai, Yanan, and Nanjing, the parallel boulevards of central Shanghai formerly known as Joffre, Edward VII, and Nanking.

In early fall evenings, the sidewalk cicadas would chirp and shrill bearing witness to us stepping on one yellow globular fruit after another, generating muffled popping sounds. They were the fallen flowers from the parasol-shaped French plane trees known locally as *wutong*: large flat leaves; broad palmate lobes. Once crushed by human heels, the small, round heads would leave their mark on the pavement as pulpy yellowish green trails. Eventually the westerly wind would ease and the sun would shine. The pulpy mess would dry up and turn into a yellow powder the texture of curry.

Uncle Fly told me that they had been imported decades before, bundles of *wutong* seedlings piled atop the trans-Atlantic freight vessels from Lyon. A "no-landing allowed" stopover would have been made along the Mekong River, then part of French Indochine and now our Communist brethren the Socialist Republic of Vietnam. Over half a century ago, the cityscape-planning-obsessed French had made sure that the part of Shanghai they administered would reflect the appeal of Paris. They held that marks left by them should be indelible.

"That's why you'll always know whether or not you are in the former French Concession," said Uncle Fly. "These *wutong* indicate its borders even today."

That fall afternoon in Fuxing Park, Uncle Fly said, "Before you came along, I used to park my bicycle outside the gates and walk around. It's the closest thing to being actually in *le Jardin du*

Luxembourg in Paris, after which this was modeled, and significantly scaled down, of course."

He referred to the site of our rendezvous as "*le Jardin de Changhaï* of yesteryear." Soaring French *wutong* and Chinese lindens flanked the winding paths. Sweet gum trees surrounded the flowerbeds with concentric water fountains. Cast-iron chairs scattered around, with large umbrellas coming out of the thick glass tabletops. Despite the revolutionary slogans written on top of the umbrellas, Fuxing Park remained for us a rare urban oasis: bucolic, poetic, and romantic.

It was during my sojourn in Hong Kong sometime later that I would hear a joke about the park's name, which used to be spelled Fu Shing (rejuvenation) following the demise of the French Concession after WWII. When China re-opened to the West in the early 1980's, Fuxing Park got some press and was quite a tourist attraction. Western writers did not realize that *x* had replaced the *sh* sound in China's new *Pinyin* romanization system. In English, when *u* and *x* are together, they sometimes carry a hint of *k*, as in lu*x*ury. Word got around among the first batches of "yellow feverish" Westerners that this prettily laid-out park was oddly called *Fuk-sing*. In one of his travelogues, a backpacker-type dubbed the Shanghai park "a Parisian-style open-air *petite mort* arena."

I failed to be amused by the joke. Fuxing Park would forever be tied to my sentiment towards Uncle Fly, especially that windy autumn afternoon we shared there. The air was damp and sultry. A weak ray of sunlight would break through the clouds periodically. We were sitting on a cast iron framed wooden chair. Across the path was an oval-shaped flowerbed with roses nestling to bud. Uncle Fly had been staring absently at it with rueful eyes. The leafy canopy of the plane trees cast patchy shadows on our torsos. Before us, the pink flowers swayed in the breeze, emitting a delicate fragrance. "This is perhaps the only rose garden left in Shanghai." He sighed. "You deserve to be in a place where a flower bud can bloom."

"Are you comparing me to a rose? You said yourself that Robert Burns was a genius to have compared his love to 'a red, red rose' but a second man who did so ..."

"... was a fool -- like me." He finished the sentence self-mockingly and turned to look at me. There was a conflicted expression in his eyes. Snapping out of his mood with a tap on my shoulder, he stood up and said, "Come, let me take you to Le Carrousel."

"Really?" I asked for a reply, excited by the prospect of riding on the only merry-go-round in Shanghai, a replica of the one in the Luxembourg Gardens. It had only recently been reopened, having been shut down at the beginning of the Cultural Revolution after failed attempts to replace "decadent" French cabaret music with the tune of "We Are the Red Guards from the Prairies". The cost – several times that of the park entrance fee – meant that there were few patrons.

After we mounted two colorful horses next to each other, Uncle Fly remarked most unexpectedly: "With a riding helmet, you'd look like an equestrian straight out of a painting."

A gust of wind hit us just as the ride commenced. I instinctively bent over, encircling the neck of the stud to cover my face. A burning exhilaration propelled me as I joined others in a joyous shriek as the menagerie of elegant creatures launched into a wavy charge.

Later we traversed out of the park and meandered in the direction of the former International Settlement, passing clusters of frayed but still charming Art Deco mansions. As we veered off onto Nanjing Road West, Uncle Fly said, "Commander K's is right up the street. We'll get you a cake if you can tell me its original name."

"Kiessling's Café, right? They have the best whipped-cream cake in town!"

"Not bad. How did you know about it?"

"Easy. I love food and pay attention to references of it whenever I can."

As we strode out of the famed Western-style bakery, I was so struck by Uncle Fly's gait while holding the cake box that I said, "You look so gallant."

"Funny that you used the same word."

"Who else used it?"

"Never mind."

"Tell me!"

He glanced at me. "Used to come here ... She'd make me carry a stack of her shoeboxes in one hand and a Kiessling's cake in another. As the clattering of her heels hit the concrete, I would trail behind and she would laugh and say that's gallantry."

I stopped walking. With the tip of my shoe, I wrote the character *Ai* over the mustard-colored crumbs on the street. Then I stamped the *heart* part.

Once. Twice. Thrice.

He looked on, not moving his feet despite the dusty cloud of dirt landing on his *Bobu* shoes. "I see you've soiled your *Huili*s," he said coolly.

"Mind your own business!" I croaked. "Why don't you go carrying boxes for your dear widowed friend in Hong Kong? One can go there again now as long as he has a financial sponsor, right?"

"Look, you persisted and I complied, so stop being childish and making a scene out here. You don't realize that I ..." his voice suddenly faltered.

I remained motionless, my eyes fixated on my *Huili*s.

"I'm torn, too ..."

"Over what?"

He didn't reply but cast a skyward look. "I'll need His guidance. Now, let's get going while the cake is fresh." He reached over and held up the cake box at his arm's length the way a Chinese houseboy would his mistress' lantern. "At your service, your ladyship."

"Oh please!" I couldn't help but to break out in a smile.

After kicking some more powdery mist in his direction, I trailed him home.

The aroma of coffee greeted us as we entered his pavilion room. "Good, Ah Fang has gotten everything prepared already," Uncle Fly said, putting down the cake box next to a stack of blue-on-white plates. They featured a pair of lovebirds kissing over a weeping willow, three men on a bridge, a sampan, and a scholar looking in the direction of several pagodas. A cake knife and silverware lay by their side along with two highball glasses, cream, and a bottle of sorghum wine.

"You like *baijiu*, too? My mother used to drink it as a substitute for vodka with our Russian meal."

"Unfortunately we'll have to use it the same way here -- as a substitute for Smirnoff. I'll show you how to mix some pseudo-White Russian here to go with the cake. Of course we've got no Kahlua, either, so you'll just have to make do with a hot one from our Yunnan beans. We can transport some of the whipped cream from the cake to top it off."

Later, as we enjoyed the Commander K's cream cake with our makeshift cocktail, Uncle Fly said, "Someday soon I hope to see you being served the real McCoy somewhere."

Since our graduation in the summer, Wang Hong had been hanging out with Condiments' circle of friends. One afternoon, I saw her loitering around the vegetable stand where we used to meet as if waiting for someone.

"Hello there," I called out. "Long time no see." She looked away and proceeded to pick out some cucumbers.

"What's the matter? You mad at me?"

She tossed the gourd back and said, "I wouldn't dare be, my Renaissance Shanghainese Princess?"

"Oh, don't be silly. We are just friends. I know lots of things have happened, but I haven't forgotten about you. Why is it that you don't come here anymore?"

"Why do you suppose I have been standing by this stall?"

"You've been waiting for me? Thanks, and by the way, you look different ... and nice." Her hair, still in bangs, appeared shinier. Her cheeks were red as ever but the dirt-caked skin she used to have was now apple-smooth. "You've got blush and lipstick on!" I cried out.

She grinned finally. "Genuine Japanese brand. Do you like it?"

"Definitely. How ...?"

"While you're busy getting even more sophisticated, I've got myself an exit visa to Japan. That's what I was going to tell you."

"Wait, wait, you're going to Japan?"

"Yes, Tokyo! Got my visa yesterday so all I now need is another one-thousand *yuan* for the plane ticket to Narita Airport. Willing to help out?"

"Where on earth can I get that kind of money? My mother is just a school teacher and I ..."

"And you are the girlfriend of the rich and regal man."

I blushed in spite of myself. "No I'm not ... and even if I were – I'd not use him that way."

Wang Hong shook her head. "Forget it. I knew it's unlikely but no harm trying. Anyway, our sponsor in Tokyo already sent us the ticket and the applications to Japanese language schools in Shinjuku, so I'm all set to go."

"Wait ... who else is going with you?"

"Condiments, of course. It's through his connections that we got our sponsor. But we're not going to be in the same school."

"You're kidding! You're just about the last person I know who wants to go back to school."

She laughed. "Yeah, right? But that's the only way for people like us to go to Japan, according to Ryu Hideo, our sponsor."

"Didn't realize that Condiments wanted to go to Japan. Are you two ...?"

She interrupted me. "He's not what you remember him anymore. He looks so different now, tall and handsome, and his hair is all spiky with Japanese gel for men. He was the one who gave me the makeup products as presents. Nice of him, right?"

Right, I thought to myself. The boy who called me a Soviet mutt and got Uncle Fly in trouble has reinvented himself and won Wang Hong as a girlfriend and they're going abroad. "How did Condiments know a Japanese?"

"You mean our sponsor?" Wang Hong cupped her hand and talked directly in my ear. "He's actually Chinese and Ryu Hideo is his fake Japanese name as he's there illegally. But he's very powerful and well-connected. He is only in his early thirties but already extremely successful."

"This is so sudden, though. Are you sure you want to go to Japan with Condiments?"

"Of course. Condiments says this is the opportunity of a lifetime. Japan is so much wealthier than China and it needs cheap labor for its booming economy. Many student-visa holders simply work and make money. And unlike the U.S., where you have to take English tests to apply for schools, anyone can go to Japan to study."

"If I were you, I would still aim at an English-speaking country."

"I'm not a genius like you who has taught yourself the 'belonging to the sewers' language, nor was I born in Hong Kong. You could go back if you wanted to. In fact, why don't you? Everybody I know has caught the 'going abroad fever' and is trying to leave ASAP."

"I know that, and it's not like I haven't thought about Hong Kong," I said, thinking of Uncle Fly's remark that I belonged in a place where I could truly blossom. "But I still need financial sponsorship so that I don't become a burden on the public. It's the same for the United States." I told her about what happened to Mother and Popov and had her promise not to broadcast this.

"That American Expert is already gone. My dad took him to Hongqiao Airport's terminal for Hong Kong. Poor Teacher Mo. But maybe just as well, since you need English in America and it'll be too hard to learn at her age. Unlike Japan, at least with the same Chinese characters we can guess some of the meaning. I have to go now. So many things to do."

I held her hand. "I would have invited you to my place again and cooked you a nice Goodbye meal but my mother has been in a horrible mood since ..."

"Don't bother. I'm busy myself. I hear they have plenty of interesting foods in Japan – they eat raw beef and seafood and poisonous blowfish, etc. Thanks anyway."

I laughed. "You're very welcome, Wang Hong. Do you realize that this was the first time since we met at four that you ever thanked me?"

"No, I don't, but I've always been thankful in my heart that you and I met and became such good friends."

Overcome with emotions, I pressed myself briefly against her next to the vegetable stand. "This is goodbye, then. Write me and do take care of yourself!"

"I sure will. Hopefully when I see you again, Condiments and I will have earned so much money in Japan that we can open a store on Huaihai Road and become rich and sophisticated like you and your Renaissance Shanghainese."

"If that's your goal in life, by all means go for it."

"Isn't that your goal in life, too – to be rich and live well?"

"Not that per se, but I certainly want to be the best that I can be, to achieve the most as a human being, and to not be judged by my appearance. Maybe that's naïve of me to be so idealistic, but I'll try my best. Let's encourage each other and best of luck, Wang Hong."

"*Bye-bye*, Mo Mo," she said, unaware that her farewell to me was bid in a common *pidgin* Shanghainese.

13 Whether My Race Is Black White Brown Yellow or Red

About a month after Wang Hong's departure, I returned home one evening to find the door to Mother's bedroom wide open. An oversized black canvas suitcase, newly acquired, lay open on her bed, the FOREVER padlock next to it. She was packing! In her crimson, form-fitting Russian dress, under the light from the flare lampshade, Mother looked striking, her silken skin translucent.

"Come over here, Mo Mo. I have something to tell you." She sat down on her bed and pointed at the spot next to her.

"Has Mick Popov proposed to you finally?"

"What made you think that? That little prick is history. Don't know where in Asia he is fooling around and frankly I've ceased caring since he left Shanghai. I'm going abroad again myself, so there're a few things you need to know."

"What? Where?"

She gestured that I stop asking but listen. "Before I start, I'd like to tell you about myself so you can have some perspective. It's my fault that I waited this long but it was out of necessity. Now – my life so far: you already know that I was raised at the Ziccawei Orphanage until Liberation when its management was taken over and the Western priests and nuns deported. The Soviet Union became our 'Communist international Big Brother' and I seized an opportunity not available to my peers."

Possessing Eurasian features was a double-edged sword. Young Mo Na-di knew what she had to do to survive and thrive. Never one who talked much, she forced herself to give speeches exposing "the imperialists' atrocities against the Chinese orphans by instilling in them Christian beliefs." She soon got noticed for "providing a living testimony against the West's cultural and religious invasion of China."

"A young revolutionary half-Russian girl like you should be able to read notes and ruffle a tutu," the female PLA commander garrisoned in the school told her. Na-di began to fumble with the pipe organ while singing songs like *Dear Comrades, Let's Meet Atop the Lenin Hills*. In a School District-sponsored event, she performed the following 1930's Soviet Union song celebrating the "international atmosphere on a collective farm":

Ren Men Jiao Ao de Chen Hu Shi Tong Zhi,
Ta Bi Yi Qie Zun Chen Dou Guang Rong.
You Zhe Chen Hu Ge Chu Dou Shi Jia Ting,
Bu Fen Ren Zhong Hei Bei Zong Huang Hong.

People proudly call me Comrade,
It is more glorious a title than any other respectful ones.
To have a title like Comrade I have families everywhere,
Whether my race is black white brown yellow or red.

In a stage play about the Soviet partisan of the Great Patriotic
War against the Germans, Mo Na-di was assigned to play the leading
role of Zoya Kosmodemyanskaya. So heroic was the teenaged Zoya
that despite torture, rape, and mutilation she refused to submit to the
Germans, who hanged her in public and left her half-naked body on
display. Na-di's knack for portraying Zola won many an accolade. By
year-end, she was chosen to be one of Shanghai's twenty "Model
Communist Young Pioneers" and declared a symbol of Sino-Soviet
friendship.

The Affiliated Middle School of the Shanghai Conservatory of
Music offered her, at age 12, a place for its fall enrollment. Over three
thousand candidates nationwide had competed for the thirty places at
this boarding school for the musically gifted.

She had dropped the Nadia Molotova part of her name at the
first signs of a Sino-Soviet ideological rift in the late 1950's. Just over
seventeen and having been included in a rare performance tour to
Hong Kong, she won approval from Municipal Cultural Bureau Chief
Chen to have "Nadia" inserted to her name in the program to appeal
to the local audience.

"That same Uncle Chief?" I asked.

Mother pulled out a box from under where we were sitting.
"Yes, him. Look, this is the program for Hong Kong:"

Nadia' Mo Na-di is the youngest musician in the delegation.
She is a product of the New China. Her rendition of Liszt and Chopin
is sure to raise eyebrows.

"How impressive, Mother, to think that you succeeded against
all odds, from an orphan to an accomplished keyboard performance

instructor," I said. "And to have raised me all by yourself, of course," I added immediately when I noticed the blank look on her face.

"You wouldn't have wanted him for your father, anyway, a man who had abused his power and taken advantage of a teenage girl well on her way to a promising career," Mother said flatly, retrieving from the box a set of 1967 newspaper clippings with headlines denouncing Bureau Chief Chen.

Flabbergasted, I simply stared at her. All my life I had imagined my father to be an elite Hong Kong Chinese gentleman fluent in English, perhaps a man who would have his photo taken under a Union Jack in a smart Western suit. But now I had been hit with a sledgehammer falling directly from the Hammer & Sickle Communist Party flag: my father was a detestable bureaucrat and I was the product of an unwanted sexual advance.

"This is not true! This is outrageous!" I screamed.

"But this *IS* true! I could never bare to tell you because I wanted to protect you. It's bad enough to be part Russian. Imagine on top of that having a rapist and a capitalist-roader who committed suicide for a father?"

"But ... but – how could you? I refuse to believe this! There must've been some mistake! Does Wang Hong's dad know about this?" I asked in rapid fire.

"No, Old Wang doesn't know about it. Nobody knows but him and me. He came into my piano room right in the middle of my practicing *The Revolutionary Étude* – I'll never forget that – and locked the door behind him. He said he had been fancying me because I was so beautiful and so Occidental-looking, and that all he wanted was to ..." she paused, fighting back a nightmarish vision. "And I was only seventeen, you know, and he said if I didn't broadcast it he would make an exception to include me in the delegation to Hong Kong. I told myself I would 'defect' – as they would call this then – to the British imperialists after the performance so I complied and got to Hong Kong. It was all well initially. I found a job teaching the daughter of this Cantonese textile mogul but he paid me peanuts. But they told their friends that I was pure white and got them all envious. When my pregnancy was beginning to show the wife wanted to kick me out. It so happened that some relative of theirs, a boy who had fled China and found his way to a church was brought over by a Shanghainese lady. That was your Ah Bu. She took me in on account of us both being Shanghainese and because my mother had also been a Christian like her."

"So Ah Bu was our savior."

"She was in that sense, at least in the beginning. After you were born I returned to the family to teach until the inevitable happened. The man kept harassing me ... the familiar story of how fascinated he was by my fair skin, high nose bridge, big eyes, long dancing fingers, etc. etc. His wife became suspicious and threatened to report me to the British Immigration if I didn't quit. I had no choice but to contact your father and told him about you. And you know the rest ..."

"I'm so sorry for what happened to you, Mother. Please forgive me if I've inadvertently said anything that hurt your feelings."

"I know I wasn't exactly transparent with you, but how could I be?"

"I'm not blaming you, Mother. I understand you wanted to protect me."

"And myself, too" she admitted, letting out a snicker. "He committed suicide to escape punishment, which suited me fine. I think it's high time you carried this cross, Mo Mo, and I'm out of here."

"It's better than being kept in the dark forever, I suppose. I think I'll be fine."

"Good. Case closed." Mother suddenly clutched the newspaper clippings and charged towards the sink. I followed her, just in time to see her pouring what was left of a bottle of *baijiu* onto the paper and lighting a match over it. The sheets were devoured by the tongues of flame in an instant, permeating the room with the same burnt smell reminiscent of the small fire involving the turtle's head gas range tube right here.

Alarmed at what was going on, I shouted, "There's a photo of him there!"

Mother used a hardened piece of the leftover *khleb* and poked at the ashes in the sink. Not looking up, she deadpanned, "Not any more. Why would you want a picture of a dunce-hatted, faceless man with a placard hanging from his neck saying 'Death to the Capitalist-Roader!'?"

"Because he was my father," I rasped. "And why did you burn that news story about his last days?"

"Because it's the best way. Now that you've seen the headlines, we can all have closure. I'm leaving tomorrow and I have no need to take all this baggage with me as I said."

"Tomorrow? And you've waited until this very last minute to tell me? And where to?"

"Japan. Tokyo, to be exact – I'm going for a symposium."

"For how long?"

"The symposium visa was for three months but thanks to Secretary-General Zhao's strong recommendation, I got a six-month visiting scholar's visa. By the way, what is your relationship with the athlete who used to live in Shanghai but is now in Tokyo?"

"Who are you talking about?"

"I don't know his Chinese name as he now uses his Japanese alias Ryu Hideo, but I'm sure you can tell me who he is."

I suppressed my instinctive desire to gasp: *Coach Long! Wang Hong's sponsor is Coach Long!*

"How did you know about him? How do you know his name is Ryu Hideo now?" I demanded.

"You tell me his real name and your relationship first," she insisted.

But I ignored her. "You tell me! How do you know about him?"

Mother backed down. "I'm sorry, but I didn't do it on purpose. I happened to be home when this letter postmarked from Tokyo came and I ... it was a wrong thought at the spur of the moment and my first thought was that maybe it's from Mee-ker and I opened it ..."

I waited for her to continue, holding my breath.

"... I had just heard Secretary-General Zhao mentioning a symposium in Tokyo ... anyway, it was not premeditated. Here you are." She handed a letter addressed to me in Chinese. The substandard, familiar penmanship reminding me of the time Wang Hong and I copied the underground novella popped in front of my eyes:

Dear Mo Mo,

> *Things have been hectic for me since we arrived here (more below), but I have something urgent to tell you. My sponsor said he knew you from his days as an athlete in Shanghai and he wanted to*

sponsor you to Japan ASAP (see the enclosed partially filled out form). Hideo-san knew the neighborhood we're from and asked if I'd heard of you and I said of course we are best friends. He said you're the smartest and most beautiful girl he ever knew. In Japan, a photo is attached to job applications and girls with Western features are highly prized. You can earn lots of yen here, I'm sure. You should fill out your part of the visa application and send to his friend's address here. Don't write Ryu Hideo on it since it's his fake Japanese name. His friend will forward him the letter.

He lives in a manshon *(I was told it's an English word so you must know it) with an elevator, it's considered high-end here but actually it's something we would call a flat in Shanghai, nothing like your fancy white house.* Manshon *is unaffordable so I share a room in the international house dorm with two other Chinese girls. My goal is to rent in a* tatami-*ed Japanese place myself eventually. For that, I need to put in many more hours in the Shinjuku restaurant as a waitress. I'm beginning to learn the concept of service. We have to yell "Irashaimas" (Welcome) every time a customer walks in. The Japanese are ultra rich by our standards. Dark-suited* salariman *(another English word you would know) spend like there's no tomorrow drinking, singing karaoke, and visiting hostess bars after work. No wonder we've been taught since our childhood that capitalism is decadent but few of us mind as long as we get compensated well. We all work like crazy but still don't have enough, as everything is so expensive.*

Too bad you don't have a private phone or I would have called you. Although international calls are expensive and even the Japanese don't do it much, I can get calling cards from people who work for Hideo-san and call from any of the ubiquitous pay phones in Tokyo for free. Obviously these are contraband cards so if you don't use it up within a few hours, the number will expire.

You probably guessed that Condiments and I have broken up. Despite what they say about male chauvinism in Japan, it's actually a lot easier to be a girl than a boy if you are an immigrant. I'm doing just fine and enjoying myself. I don't need to have him burden me anymore now that I'm here.

Got to go now. Remember to send the application back ASAP so I'll look good before Hideo-san. He's really a powerful man here.

Hope to see you soon in Tokyo!

Yours affectionately,

Wang Hong

"I'm speechless ... This is so beneath you! Do you seriously believe that I would tell you about him after you did this to me?"

"Come on, Mo Mo. I gave birth to you, sacrificed for you and protected you all these years. This may be my only chance, and all I want is a contact in Japan ... to know who this powerful man is, just in case I have to ..."

"... overstay your visa to become the most sought-after Eurasian in Tokyo? What has gotten into your head, Mother? You've not learned anything from life. You still think you can play your good looks card?"

She charged towards me, snatched the sheets from me, tore them up into pieces, and tossed them over my head like confetti. "Forget it! Forget about Ryu Hideo! I've come along all by myself and nobody ever helped me. I've come this far and I'm not turning back! Don't you dare follow me and show your repulsive little face in Japan!"

Surprising myself, I stood there, collected. "What made you think I'm interested in going there?"

Her pale face flushed scarlet, Mother reached over to help dust the scattered paper off of me. "I'm sorry, Mo Mo ... just promise one thing, my child, do not tell anyone we had this conversation. I'll be back on time after the symposium."

I clasped her hands. "Don't you worry a thing, Mother. Please believe I am genuinely happy for you for this opportunity and I will not ruin it for you. You've earned it the hard way and you deserve it. Have a good trip ... a good journey. I'm grateful for everything you've done for me. Thank you. Take care of yourself, and best of luck!"

14 *Like Sleeping in Heaven*

A woman had left for the foreign city where a younger man I had once loved and now loathed also lived. A long dead man of whom I had little memory had newly shattered my dream of the sanctity of fatherhood. The younger man had made it big and now sought my return. The woman wanted me out of sight. Never had I felt so orphaned yet so grown.

The Conservatory would repossess our two-room flat as soon as it was established that the woman would not return. I needed a roof over my head elsewhere, somewhere, near or far.

If I filled out the forms and mailed them out, I could be in the presence – and arms -- of my onetime hero.

Simple.

But I would not be the lamb to this wolf again! Coach Long, or Ryu Hideo for that matter, had long been out of my system. Even though there would be no elite Hong Kong Chinese father to be found, I still wanted to return to my birthplace, where the lingo I had taught myself was an official language and where people would judge me not on the basis of my appearance but my abilities. There, I could bloom like a flower bud professionally, Uncle Fly said.

Helen Jen came to mind as the only possible financial sponsor. Uncle Fly's home telephone service disconnected since the Cultural Revolution had just been restored and he had exchanged calls with her. When I went to Uncle Fly's to explore this possibility, Ah Fang answered the door and warned me about his foul mood.

"Daisy has been missing for two days and we've searching all over. I asked around at the market and this Ah Zheng said that a neighborhood young man who had returned from Tokyo with some dough is starting a game restaurant. Last night he treated his buddies with a bizarre feast and one of the dishes was 'Soy Canine'."

From Ah Fang's gesticulating description I could almost hear Ah Zheng's screeching voice coming out of her head of plastic curlers.

"What? She meant Daisy could have been ...?"

"Wait, there's more. Ah Zheng said the boy who lives on our first floor is a member of the clique. She thought he might have snatched Daisy... anyway, they smoked and quaffed pitchers of draft Tsingtao beer until early this morning ..."

I couldn't bear to hear more. "Did you tell him that yet?"

"I had to. He was aghast and promptly asked me to leave all her shoes in a sack outside for the trash collection. There's no point keeping them as gnaw-bones anymore, you see."

The irony of Helen's fancy pumps being kept for years to serve that purpose was not lost on me. Her *cheongsam* would be the next to go, I thought to myself, *after* I secured the sponsorship.

"That's right, Ah Bu Fang. Thank you."

I went up the stairs and knocked on the door.

"Come in," he said, listless.

The gabled room was nearly dark but for the pyramidal stream of light thrown from the lamp-shaded bulb. He did not move from his wing chair.

"It's me."

He shot up and turned. "Darling ... oh, I ... I was just thinking about you."

I met his intensity with a smile. "Sorry to disturb you."

"You're not disturbing me at all. Welcome." He walked towards me, somewhat recovered.

"I heard from Ah Fang ... I'm so sorry, Uncle Fly ... Daisy was our 'matchmaker' when we reunited ..."

He smiled faintly. "That's a good way to put it. She was a sweetheart, but gone like that ..."

"It's not confirmed yet ... some aging dogs will go off to die by themselves and she was getting old. Anyway, you doted on her and took good care of her ... may she rest in peace."

"Thank you. I'm not blaming myself. Now, what's on your mind today, my dear?"

"Actually I'm here to ask for a big favor. Next time when you talk to Helen, I wonder if you could ask her to be my sponsor to Hong Kong."

He studied me, wistful. "I've had the premonition that this was going to come sooner or later. 'It never rains but pours.'"

"Meaning?"

No reply.

"I'll look into that for you," he said finally.

"And you don't even ask why I want to leave?" I shot back, suddenly offended.

"*Ecclesiastes* says there is a time for everything: a time to get and a time to lose, a time to keep, and a time to cast away. Perhaps it's time for you to see the world. You are beautiful and intelligent and you deserve better. As much as it hurts me to see you go, it is the best thing for you. That's what I was thinking about when you came in just now."

My eyes well up. "You are my guardian angel, Uncle Fly."

"Thank you for thinking of me this way, but I'm afraid I don't deserve it. Helen may not be the right person. I'll try my best to find you a suitable sponsor."

"Whether or not a sponsor could be found, I'm forever indebted to you, Uncle Fly. I thank you from the bottom of my heart."

"You're most welcome. What would you do if you managed to go there?"

I poured my heart out to the most trusted person in my life. "Getting my Hong Kong-born status validated will be a priority. I can then live and work in Hong Kong legally. I want to maximize any opportunity to build a resume and apprentice in a field that can utilize my training in performing arts. I want to improve my English so that I can work with both the Chinese and Westerners in the future, and who knows? -- some of my former schoolmates who are in Japan plan to return to start a business. I may end up doing the same."

"Or simply being homesick:
Perhaps the self-same song that found a path
Through the sad heart of Ruth, when, sick for home,
She stood in tears amid the alien corn."

"Are these lines from a famous poet?"

"Yes, from John Keats' *Ode to A Nightingale*, but the story about Ruth is biblical."

He went on to tell me the story.

"But I don't think I would be in tears like Ruth," I said. "If I decided to return, it would be for a bigger reason, like having my own venture and realizing my own dreams."

"And what kind of a venture do you have in mind?"

I considered for a moment and said, "I love food so a restaurant that serves Western as well as Chinese food is a possibility.

It will be the type that will reflect the genuine international character of Shanghai."

He walked to the closet and reached for something on the bookshelf inside. I was delighted to notice that all of the *cheongsam* dresses were gone.

"Here's an old copy and you can use it until you can get a newer edition," Uncle Fly said, handing me a calf-hide bound pocket-sized dictionary with golden cover protectors. The embossed printing read *PENGUIN'S CONCISE DICTIONARY OF ENGLISH-CHINESE. Copyright © 1949.* The lower spine oval logo showed the profile of a short-legged southern hemispheric bird looking due west. Pages had become brittle, its glue on the spine having hardened into yellow crusts.

"Thank you so much. I'll treasure it," I promised as my hand caressed its leather cover like a piece of glove-soft flannel.

"And use it."

That late afternoon, I was in the bedroom editing my journals in English with the help of the pocket dictionary. I had moved into Mother's former personal space which had a desk and a chair. She had taken the FOREVER padlock for her suitcase and I certainly didn't miss it.

Then I had an unexpected visitor.

"Oh, good afternoon, Uncle Wang. Please come in. What brings you here?"

Old Wang replied with a dry chuckle and looked up and down our home, his very crooked teeth flashing a grin. "Really nice, so big, separate room with a door and flush toilet as well. Nicer than I remembered the last time I saw it – I carried all the stuff here the day you and your mother moved here, remember?"

"Yes, Uncle Wang. It was a long time ago. How have you been since Wang Hong left? Do you have a message from her for me?"

Without asking, he sat down on my bed next to the turtle's head gas range and rocked himself. "So this is how a *ximengss* mattress feels – like sleeping in heaven!"

"Is there a message for me, Uncle Wang?" I asked again.

"Yes, from that Buddha-forsaken girl of mine and from Teacher Mo, too and that's what I'm here for."

"You heard from my mother? What did she say?"

"She confirmed our agreement so now is the time for you to hand over this flat to me since she has found my girl's sponsor. She promised that to me before going to Tokyo."

"What are you talking about? Have you or haven't you heard from my mother since she went there?"

"I have. My girl called Secretary-General Zhao's office this morning and asked for me. Teacher Mo also got on the phone briefly and said our agreement before she left is now official. You should come to the School to process the transfer immediately."

"You really confuse me, Uncle Wang. How's my mother doing? You said she found Wang Hong's sponsor. Did she say anything about him? Did she give you her contact information? Did she ask of me?"

Old Wang shook his head like the pendulum on a grandfather's clock. "No-no-no. She only spoke one sentence to me. She said our deal is official now. She came to our place very late the night before she went to Tokyo and asked about getting in touch with our girl's sponsor. I said since she was leaving, we'd have your flat and she'd have our girl's sponsor's information. I said I would keep it a secret that she did not plan to return from Japan. She knew I could keep a secret well. A deal is a deal."

I wrung my hands and said, "But this is so ... unexpected. I had no idea. Let me think about it and I'll give you a reply as soon as possible. By the way, how's Wang Hong doing? Did she ..."

Old Wang interrupted me. "I don't have time! If you don't come in to do the transfer by the end of the week, I'll tell everyone about Teacher Mo's shenanigans with my old boss Secretary-General Ouyang and ..."

"Wait a minute! She and Ouyang ...?"

"He-he, Mo Mo, I know everything and you better give us the flat fast. Teacher Mo is not returning so you can't stay on anyway. You might as well be smart like she always is and I won't let you lose face."

Although Mother said only she and my father had known about their relationship, I wasn't sure now if Old Wang knew about it too or if he was just bluffing about Ouyang. But since both Chen and Ouyang were disgraced former bosses of his, he could have easily used Chen to blackmail me had he known I was his child. But either way, I was not going to take chances.

Just as these thoughts went through my mind, Old Wang caught sight of the rubber hose connecting the turtle's head gas range and got up from the mattress. "I'm bringing this back," he said, disconnecting the tube. "I gave this to Teacher Mo to use for free and it belongs to me. I'll put it back again when I move in!"

With that he walked out of our flat, leaving the door opened behind him.

"Hello, Beautiful ..."

The sarcastic voice gave me a start as I walked up the stairs the following evening.

"Who is it?" I asked, clutching onto my key, ready to use it as a weapon to poke his eyes if necessary.

"Why, our great beauty cannot recognize her long time admirer's voice?"

"Condiments? You're back from Tokyo?"

"I am indeed, but that's not important. I'm here today for poor ol' Master Worker Wang."

"Wang Hong sent you? Is she back, too?"

"No, but if I get her old man what's due him, I stand a good chance of convincing her to return as well. Let me get to the point: you go process the transfer of the flat tomorrow or else."

"Or else what?"

"Look, my beauty, do not choose to do things the hard way. I didn't go to Japan for nothing. I'm a businessman now, and if you're smart as we all know you are, I can get a few buddies around to help you move out for free. Otherwise, Master Worker Wang knows the Conservatory inside out. Enough said."

There was silence for a moment.

"Fine, I'll move. But only the flat itself belongs to the School and not the furniture in it, I want a two-month extension to vacate and he can have all our things in it."

"Including the storied *ximengss*?" Condiments asked excitedly.

"Yes, both of them, plus a desk, all the chairs, a small table and everything el..."

"Deal! I'm sure he can wait two more months to upgrade himself and his wife to the *ximengss*-sleeping class. Lucky Old Man Wang! Even in Japan we had to sleep on the *tatami* mats."

I remembered the description of Wang Hong's living quarters in her letter. In my head, it looked like Coach Long's *tatami*-dorm with the "coffin" bed and the plastic lasso noose.

Ryu Hideo.

"So how is Wang Hong doing in Japan?" I asked.

With a crinkle of his nose Condiments answered, "She's fine ... and thanks for asking."

I was a bit taken aback by the "thanks for asking" part and wondered if I had inadvertently touched upon a sore spot in his heart, or if Condiments had finally learned some basic manners from his stint in Japan.

"And how's your sponsor ... eh ... Mr. Ryu?"

Condiments flashed me a weird look and shot back at me, "It's none of your business, now I give you two months!" At that, he ran down the stairs.

Manners were not one of the things he had learned in Japan, I concluded.

Late that night Old Wang came again. He brought back the rubber tube and hooked it up for me so that "You can make tasty late night snacks for yourself." He also gave me half a catty of salt baked sunflower seeds. "My woman would be offended if you think too low of us and don't take it."

"I'll accept, then, Uncle Wang. Please thank Mrs. Wang for me."

"Can I sit on the mattress again?" he asked this time. "I want to be used to it in two months."

"Be my guest."

Before he left, he apologized for Condiments' immaturity. "*Ai-ya!* The boy may know oil, salt, sauces, and vinegar well but even after Japan he still doesn't understand the proper way to handle things. I would have agreed to three months if I knew you'd include both *ximengss*. Please understand because he's too anxious to please me for our girl."

"Don't worry, Uncle Wang, I understand. You've practically seen me grow up, and you've helped me and my mother over the years and I'm grateful. I'm glad you and Mrs. Wang can live here soon."

"You people *are* different and all so smart," Old Wang said upon leaving, carefully closing the door.

15 Until Daybreak It Sheds Its Tears

We were strolling towards the Pushkin statue newly re-erected on the site where the Red Guards had overthrown it. The onetime "graveyard" was now a manicured garden with a freshly planted maple. Uncle Fly looked on as I ran my hand over the Russian poet's bust on a five-meter slab of granite. We now flanked Pushkin, in quiet reminiscence.

China had undergone rapid changes since the time we first noticed each other right around this spot. These days, government-sanctioned "patriotic" religious activities were beginning to take place in Shanghai. Decades-old copies of the Bible, their pages yellowed, were seeing the light of the day again, albeit mostly in the shaded corners of private homes.

After we started walking again, Uncle Fly said, "I'd like to take you to another place that was also built in the 1930's. Do you know the former Russian Orthodox Church?"

"I know where it is -- that cream building with five aqua-blue onion domes and cusped turrets, but I've never been inside."

"I was only there a couple of times myself years ago, with Peter."

"Your Christian friend?"

"Yes. Peter recently went to take a look inside. Since the last priest died in the beginning of the Cultural Revolution, the place has been deserted except for the occasional revolutionary meetings. But now some people are back, mostly curiosity seekers, though."

When we got there, the gates of this Moscow-style church were closed but not locked. Part of the stucco on the exterior walls was crumbling. Inside, we walked on the loosening hardwood floors with care. Dust covered the rows of long benches made from pomelo trees. Uncle Fly pointed out to me a barely discernable portrait of Madonna and Child in an alcove, explaining the mostly discolored frescoes. "If you can, try to picture their splendor when they were first consecrated," he said.

I did. And despite its rundown condition, I was in awe of the hallowed 2,000 square meter sanctuary with a soaring, twenty-eight-meter vault. To me, the structure was love at first sight.

When Uncle Fly spread out a piece of plastic paper he had for us to sit on, I asked, "So you had this planned from the beginning?"

He only replied, "I've been giving things a lot of thought lately."

I tucked up my knees under my chin and stared into the space before me, picturing its former grandeur and envisioning the future it could become with proper renovation.

He watched me as though savoring. "Do you feel your grandfather's spirit?"

"Sorry to disappoint you but no, not really. My generation was raised as Marxist-Leninist atheists, remember, my dear Mister Pious Christian?"

He laughed, shaking his head in self-mockery. "What was I thinking?"

"How many White Russians came to China as a result of the Bolshevik Revolution?"

"About a quarter-million, I believe. They crossed the Steppes on camelback and in caravans, or traveled as stowaways in the Trans-Siberia Railway cargo sections. Those 'stateless people' ended up largely in China's Northeast, Xinjiang, and of course, Shanghai."

"I didn't know they went to Xinjiang."

He lifted his eyebrows mischievously. "No? But weren't you supposed to be a native of the Muslim land?"

"Can you not rub it in? I didn't make it out there because the movie never went on location."

"I know, my darling. You know they shouldn't have cast someone as refined as you as a frontier girl to begin with. With the pose you're striking just now, if you were wrapped in ermine over a *cheongsam*, you'd be straight out of a 1930's 'beautiful Shanghai calendar girl' poster."

"I'm not sure I'll take that as a compliment. I think perhaps you just spoke to Helen Jen, for she's more likely to be associated with that kind of image. Am I not right?"

"You're just as sharp as ever. I did talk to her concerning you and here's the situation: she said she's like a clay Buddha figurine trying to cross the river -- she can't even save herself at this stage, but she may be able to find you somebody else as a sponsor."

"What kind of a person?"

"Well, first let me ask you this: can you see yourself working as a fashion model cat-walking up and down the runway?"

"As a job in Hong Kong? And she can get me a work visa doing that? Absolutely! Just watch."

Before he could speak I stood up, threw my shoulders back, and began sashaying into the beam of light cast on the aisle through a tall stained glass panel featuring a biblical scene. Taking one step back at the end, I pivoted on that back foot to complete the turn, returning in his direction and looking straight forward.

"Bravo!" He clapped as I stopped before him and struck a pose.

I did a curtsey and said, "Thank you. Do I have a work visa sponsor now?"

"I cannot tell you just yet. Let's talk details over dinner. Maison Rouge has a new menu if you care to try," he said, standing up.

Taking one last survey of the church, I said, "This would make one gorgeous place for dining if it were properly fixed up."

"And it could be named Maison Jasmine."

Facing competition from private entrepreneurial startups that until recently had been banned, Shanghai's existing service sector was slowing getting in shape. Traditional items such as escargots, foie gras, and crème brûlée, long absent from the Maison Rouge menu, had reappeared. The French Onion Soup was now graced with cheese.

Returning to the venue of our first meal together, we were seated at the same table by the wainscoted window. I clutched onto my napkin and whispered, "Details, please. What kind of a sponsor?"

"His name is Hua Wen and he owns a dining club where Helen's *mahjong* partner and high tea companion is a member. Mr. Hua is British-educated and also operates a boutique department store chain. The ladies approached him and he has agreed to sponsor you for a work visa although actual employment is not promised. He'll arrange to put you up initially though."

"This certainly sounds promising although it's a lot to swallow. You mentioned catwalk earlier. Does that mean that I'll be working as a model if I can convince Mr. Hua to hire me?"

He didn't answer directly but said, "Another food metaphor."

"What?"

He gazed at me, eyebrows knotting. "There's indeed a lot to absorb, isn't there? What if Mr. Hua turns out to be not as uninterested in you as Helen makes it sound?"

I inched my hand across the table to clasp his. "I understand your concern and I appreciate it. But I can assure you that I will not be taken advantage of. Nothing will stop me from going to Hong Kong, not the least the potential of having to fend off men like him. You said the other day that it's time for me to be tempered in the outside world. I can only come out stronger and better. Please tell Helen I agree to this arrangement, and thank her, and you, so very much. I'll go visit her and thank her personally as soon as I get to Hong Kong."

"Let me pass on your gratitude over the phone. I think it best that you two do not meet."

"No?"

His eyes were on the snail tongs he was holding. "And here's why ... Helen ... two decades and still the same temper," he said, poking an escargot in the garlic and parsley butter sauce with a fork. He suddenly looked up. "We won't have anything else to bother her with after this anymore."

"We? Did you get into an argument with her on the phone because of me?"

His face fell. "Nothing to do with you, darling, but we did have ... arguments from time to time ... anyway, I respect your decision and will do my best to help you live your life well. Godspeed."

Our desserts had arrived. My crème brûlée was vanilla custard topped with caramelized brown sugar. He had ordered a napoleon.

Two cups of coffee.

Black.

"This sugar looks like a perfectly shining moon. I hate to break it."

He smiled. "It's just sugar. Now dig in and see how you like it."

"I want to treasure the last course of our last meal in our first restaurant," I said, choking up.

"Don't be silly. There's nothing 'last' about this. If the Lord will answer my prayer, we shall be able to dine together again in the foreseeable future."

A teardrop landed on the surface of my crème brûlée like a pearl glistening on a moonlit lake.

Gazing at the black and white passport photo I had just picked up from the photographer's, Uncle Fly said in English, "*Here's looking at you, kid,*" complete with a suggestion of the Humphrey Bogart lisp.

My throat tightened.

Within a week of being issued a Chinese passport, my Hong Kong work visa was granted. He would be buying me the plane ticket as a present. I had my passport photo blown up and inscribed it on the back -- my going away present in return.

Ah Fang had left in the pavilion room a stack of rice paper and a Chinese ink and brush set on the rosewood desk with brass-handles. Uncle Fly smoothed the paper and put a pair of marble lion paperweights to secure its corners. He then wrote down the canto "*Zeng Bie*" (Presented upon Departure) by the Tang Dynasty poet Du Mu in elegant classical Chinese calligraphy:

> *Duo qing que si zong su qing,*
> *Wei jue zun qian xiao bu cheng.*
> *La zhu you xin hai xi bie,*
> *Ti ren chui lei dao tian ming.*

> So deep is my feeling that it is devoid of it all,
> Gazing long at the wineglass brings no smiles at all.
> Candle's wick, like my heart, is reluctant to see us part,
> Until daybreak it sheds its tears on our behalf.

As it lay drying, I forced a smile and said, "Thank you for this precious gift. I'll hang it in my personal space."

"This is no penmanship to be on display. It is a keepsake if you care to see it that way. And here is the ticket." He stepped closer, handing me the folder.

"Thank you again so much ... thank you for everything," I said, overwhelmed by his magnetism.

"Airports are sad places, darling, so I won't be seeing you off. Do call once you get to the flat. And one more thing: you'll be in cars and taxis in Hong Kong from now on. Remember to fasten the seatbelt. It's the latest safety item they've added in a car according to Helen."

My eyes reddening, I nodded firmly. The Renaissance Shanghainese I had adored since the moment we met wrapped his arms around me. There was a hint of cologne. I tilted my head. He traced my cheek with a finger, bit by bit, as if to etch its contour into a sculpture of memory. Then, resisting the urge, he released me with a sudden push.

"Let us make this an *au revoir* and not *adieu*. Remember General Douglas MacArthur's vow upon leaving the Philippines in 1942: 'I shall return.'"

"*Au revoir*, then, dear Uncle Fly."

"Take good care of yourself, darling."

16 From Pravda to Prada

Hong Kong, Cantonese for the "Harbour of Fragrant Joss Sticks", was among the few territories outside of the British Isles still flying the Union Jack in 1995. By July 1997, it would be returned to China.

After the legendary *kamikaze*-style landing at Kai Tak International Airport, I was greeted at the Arrivals by a small-framed man with a sign that read "Jasmine Molotova", the name I used to process my reentry into Hong Kong.

"Hello missee, I picked you out of the crowd as soon as you came into view, so white lady-like," said Ah John, the chauffeur. His weather-beaten skin contrasted sharply with the white shirt which, despite being crisply laundered, appeared oversized on him. People dressed smarter in Hong Kong, although it would take just a short few years before Shanghai folks were back on top of the game.

Taking my luggage, Ah John hurried to a parked car that sparkled under the sun at the curbside. "Private vehicles are not allowed here, but they recognized Boss Wah's plate so they gave me a break. Let's hurry, missee."

Wah must be the Cantonese pronunciation of Hua, I noted to myself as Ah John held the door open for me to enter. He pressed some buttons next to his seat and both our doors closed automatically. That reminded me of the seatbelt which I figured out how to buckle.

Dear Uncle Fly, I've arrived!

Once the car got rolling, I asked, "How could they memorize people's plate numbers?"

"Because Boss Wah spends big money in the government's auction to get the most auspicious number for this Rolls Royce Silver Spur. Only the fleet at The Peninsular Hotel has the same model. Boss left word for me to pick you up in it while he is in New York."

"On a business trip?"

"I won't know but Boss Wah is always looking to expand Mandarin World."

"That's the name of his boutique chain?"

"You are its model and you don't know? Sure, there is the boutique and then the club."

Ahh, I thought to myself, remembering that the club must be where Helen and her friend met Mr. Wah. Looking outside the window as we passed through the tunnel from Kowloon to Hong Kong Island, I tried to recall the place I had left when I was a mere child of four. The streetcars were still there, as were the European-style buildings recalling Shanghai's former European concessions. Most of the glassy skyscrapers, however, had mushroomed in the more recent past. When Ah John began driving the winding roads up the hilly terrain, I no longer felt a sense of familiarity with the place.

Her Majesty's Court, the twin-towered high rise on Old Peak Road, was our destination. A pair of stone-faced sentinels opened the cast iron gates. Ah John nodded at them and swirled the car around the fountain at the center of the complex.

"The guards aren't Chinese, are they?"

"Oh no, they're all Nepalese Gurkas, the bravest and the most loyal security guards in Hong Kong, along with the Sikhs – you know, those Indians with turbans on their uncut hair. Boss Wah taught me that they belong to the Martial Race. That's why they're the best at this line of work."

"Which race is that?" I asked as he parked the car and headed toward the elevator banks with my luggage.

Ah John laughed nervously and replied, "Oh, I don't know for sure, missee. I dropped out of school in Form II to work as an errand boy. I suppose different races are different is what he meant. The Martial Race is good at military things just as white people are better than us Chinese and fair-skinned girls like you have better fortune than the rest of us."

I could not believe my ears.

My flat faced northeast and had a sweeping view of the Victoria Harbour. Equipped with 16-feet floor to ceiling draperies operated by electric switches, the unit was outfitted with stainless steel fixtures, marble countertops and built-in chestnut dressers.

According to the brochure left by the leasing agency, Old Peak Road used to be the only route to the Victoria Peak, the highest point on Hong Kong Island. Straw-shoed Chinese coolies carried on bamboo poles everything from sedans bearing their British rulers, to water, coal and ice. Today, residing in Her Majesty's Court was "the

ultimate city-living experience befitting the royals." Gone was the era
when the good women and men of the Peak and the Mid-Levels had to
be transported on the backs of local laborers. "Her Majesty's Court
provides shuttle buses ferrying residents and their servants up and
down the steep mountainous roads to Central and Queen's Pier."

I soon learned that the majority of "the servants" were workers
imported from the Philippines and Indonesia. In contrast to the
brochure wording, the English language *South China Daily Mail*
referred to them euphemistically as "foreign domestic helpers." Like
neighboring Dynasty Palace, Her Majesty's Court had a clubhouse, a
heated, kidney-shaped pool, saunas, gym, basketball and squash
courts, a mini mart, and a reading library.

A giant lime green colored gift box with a fuchsia bow sat on
the coffee table. The attached card read:

*Welcome to Hong Kong. Make yourself at home. I'll see you in
a fortnight.*

M.W.

The box contained a Mandarin World wardrobe for me. A
membership card to the Ladies Entertainment Club located across the
street was also left for my use.

A glossy magazine whose cover featured an Andy Warhol-style
headshot of a Chinese man in a black Mandarin jacket commanded
my attention. I scanned the contents of *The Mandarin Literati* : a
Chinese-Canadian returnee's essay on being Hong Kong Chinese, a
"conceptual piece" by the Mandarin World Boutique's Milan-trained
Malaysian-Chinese creative director, and photographs of Asian
landscape and people in various shades of gray. The "Initial
Impressions" column solicited readers' stories. I immediately jotted
down my thoughts of Hong Kong in Chinese shorthand, thinking that
I might want to translate them into English and submit them to the
magazine once I had settled down.

I next called Uncle Fly, who picked up at the first ring. I gave
him a quick rundown and said, "So far nobody stared at me and the
driver made the usual comment about how the way I look made me
stand out in a crowd. I suppose Hong Kongers are used to seeing the
non-Chinese. In the short few hours here, I've already come across
Caucasians, Filipinos, Indians, Japanese, and Nepalese."

"I'm glad you find Hong Kong more tolerant in that sense but don't be surprised if this is only an illusion."

"You're so right, Uncle Fly. I already noticed that the locals are obsequious to the British to a fault. It's very disappointing."

"You've got a lot to learn and to experience there, so don't jump to conclusions yet. Are you going to contact the hospital?"

"Yes, as soon as I hang up with you. Guess what? Miss you already."

There was a pause.

"Go make the call ... and best of luck, darling."

I telephoned Canossa Hospital and set up an appointment for the following morning. It turned out that the hospital was located just down the hill, at the beginning of Old Peak Road. I experienced an eerie excitement to be so physically close to the place of my birth.

The birth record of "Baby Mo" was found, complete with a set of the newborn's footprints. DNA testing was ordered. A match would enable me to live and work legally in Hong Kong and render Mr. Wah's nominal work visa sponsorship unnecessary.

Upon returning to the flat, I dispatched a brief letter to Mother in care of "Hideo's friend", giving her my contact information in Hong Kong.

The Ladies Entertainment Club, its name notwithstanding, welcomed both genders. It embraced both dues-paying locals and expatriates, almost all having endured a long waiting period. Multinational companies swallowed the hefty price tags for their professionals in exchange for a corporate tax write-off. Some two thousand members enjoyed the sumptuousness the LEC offered: aquatics, bowling, café, dance hall, function room, massage parlor, restaurant-bar, tennis courts, swimming pools, and yoga studios.

Set up by the British in the 1880's, the LEC had for decades prohibited Chinese from becoming members. Even today, as I made my way to its entrance, I was struck by the shining brass plaque stating, in English only, that chauffeurs, servants and other service personnel were not permitted on the premises. Ah Bu, my childhood nanny here in Hong Kong or for that matter Ah Fang back in Shanghai would surely be chided and scuffed away if they were to come here.

Not until I visited my old North Point neighborhood a few days thereafter did I know that my beloved Ah Bu had already passed away. Her last wish of dying in Shanghai "like a fallen leaf that returns to its roots" was never realized. Ah Bu was interred by friends from the church at the public cemetery near Hong Kong University. I visited her gravesite to "sweep the tomb" and pay my respects, bringing as offerings joss sticks and cooked hairy-peas with pickled vegetables, the Shanghainese signature dish she had perfected. A tingle of satisfaction surged in me as I saw her epitaph identifying her as "a devout Christian originally from Shanghai". As my fingers traced these chiseled words on her modest stele, I made the wish that Ah Bu would meet my maternal grandmother Nga Bu, a fellow Christian from Shanghai, in heaven.

Now rewind back to my initial visit to the Ladies Entertainment Club. By far the most attractive feature there to me was the swimming pools. The outdoor competition-sized one with a three-tiered high diving platform was ideal for lap swimming. The two indoor ones were perpetually ozone-heated.

This facility naturally reminded me of Coach Long. *Ryu Hideo.* I willed myself to drown the thoughts of my former hero by diving into the pool. I had forgotten how much I loved swimming!

After doing laps, I lay on a deckchair and began reviewing a draft of my intended submission to "Initial Impressions", which I had inserted in the copy of *The Mandarin Literati* I had brought along with me. The gentle splashing sound from the pristine water and the scent of the insect repelling sprays from the poolside shrubberies proved to be a constant yet not unpleasant distraction.

A man and a woman, both Caucasians, were swimming freestyle but my eyes followed the one Asian in red swim briefs doing the breaststroke. At about five feet five, he had a lean athletic torso enhanced by a glistening tan. He was advancing at a good speed and made passable turns as well. But the way he swam betrayed him: he was not taught by a professional when he was a boy.

As he emerged from the pool, the image of Coach Long again came to mind. Trying to snap out of it as I saw him walking in my direction, I pretended to focus on my magazine as he took the deckchair next to mine. "Bottle of Perrier, chilled," I heard him order in impeccable British English with only the faintest hint of a Cantonese accent. A white polo-shirted server brought out a silver tray and placed it on the side table between us. The man swung to the side and poured the water into a tall glass garnished with a wedge of lime.

My peripheral vision caught him taking a sip.

I sensed him watching me. There were butterflies in my chest. I put the journal closer to my face.

"I see I'm already in your hands," he said.

I flushed. "Excuse me?"

"That," he pointed to the cover of *The Mandarin Literati*, "is supposed to be me. Artists. They make their subjects appear more handsome than they are in real life, don't they?"

"..."

He extended his hand. "I'm Man."

"Oh. I'm a woman, then," I said, shaking his hand, amused despite myself.

"Now there's one I haven't come across before. Man Wah, or as they say in Mandarin, Hua Wen." His Mandarin Chinese pronunciation was equally impeccable.

I sprang from the chair. "Mr. Hua! I'm Mo Mo, from Shanghai. I thought you would be in New York a few more days."

"Just got back this morning. Change of plans. How's Hong Kong been treating you so far?"

"V-very well, thanks to you ... and thank you, Mr. Hua ... I mean Man."

"You are welcome. Why don't we go get changed and meet up at the Café in half an hour for some proper talk?"

"Certainly."

Air-conditioned to the degree of chilliness, the LEC Café was empty when I entered. The overhead television was on mute showing a rerun soccer game between Manchester United and Real Madrid. I sat down at a corner table and waited for Man.

When he returned, Man Wah was clothed in a black taffeta shirt inlaid with a white Mandarin collar, tailored trousers, and boat shoes. A cream-hued fedora was in his hand and a flaxen kerchief in his chest pocket.

I was about to stand up when he said "Please remain seated," and planted himself across from me. Switching to Mandarin he asked, "*Xihuan zheli ma*?" (Like it here?)

I replied in kind, "Yes, very much. Thanks so much for having made everything possible, Wen."

"Stick to Man, please. Wen sounds unnatural. Here, quick Cantonese lesson: my first name -- the Chinese character for language, culture and literature -- is pronounced *man* and my surname, which happens to be the character for China, as you know, is pronounced *wah*."

"I see. You must have derived the name The Mandarin World from its approximate Cantonese homonyms Man Wah."

"You are the cleverest and most beautiful girl I've ever met. We'll have to get you started being a screw of the Mandarin World revolution machine as soon as possible," he chortled.

I turned red at the double entendre and was simultaneously dumbfounded. I couldn't imagine anyone with such immaculate Queen's English was capable of making that allusion. *"I'm happy to be a mere screw in the great revolutionary machine"* was a well-known quote from Lei Feng (1940 – 1962), a People's Liberation Army solider whose allegedly selfless and modest personality prompted Chairman Mao to start the 1963 nationwide "Learn from Comrade Lei Feng Campaign."

"You must be wondering how I knew that reference. Well, I was a pupil in Guangdong until I swam over here at eleven, so I knew all about becoming a young revolutionary successor."

"Wait! You *swam* to Hong Kong as a kid ... alone?"

"Yes. *Pravda* (Russian: truth) was indeed stranger than fiction in my case -- not entirely alone, though. I was accompanied by eight watermelons. The lucky number helped me, you see."

"How did you do it? Why did you risk your life to do such a thing?"

"How? I dug a small hole in each of the watermelons stolen from the people's commune, scooped out the flesh, strung them together to make a life preserver and doggy paddled my way across. And why? Because my family was branded 'class enemy' after Liberation, and by the early sixties, everybody was starving. I had no future staying. An older clansman who'd gone to Hong Kong a decade earlier had struck it rich with a sizable garment operation so I took a chance."

"And made it! And would you believe that I met a 'class enemy' stealing watermelons from the people's commune once before, in a film script I was slated to star in right before the end of the Cultural Revolution?"

"Right, as though such a propaganda film would have made it into the Tinseltown hall of fame if it had been made," Man said flippantly.

"I agree, although it did end my prospects of getting a career going."

"No worries. You're still young and beautiful and you're now part of the Mandarin World family. There'll be plenty of opportunities to become a star if you know how to act."

Avoiding the bait, I asked, "Did you find the relative right away after you swam ashore?"

Man shook his head and said, "Helen was right. You are a character. Well, I'll tell you everything if the policy of *Be lenient with he who confesses and severe with he who defies* is applied."

I couldn't help but laugh out loud. "You are too much, Man. You remember every single revolutionary slogan in China. Don't worry. You're not a 'class enemy' to me. Just tell me how you started here."

"It's fairly unexceptional. The rich uncle took me in and sent me off to a public school outside London. Jim Callaghan was the Prime Minister and England was deep in recession. I remember Piccadilly Circus with heaps of overflowing rubbish and chanting laborers on strike, much like a 'struggle meeting' scene at the height of the Cultural Revolution."

"I can almost picture this: *Man amid the alien trash.*"

"I can't believe you know that reference – another clever one. And you're right, there I was, barely had time to transition from Communist China to capitalist Hong Kong before I was thrown into the English country, speaking not a word of its language and being the only Oriental eyesore in the class of towheads with freckled faces and pre-pubescent whines. But having risked my life to come to the free world, I knew instinctively how to appreciate it. Although adolescent follies were an integral part of the boarding school experience, few if any would be interested in any hanky-panky stuff with a Chinaman, and that turned out to be a blessing in disguise. I was a serious and studious boy from day one and began getting high marks in my third term there. As I always had an entrepreneurial streak in me, I chose the London School of Economics in central London over Oxford or

Cambridge, and returned to Hong Kong as a graduate to start Mandarin World."

"And the rest, as they say, is history."

"I'm afraid you flatter me, Miss Mo. Now that you know everything about me, can you entrust yourself to your sponsor?" he asked, taking my hand.

Withdrawing with a wince, I said, "Please don't, Mr. Hua! I'm not the kind of girl you think."

"No? And what kind of girl are you?"

I sat up straight and folded my hands over my lap. "Mr. Hua, it was very generous of you to have arranged for my work visa and put me up for the past week, but I intend to realize my goals in life through legitimate means. A casting couch is not something I will crawl on to. You may already know that I was born in Hong Kong and shall be able to reclaim my status soon."

"Good Lord, looks like Hua Wen has just met his match," he said with a self-deprecating snicker. "You know what they say: No concord without discord first. I have to say you are a real 'Shanghai Surprise', Miss Mo."

"I take it as a compliment, then. Thank you. If you care to indulge me for a moment, I'll show you my first impressions of Hong Kong. Perhaps it'll surprise you some more."

Dear Editor:

My initial impression of Hong Kong was one of familiar sights: dark-haired people, remnants of European colonial architecture, and a general pragmatic attitude towards life similar to that held by my home city folks in Shanghai. Then came the shocking remark by a working-class man that "They are better than us Chinese," referring to Caucasians in general and the British rulers in particular. Empirical evidence suggests that his view is representative of not a small segment of the Hong Kong Chinese populace. The upper middle-class stay-at-home wives, for instance, try their utmost to emulate the Britons: they have supper not dinner, sample puddings not desserts, and take tea not coffee – in little fine porcelain cups with saucers, no less.

Within hours of my arrival in the Territory, I was introduced to the Martial Races Theory that the Nepalese and other South Asians are inherently more militant than the Filipinos due to the latter's fun-loving nature. Such racial stereotyping is appalling to me. As a rare Eurasian in China, I have endured my share of appearance discrimination, although that is changing in Shanghai and my gawk-worthiness is fast on the decrease. Although I haven't exactly been stared at here in Hong Kong, I have been greeted with fleeting glances not entirely devoid of judgment.

As entertainment in English is not available in Shanghai, I was particularly intrigued by the dubbing into English of the Cantonese *kung fu* stars and the equally incomprehensible yet rapid fire Cantonese-English spilled out by the celebrity TV chef of "Yan Can Cook" fame. Complimenting triad-fighting and stir-frying was a third genre -- programs beamed from America. There was the rerun of the 1991 William Kennedy Smith "... then I ejaculated" in the back bushes of the Kennedy Compound in Florida drama, the Clarence Thomas and Anita Hill public interest, pubic hair, soft drinks, hardcore, he says she says soap opera; and the more current and juicy, O. J. "Juice" Simpson double murder trial, where celebrity lawyer extraordinaire Johnny Cochran donned a ski cap to save the life of the erstwhile American footballer, along with Marcia Clark's metamorphosis from an overworked and undersexed Los Angeles County prosecutor to a made-over look-alike of the homemaking queen Martha Stewart.

Hong Kong is where the Orientals meet the accidental Occidentals.

Jasmine Molotova
Mid-Levels

"Umm, a bit rambling but interesting perspective and keen observation, rather insightful for someone so new to this Vanity Fair. By the way, your English is excellent. I'll see to it that this gets in the next issue."

"But it's only a draft and I'm still tinkering with it. Are you in any way connected to *The Mandarin Literati*?"

"Connected? I *run* it. You can say it's a labor of love. The people on the ad side help put it together visually."

"Really? I'm surprised that a businessman like you is actually running a magazine. I'm really lucky to have met you. I have been doodling things about my life for years now."

"And now you can write your autobiography. How about *From Pravda to Prada* for a title?"

"You really are obsessed with Communism, aren't you? What's *Prada*, by the way?"

He laughed. "Ah, how interesting. For most girls here in Hong Kong it would be the other way around. Nobody would know that *Pravda* is the official Soviet Union Communist newspaper *Truth* but everyone knows that *Prada* is a luxury Italian brand and one of the most hankered status symbols."

"Just like The Mandarin World."

"Nice one."

"So what time do I report to work, Boss Wah?"

"What work?"

"Does Mandarin World have a modeling program?"

Man displayed a wicked smile. "Oh y-ye-ss, but casting couch is a prerequisite. Still interested?"

"Honestly I am disappointed. One would hope that someone who had floated to Hong Kong on stolen watermelons would have some compassion for a fellow youngster fresh off the plane from Mainland China, but then who can compel empathy?"

"Gotcha!" Man cackled with an American expression. "You are even more alluring when you're mad. Why don't you start tomorrow at Club Mandarin as a management trainee to learn on the job."

"Club Mandarin?"

"My Shanghai-themed club in Central, perfect for a Shanghai Surprise."

"Well, thank you, Man!"

He glanced at his watch and stood up. "Ah John should be at the car park now. May I give you a lift?"

"Thanks but no thanks. I'll just walk across the street to Her Majesty's Court. By the way, do you have a unit in there?"

"Yes, and you're staying in it. But don't worry, it's yours for now and I won't bother you. I've got a house each in Kowloon Tong and Sai Kung."

17 The Long Long Life Bar and The Pen Ball

Situated in the heart of Hong Kong Island, Club Mandarin occupied the top floors of one of the grandest contemporary buildings that had only recently been dwarfed by newer arrivals. Its concept was to marry the stylish seediness evocative of Shanghai's colonial heyday with contemporary European chic. The decorations were typical of a Chinese eatery, with wax-polished wood floors, retro furniture, slow-spinning ceiling fans and lighting reminiscent of 1930's Shanghai. Paintings and sculptures by avant-garde Chinese artists were on display throughout.

Marketed as a high-society hangout, it targeted expatriate executives with their often Asian but not necessarily first-time significant others or spouses, Sinophiles, and self-styled East-West relationship experts. The restaurant served home-style southern Chinese and fusion European haute cuisine. Club members spoke of intentionally ungrammatical and misspelled fortune cookie slips dispensing tongue-in-cheek classical Chinese wisdom.

A sampler:

Club Mandarin say No to greasy wok'n'eggroll.

Brown lice (the Cantonese, like the Japanese, confuse the *l* and *r* sounds) *and white powder -- just do it!*

Grand Master Hung sayed 'Mandarin doll obey father, grandfather desires! (Confucius, incidentally pronounced Hung in Cantonese, was the Grand Master in question.)

The most talked about feature of Club Mandarin was the Long Long Life Bar. Knowing Man, I gathered that he got his inspiration from the slogan we as children were required to hail daily: A long long life to Chairman Mao! (literally: *With the utmost respect we wish Chairman Mao ten-thousand boundless lives!*) A replica of the former Shanghai British Men's Club's L-shaped mahogany bar, then the longest in the world, Club Mandarin's version conjured up the image of Shanghai as the "Paris of the East" populated by Hongkie Shangkie merchant bankers, zuit-suited triad members, turbaned Sikh bodyguards, and cigarette-puffing European film star wannabes.

At this moment, as I slid my hand along the smooth shiny edge of the Long Long Life Bar, I could hear the pre-Communist Shanghai nightclub duet numbers played by my grandfather Kirill Molotov and his Filipina partner Coco; I could see my beloved Renaissance Shanghainese dancing to the strains of jazz music and drinking White Russians mixed not with *baijiu* but Kahlua.

As I studied *Mandarin & Mao*, the painting coupling a mandarin headshot with that of a Chairman Mao which Man had commissioned for the Bar, a déjà vu sensation of my menstrual onset at the Mao memorial service hit me. The artwork showed a Qing Dynasty official in a black velvet cap with a finial and bright tassels, but it was the scarlet red allocated to Mao that overwhelmed me.

Just then, the bartender offered me a drink on the house and I picked the first one on the bar menu, a *Bloody Mao-ly*.

That evening after returning to the flat I did some emotional unpacking. Boiling rice to the exact consistency for glue, I paper-mounted Uncle Fly's calligraphy of Du Mu's *Zeng Bie* (Presented upon Departure) so that it now had the texture of parchment and spread the scroll on the lacquer altar table below the tin mirror. I read and reread the following couplet, written in his graceful classical Chinese lettering:

> *So deep is my feeling that it is devoid of it all,*
> *Gazing long at the wineglass brings no smiles at all.*

An *objet d'art*.

An object of the heart.

Since arriving in Hong Kong, I had been carrying in my purse an English-Chinese dictionary purchased in a D'Aguillar Street bookshop. At this moment, I took out the 1949 Penguin's dictionary from Uncle Fly and examined its cracked binding. With a trembling index fingertip, one dab of mashed rice at a time, I fixed the pocket-sized learning tool, smoothing the pages its original owner had fingered before, thinking of my Renaissance Shanghainese.

Also in my thoughts was of course Mother. Either she had never received my letter or she did not wish to contact me. Recalling how she viewed me as a potential rival in Japan, her not wanting to be in touch with me was understandable.

Finally, Wang Hong. I longed to hear from her. I could have called Secretary-General Zhao's office and asked for Old Wang but with Mother not returning to the Conservatory, I couldn't bring myself to face whoever would answer the phone.

And then, there was this pompous, British-accented "Hallo" from a schoolgirl, which was how I found out about the glitterati-filled opening of the Mandarin World branch in the Kowloon landmark The Peninsula Hotel.

The other day, I was strolling up Hornsey Road off Her Majesty's Court, a popular dog-walking path for Southeast Asian domestic workers taking their employers' pets for fresher air. This was the United Nations General Assembly of canines: English terriers, French poodles, German Shepherds, Maltese, Pekingese, even Russian borzois, many of them born in lands afar and flown in with birth certificates of blue blood. The maids carried with them their employers' *South China Daily Mail* to use as fans for themselves while their charges behaved and as toilet paper when they fouled.

Chris Patten, the last Governor of Hong Kong, had arrived in the Territory in July 1992 with the Queen's historical mandate, his family and Norfolk terrier cousins Whisky and Soda in tow. From the outset the two top dogs and three first daughters seized the imagination of Hong Kong Chinese and Western expatriates alike. Worcestershire, England by birth, the Patten pets were of immaculate pedigree with proper human names. Soda, the "canine first lady of Hong Kong", was legally Alice Hanley Castle. Not all Hong Kong dog owners aspired to having their dogs included in the same league as those of the Governor's, but some Mid-Levels residents certainly had their live-in pooper-scoopers go out of their way to try.

Being on Hornsey reminded me of the now departed Daisy, the matchmaker for me and Uncle Fly. The contrast was stark. Daisy's breed was uncertain and her exact cause of death unverifiable. I wondered about the fate of that game restaurant and whether establishments like it should be allowed to operate at all considering the way they sourced their raw material.

Located at the beginning of Hornsey was The Mid-Levels Grammar School, the feeder school to Hong Kong Island English School where the Patten's youngest was a student. As I passed, I couldn't help but be distracted by the sobbing of a Eurasian girl in the School's blue and white gingham uniform. Looking perplexed next to her was a Filipina, leash in one hand and newspaper in the other. On her shoulder was the girl's "Hello Kitty" school bag.

"No use cry, Sarah! We go home. Later Ma'am will scold me."

"No fair! No fair! Mr. Wah's party at The Pen is the biggest in Hong Kong this year. The Governor's daughter is going and so is Matilda. I want to go too!" Sarah, whom I now recognized from the premises of both the LEC and Club Mandarin, continued to wail.

"Matilda go because she is debater. You go also when you get old to Island English School," her forty-something chaperone with several gold-capped teeth said.

"Not 'debater'. *Debutante*! It's French!" Sarah corrected her.

"Okay, okay, I don't know fancy French word but Sarah, please, we go home now!" the helper pled as she led the dog to the curbside to do its business.

The girl turned away from the sight and saw me. "Hallo, I'm Sarah. I've seen you before. Aren't you Mr. Wah's new model?"

"I work with him, yes."

"So you can get me an invitation, right?"

"About The Pen Ball, ..." I said casually the next time I spotted Man.

He looked at me with jovial amazement. "What about it?"

"I'd like to be involved -- to learn on the job, as you said."

"I like it when you take the initiative. I'll let you talk to a few people and go to some meetings, then."

I took in the sights and sounds of the soirée like a sponge soaking water. The gala would later play back in my mind's eye like a movie, a skill I had acquired at the Film Studio from being ordered to commit to memory for later emulation every detail of the revolutionary film *The Brightly Shining Red Star*. This was an excellent chance for me to "learn on the job," I told myself. I would eventually adapt some of the things I observed there to my own professional endeavors.

Eight hundred guests in formalwear swirled in the marble Peninsula Hotel lobby to the accompaniment of the Hong Kong Philharmonic, scintillating gems, clinking champagne flutes and all. There was a concurrent launch of the *Changhaï Cheongsam* line of apparel inspired by the 1930's Shanghainese calendar girls, beauties in high heels and permed hair known for their flirtatious smiles, seductive poses, body-hugging cheongsams, and state-of-the-art European accessories.

The Pen was wrapped in silk drapes in the Mandarin World signature colors of lime green and fuchsia, descending from the mezzanine Shopping Arcade. A pair of giant mannequins bent into the shapes of *M* and *W* was hung from the ceiling, complementing the magnificent chandeliers. Seventeen-year-old debutantes outfitted in a new His and Her *Changhaï Cheongsam* line, young couples handpicked from Hong Kong Island English School, were formally introduced to the society. The debs wore shimmering silver silk gowns and long, black velvet gloves, and their beaux wore white silk bowties and black silk tails with a subdued "double happiness" character logo.

The Pen Ball went smoothly as planned. Man's introducing me as "la jeunesse de Changhaï" led to a cameo of me in The *Island Tattler*'s coverage of the night. Of him, reporter Siobhan Foley wrote: "Man Wah has managed to transform his fifteen minutes of fame into a timepiece that tick-tocks around the clock. ...... The Pen Ball was in every sense of the word a triumph." By contrast, *South China Daily Mail* published an account about Mandarin World's failure to open a branch on Madison Avenue in New York.

It was by far the most educational event I had ever attended. With the *China Mail* article in mind, I thanked Man for the opportunity and asked if it was true that he had been doing the feasibility study in New York when I first arrived in Hong Kong but decided against it.

"I haven't ruled out anything, but from a marketing standpoint, it is much harder to establish an Asian brand name in a Western metropolis."

"Right. However, I couldn't help but notice that almost all the debutants at The Pen Ball were white, yet 95% of the Hong Kong population is ethnic Chinese, not to mention the highly visible groups of Indians, Pakistanis, Nepalese, and the small segment of Eurasians."

"They aren't sophisticated enough to be our targeted market and the half-breed's numbers are miniscule."

My face fell. Since arriving in Hong Kong I felt largely liberated from the unwanted attention associated with my appearance. But Man's slur betrayed the locals' prejudices. I realized in that instant my naïveté at believing that Hong Kong was the colorblind place where meritocracy ruled. Even back home in Shanghai, with the gradual returning of Western influences now, a face like mine would be more accepted and even welcomed. Uncle Fly's advice over the phone that I shouldn't jump to any conclusions in Hong Kong resounded in my ears. How I wished I could have him with me to give guidance!

Man was quick to apologize. "Sorry that was a slip of the tongue. I didn't mean it disparagingly. I was just saying the demographics ... the demographics ..." I had never seen him so incoherent.

"Don't worry. I'm above that."

"Uncle Fly!"

"Darling! How have you been? All settled down?"

"Can't say all but I'm getting there and doing well, very busy though. Just want to tell you that my Hong Kong birth has been verified so technically Hua Wen's sponsorship is no longer necessary. However, he did hire me to be a managerial trainee and I got to attend a ball at The Peninsula where he just launched a new clothing label."

"Congratulations on your birth verification and on getting the job. Are you still at the same flat?" his voice trailed off.

I knew at once what he was hinting at. "Yes, but I've always been here by myself. I made it clear to him from the beginning that I'm an independent girl ... he's actually a decent guy and I'm really learning things on the job here."

"You rent from him, then?"

"N-not yet ... this place is beyond my budget b-but ... I'll look for another place ... soon."

There was dead airtime.

"Did you dance at the ball?"

"No! Oh, please understand, Uncle Fly, it was all work for me as a junior staff member and I had taken the initiative to be included. It was a great eye-opener for me to see how things are done from planning to execution. I observed and kept mental notes of everything as one day I want to be on my own ... I told you that before."

"I see."

"I ... I was actually thinking of you while at The Pen ... what it might have been like for you as a boy staying there."

"You still remember." His tone of voice softened.

"Of course, Uncle Fly. I remember everything you told me. Anyway, h-how are you? What's new in Shanghai?"

There was a pause. "It's not the same without ... y-you ... and what's new? Lots of gentrification going on in the former concessions and the Orthodox Church has finally fallen into private hands."

"Really?" I asked excitedly. "Do you know who and what are they going to use it for?"

"Ah Fang heard that the money came from Japan, a few returnees running the show."

"Was the one who had wanted to open the game restaurant involved?" I asked, thinking of a possible Coach Long connection.

"I don't know, but the restaurant is defunct. Supply problem."

"Good." I stopped, knowing we were both thinking of Daisy.

"They're gutting the church and seem to know what they're doing. I went over the other day with Peter to take a look and ... it's a shame you weren't here."

"You mean Shanghai or the church?"

He answered irrelevantly. "You were bedazzling that time we were there."

I curbed the urge to tell him the possibility that Coach Long could be the backer and that Condiments and his clique could be the ones doing the work. It was best that Uncle Fly never knew about Coach Long, or Ryu Hideo's existence, I thought. "Someday I will make it big and become a real hero," Coach Long's voice echoed in my mind. He may in fact be finally pursuing a business venture in Shanghai.

"Also," Uncle Fly suddenly resumed, "several municipal officials before the Cultural Revolution got de-purged and had their stripped Party memberships reinstated. Apparently they had been wronged, can you believe that?"

Ignoring his sarcasm, I asked in an urgent voice, "Was former Cultural Bureau Chief Chen who committed suicide included?"

"Yes, I believe he was on the top of the list. What else ... well Peter mentioned that the Russian violinist ..."

I dropped the phone. Hastily picking it up, I apologized. "Sorry about that, the handset slipped off. You were saying – "

"Yes, this bloke called from Tokyo to inquire about your mother after not getting an answer from his letter to her in care of the Conservatoire."

"Mick Popov ended up in Tokyo, too?"

"Seems like it. He may just as easily bump into her at some concert. By the way, any word from her?"

"No. I wrote her right after I got here but never got a reply. I don't think she wants to be in touch anymore. She couldn't leave me faster enough. I have always been an orphan emotionally ... until I met you, that is."

There was another spell of silence.

"Thank you, darling ... it was so nice that you called. Take care of yourself ..."

My voice cracked. "You too, Uncle Fly ... *Au revoir!*"

"*Au revoir!*"

18 A Query from Tokyo

Although Man came to Club Mandarin regularly, he and I rarely had the opportunity to talk. I had seen him going into one of the private rooms with a tastefully bejeweled lady I was convinced was Helen Jen. Both Man and the modish woman with a defined yet slightly sagging chin appeared to be avoiding eye contact with me. Keeping in mind Uncle Fly's wish not to have me meet Helen Jen, I held back my urge to verify her identity.

I tried to learn as much as I could about the Mandarin Club's daily operations and jotted down its managerial procedures, fanticizing that the new owner of the former Russian Orthodox Church in Shanghai, whether or not he was connected to Ryu Hideo, would convert it into a restaurant. If that were to be the case, I might make a special trip to see the venue and talk to the people there, not to mention seeing Uncle Fly. Remembering Condiments' rude avoidance of my question about Ryu Hideo, I wondered if he was one of Ryu's "buddies" in Japan that was sent packing by the big boss.

Listening to music was a new hobby after buying a second hand CD player from Apliu Street, the Kowloon electronics bazaar. The stall vendor gave me a few "throw-in" CDs, one of which was The Byrds' *Turn! Turn! Turn!* I was surprised and thrilled to discover that its lyrics were almost verbatim from *The Ecclesiastes*.

I knew I would wait for the right time to see Uncle Fly again.

From the same source came an electric typewriter, as a personal computer was beyond my budget. Unlike Mother, I never laid my hands on a piano. Learning to touch type was the closest to it.

From the dictionary, I had the words down -- *abasement* to *azure*; *zeitgeist* to *Zen*. *Dao De Jing* and the Taoist concept of *Wu Wei* -- knowing when and when not to act or to believe.

And The Byrds were singing in the background:

To everything - turn, turn, turn.
There is a season - turn, turn, turn.
And a time for every purpose under heaven.

The latest issue of *The Mandarin Literati*, a complimentary copy of which I saw in the Club, printed my "Initial Impressions" entry with little editing. With that I became a published (letter) writer, in English at that! I could hardly contain my excitement when I next saw Man.

"Thanks for using my two cents in the first impressions' column," I said. "You should have told me beforehand so I could have been looking forward to it."

"Sorry I never got a chance. Glad you liked it but next time we may print some letters rebuffing your opinion."

"I'll definitely want to read those. By the way, how have I been doing on the job front, Boss Wah?"

He laughed. "You're doing just fine so keep up the good work."

All at once I couldn't wait any longer. "By the way, was the lady I saw you with in the private room Helen Jen?"

"Ahh, y-yes. Now if you would excu..."

"I'm sorry but is there something that I should know about her that I'm not being told?"

"N-nothing I'm aware of. Incidentally, do you know anyone currently living in Japan?" He asked as an afterthought, clearly trying to change the subject.

"Yes, I do. Why?"

Man stared at me funny, weighing whether to resume.

"My mother contacted you?" I ventured.

Man's tone of voice became tense. "She lives in Japan?"

"Yes, in Tokyo, as far as I know. Her name is Mo Nadi, or Nadia Mo. Did she contact you from Japan?"

"Nadia? Wait, you are that ille- ... that child of Miss Nadia, the one who taught piano at the Wah residence years ago?"

I stared at him. "I can't believe it! You were the rich brat that she used to teach? She got in touch with you recently?"

Man shook his head and muttered under his breath "Christ!" He wrapped his arm around my waist and steered me over. "Come with me to my office," he said.

As we entered he said, "You might want to take this sitting down."

I sat on the edge of the lime green upholstered sofa across from his desk as he searched in a drawer. As though to quell misgivings in himself, he said, "You know when you print a small pamphlet, people send you all sorts of crazy things ... and this one crossed my mind when it first came in and then ... well, anyway, here it is." He passed me a letter and clasped his hands together.

The Editor
The Mandarin Literati
P. O. Box 10280
Central Station
Hong Kong

Dear Editor:

I am writing with an idea for a feature story. I hope that my suspicion that a Chinese friend of mine was the victim of cannibalism here in Japan will be proven false but trust that you can help bring about an awareness of this most distressing incident if it proves to be true.

Two weeks ago, during a routine search of Aokigahara, a lush forest nestled at the foot of Mt. Fuji famous for Japanese seeking to commit suicide, police discovered six sections of a female human body stuffed in two heavy-duty garbage bags and squeezed into a large black canvas suitcase closed with a FOREVER brand padlock. Both of the last items were made in China and neither was available in Japan. It was apparent that the corpse belonged to a homicide victim rather than a suicide one as parts of the flesh from the breasts, biceps, inner and outer thighs had been sliced off sashimi-style. The severed head has not yet been located but her arm pit hairs and pubic mound were a smoky brown. The forensics experts have concluded that the corpse belonged to a female 35-45 years of age who was fifty percent Caucasian and fifty percent Northeast Asian -- defined as being of Chinese, Japanese, or Korean race. The Yamanashi Prefecture Police have not conclusively determined the identity of the deceased although they have named Japanese national Matoko Mori, who himself was later killed, to be the suspect responsible for the murder-cannibalism of the female victim. They also pressed murder charges against a Chinese man living illegally in Japan under the alias of Ryu Hideo for Mori's death.

Like millions of other Greater Tokyo residents, I learned about the murder-cannibalism in grotesque details from the media. It immediately reminded me of Kazumasa Sagawa, the acquitted Japanese cannibalistic murderer popularized by the 1983 Mick Jagger song Too Much Blood:

> *A friend of mine was this Japanese.*
> *He had a girlfriend in Paris.*
> *He tried to date her in six months and*
> *eventually she said yes.*
> *You know he took her to his apartment, cut off*
> *her head.*
> *Put the rest of her body in the refrigerator, ate*
> *her piece by piece.*
> *Put her in the refrigerator, put her in*
> *the freezer.*
> *And when he ate her and took her bones to the*
> *Bois de Boulogne,*
> *By chance a taxi driver noticed him burying*
> *the bones.*
> *You don't believe me?*
> *Truth is stranger than fiction.*

The publication of Sagawa's memoirs ("The flesh of her butt is incredibly soft and juicy like genuine filet.") and a self-illustrated comic book each chronicling the murder of his girlfriend has turned him into a media darling, with critics calling his illustrated *manga* "a *sashimi* epicure's ultimate gourmet guide." His books' reception has been phenomenal. The police have not ruled out the possibility of a copycat Makoto Mori imitating the murderer-turned best-selling author. The murder victims had one thing in common -- being Caucasian, either pure or partial. Mr. Sagawa's victim at the Sorbonne was Dutch. Sagawa admitted in his memoirs that he had always been fascinated by Caucasian women's "snowy white flesh" and wondered how it would taste.

A brief background of myself: I was a violin instructor for young adults in New York City before completing a one-year teaching assignment at the Affiliated Middle School of the Shanghai Conservatory of Music last summer. I fell in love with Asia and decided to stay in the region. After some research in Hong Kong, I went to Japan, the empire of the sun, the

Shinkansen bullet train, and the Suzuki method for music, and became one of thousands of *gaijin* (foreigners) in Japan working as a "Native English (euphemism for Caucasian) Teacher". American English, not its British counterpart, is most enthusiastically embraced here, so good luck was waiting for this 29-year-old yours truly, known as the *Amerika-jin* Popov *sensei* (teacher).

It is my freelance work, not my English teaching that enables me to rent a 6-tatami-mat-sized room in Tokyo. I put on a robe of a Western clergyman and perform wedding ceremonies for young Japanese couples in front of makeshift hotel lobby altars in *Amerika-eigo* (English). Strange as it may sound to folks in the West, a Caucasian face has been known to sell everything from canned sodas to votes here in Japan. A balding Bruce Willis is featured in practically every automated vending machine sipping a popular carbonated drink bearing the name *Calpis*. Don't ask. Richard Gere, the star of "Red Corner", in which he played a hotshot American businessman in China engulfed in a one-night stand with a Chinese sex kitten, would know the feeling first hand. This actor of "American Gigolo" fame, with his squinting eyes and wavy mane, epitomizes the ideal looks obtainable by aspiring Japanese. A household name since starring in Akira Kurosawa's "Rhapsody in August" as a Hawaiian *nisei* Japanese-American, Gere has been linked to "the best Western-style suited man", the politician Junichiro Koizumi, who sports a wavy salt-and-pepper hairdo much like Gere's.

Last Wednesday afternoon, a Chinese woman whom I'll refer to as WH appeared in my English class and broke the ice with an outrageous proposal. "Popov *sensei*," she began, looking straight into my eyes. Such boldness would be inconceivable from Japanese women who are culturally conditioned to avoid eye contact with men with a kind of affected coyness. "I can make you the richest English teacher in Japan. You must have heard about the body in Aokigahara, the man who ate parts of her, and his murderer. I know everything about the woman who was killed, the man who killed her, and the man who killed her killer. I can give you all the information for one million *yen* (about US$10,000), cash, and you can sell it for a lot more and keep the difference."

"Excuse me, I have to go," I snickered.

"Mo Nadi, your co-teacher in Shanghai!" WH called out.

I stopped in my tracks. Mo Nadi, whose Western name was Nadia Molotova, was the half-Russian half-Chinese colleague I had an affair with at the Conservatory.

"I see I have your attention now. You don't know me but I know who you are. Do you think I would just go to any English teacher in Tokyo to propose this? I practically grew up in the Conservatory and maintain close ties to it today. Your letter to Teacher Mo was never answered, was it? And that's because she was in Japan herself."

"She was?" I blurted out, astonished. "Since when?"

"That's not important anymore as she's already been slain and mutilated. If you want to hear more, agree on a number first. Three quarters of a million?"

"Wait. Tell me first about how I can get in touch with her."

"I told you she's dead -- murdered and partially eaten by Makoto Mori. It's all in the press." She stuck an open palm before me.

I couldn't bear to hear this but I wanted to hear more. I handed her a 10,000-*yen* note and said, "But they haven't positively identified the victim."

"I have. It has to be Teacher Mo. She had fights with Hideo over him not loaning her money to buy a piano. The money she made from Snow White Saloon was not enough. And Hideo had been furious over her forbidding him to sponsor her daughter to come to Japan. Teacher Mo had threatened to expose Hideo's identity to the Immigration Bureau of Japan if he did. Anyway, Teacher Mo got picked up by Mori-san and put up in this *manshon* in Hiroo. It must've been during their Hakone hot springs trip that Mori-san sliced her up for *sashimi* and sent her decomposing body off to Aokigahara. When Hideo realized that Teacher Mo was missing, he tracked Mori-san down and killed him but now he is on death row for that."

"Sounds like a lot of it is your speculation. How can you be certain?"

"Just the instinct of a girl from Shanghai," WH piped snappily. "Besides, how many people in Japan have *sekushii* (sexy) natural wavy and smoky brown hair like her?"

I swallowed a breath of air. "Have you filed a missing person's report?"

"No, and I don't plan to. I'm not stupid enough to 'beat the grass and startle the snakes,' – the Immigration, you know. Anyway, with all these unexpected happenings I may be forced to return to Shanghai before they deport me. I've told you everything and my own circumstances. Now you pay the balance, please."

WH was really not that sophisticated after all, I thought to myself, not without glee. "Not so fast. How do I know anything you claimed is true?"

"Swear to Buddha it's true. I know because Hideo asked my old boyfriend to go talk to Teacher Mo at The Snow White but was scolded by the Mama-*san* as this 'was no place for a Chinaman to show your filthy face.' He was so enraged that he hit a Japanese bouncer there and left. Hideo was in turn angry with him for risking us all and arranged to have him sent back."

"Sent back?"

"To China. Anyway, Makoto Mori made lots of money in real estate during the bubble years and he was hooked by Teacher Mo's Caucasian looks from the start. You would know, right, that her skin was as smooth as the surface of the cheese cakes they sell at the Mitsukoshi bakery, only whiter and smoother."

I uttered a sigh of recognition, remembering Nadia's silky skin that I always associated with being Oriental. At this point I began to take WH seriously. This had been an all too familiar a story: some Japanese man meets a Caucasian woman in a hostess bar and pays her upkeep in an upscale neighborhood. It is common knowledge that Caucasian hostesses, rather than their Asian counterparts, are paid significantly higher due to sexual fantasies associated with their race. WH's depiction of Nadia sounded like it was straight out of Kazumasa Sagawa's books. The Japanese and many other Asians share the same aesthetic attitude towards facial and physical appearances: the more Caucasian, the more desirable. In a Japan that obsessed over appearance and worshiped Caucasian looks, it was not unthinkable that Makoto Mori's victim was indeed ...

I froze at the thought, horrified by the morbid conclusion. I came to an uncanny realization that Mori, while a common Japanese last name consisting of three characters for *wood* stacked together to indicate a *forest,* was also the Latin word for death.

Memento mori -- Be mindful of death.

I shelled out another 40,000 *yen* -- all the cash I had on me save change -- to WH for the information, adding that it was the maximum sum I could give without having her invited to the Tokyo Metropolitan Police for interrogation. Her parting shot was not something I would have expected from our conversation up to that point.

"You don't have to sink so low. We both know you would have nothing to gain to report me to the Japanese. Count yourself lucky as a white man who enjoys all the privileges in Asia. Fifty-thousand *yen* can do little for me and you Western imperialists are known for your stinginess, you pathetic white prince riding on your moral high horse. If you had any feelings for Teacher Mo, if you have any conscience at all, you shall pay for the rest of your life knowing that you could have prevented her from this tragic ending to her life. Now *sayonara*, Popov-*sensei!*"

When I recovered from WH's outburst, she was out of sight. I convinced myself that it was Nadia's own unique heritage that proved to be the real curse of her life among predatory Asian men, and that I had nothing to do with her ultimate downfall, if indeed she had fallen. I believe that Asian men have a sexually charged fascination with Caucasian looks. To them, a salad of racial genes was tastier than a steamy hot bowl of rice. North Korea's stout, bespectacled, and illusive "Dear Leader"-turned-"Great Leader" Kim Jong Il, notwithstanding his being perpetually clad in a drab olive leisure suit, is legendary for his taste for Caucasian women and is an avowed Liz Taylor fan.

Ever since my encounter with WH, images of Nadia Mo kept penetrating into my consciousness. I cannot help but wonder about the goings-on in a high-end hostess bar catering to an almost exclusively Japanese male clientele – the ice-breaking, the *sake*-pouring, the bowing, the half-smiling, the chit-chatting, the fondling, the picking and choosing of the "ordinary" girls versus the "extraordinary" white girls, and the cut-throat, behind the scenes rivalry for top customers. I speculate on Mori's fantasies for Nadia and his expectations from her, however perverse.

Pudgy, muscular, one-earringed, with dark chin pubes and plucked eyebrows? I try to picture Mori as if he were still alive and an archrival in my winning back Nadia's affection. A man infatuated with the West, no doubt, or the image of it. Was Mori the kind of Tokyo man who, as I have regularly read about here, would make weekly visits to salons to have his hands massaged, cuticles trimmed, nails scrubbed, bluffed, and transparent-lacquer polished? Would Mori be showing off as well his bleached, frosted, and permed wavy locks à la Richard Gere? Would he be wearing those white patent-leather shoes with shiny metal logos and custom made two-inch heels to compensate his height? Would he, in fact, be so obsessed with approximating the Caucasian physique as to have sought intrusive augmentations as some here men have done?

Yesterday, I found myself in the Aoyama Reien Cemetery, strolling along a myriad of trails paved with ancient stone slabs smoothed by many a passerby before me. Under the lazy winter sunlight filtered through the maple trees and pines, I drifted aimlessly, thinking about Nadia and curiously, Ryu Hideo, the Chinese man who has killed Mori for Nadia. Jealousy surged in me.

Then I laughed at myself. The guy is on death row in a Japanese cell with no television and a maximum of three books, for goodness sake, not that I would assume that he is any kind of a reader. One thing is clear: there is no crime of passion argument in Japan. Capital punishment is standard for such offenses and executions are carried out by hanging.

Family and legal representatives will only be informed of the condemned convict's death afterwards.

The sun, devoid of warmth, streamed through the foliage upon me. I was thrown back to an afternoon I spent with Nadia in our favorite piano practicing room when she tried to explain to me a 300 A.D. love song written by the Chinese poetess Tzu Yeh. Nadia at these moments epitomized for me the most charismatic qualities of the "East meets West" Shanghainese femininity. I later managed to find an English translation of the song in The Hong Kong Library, and here it is:

> *I let down my silken hair*
> *Over my shoulders*
> *And open my thighs*
> *Over my lover.*
> *"Tell me, is there any part of me*
> *That is not lovable?"*

Dear editor, I am in a cauldron of emotional turmoil and moral dilemma. Part of me wants to alert the authorities that the Aokigahara victim could be Nadia Molotova even at the risk of endangering WH and potentially other Chinese residents in Japan. Another part of me is praying and making believe that Nadia is still alive and that this appalling case has nothing to do with her.

Whereas this query may appear unconventional, it fits into your guideline that "it has a strong Asian theme or connection." Whether or not Mo Na-di will prove to be the victim, my unique relationship with her and the experiences we have shared in Shanghai should make a fascinating read.

Sincerely,

Mick Popov

Tokyo

At some point of my reading, the typed writing grew so misty it felt like I was deciphering the tiniest prints down an optometrist's chart. When I finished, tears had stained the pages as I sobbed "Mother, oh Mother", drawing a blank to my surroundings.

Man came over and gave me a consoling hug. "I am sorry ... I was so buried in work that I didn't give it a second thought when I first received it."

"So you were the one she taught?"

"No, it was actually my cousin that Miss Nadia taught, and of course with all the seduction thing and then my uncle sending me off to England, I never did know her."

"Seduction?"

"Oh, cat out of the bag again, I'm sorry, but that's why she had to leave Hong Kong. It was my auntie's condition for not going to court, and of course Miss Nadia had failed to put you up for adoption ... you know how some Hong Kongers think, a girl and mixed-blood on top of it."

"Well, thank you for enlightening me," I snapped, shaking. *My mother has just been murdered because she was Eurasian and I'm hearing this kind of nonsense!*

"Sorry, Mo Mo," he said, glancing at his watch. "I'm as shocked as you are and you have my complete sympathy, but I have an appointment outside now. Why don't you come with me and Ah John can drop you off afterwards. Take the rest of the week off to sort things out and call if there's anything I can do."

"I'll be fine. Thank you. Sorry, could I have the letter for now?"

"Yes, of course. You can keep it. I just wish its content were different."

"So do I. I think I'll just go home myself. Thanks again for everything."

19 Fortune Alley Revisited

I did not return to the apartment right away. A taxi dropped me off in Sheung Wan's Fortune-Telling Alley. I came to the place where Mother had sought to have our future told.

Our fate.

Hers, mostly.

I looked at the fortune-telling stands before me, seeing but not registering.

Montages:

May 15th, 1962. The Royal Hong Kong Observatory forecast 70 millimeters per hour of rain falling on the Crown Colony.

By late morning, the sky was the color of steel and pedestrians were seeking shelters. The cloth umbrella she brought from Shanghai was flipped inside out. She waved it like a flag for a cab. Many whizzed by her until one finally stopped. The driver took pity on the frantic Eurasian chick who by then looked more like a drowning hen. She realized that her own water might soon break and converge with the downpour.

"Quick, please, to that Catholic hospital on Old Peak Road!" she called out in Chinese.

"Missee richee En-ga-leash lay-dee. Big rain big wind. You pay now, three time." The Cantonese cabbie negotiated in his broken English based on the face he saw rather than the tongue he heard.

"I'm neither rich nor English but I'll pay you three times the fare now. Here, just go, please! Only a church hospital will take me in for free."

My mother was put on a gurney when she arrived at Canossa, skipping the front desk registration altogether. At one point during her contractions, she sensed a nurse drifting about her bed, a clipboard in hand.

"How old are you, Mrs. ...?" the sister asked, staring down on the contorted young face, expecting a European surname.

Beads of sweat rolled down from the unwed girl's forehead, blurring her vision. "Mo!" she heaved at the figure whose nurse's cap was floating in front of her like a large dumpling. "I'm Mo Na-di, Miss

Mo!" A brief hesitation later, she added, "I'm eighteen and I'm by myself!"

The Cantonese nun's surgical mask concealed whatever feelings of disapproval she might have. She dutifully jotted down the information before making a name tag for the maternity ward. It had me down as "Baby Mo."

When the moment finally arrived, the starched *wonton* cap declared, "It's a girl."

"I knew it wouldn't be a son," sighed my mother in resignation. "Perhaps it's my retribution."

"Oh, please don't say that, miss. All children are our Lord's creation."

She did not concur, biting her thin shapely lips to refrain from a rejoinder. What Chinese family wouldn't want a son if it were to resort to adopting? -- this accidental mother retorted in silence. Back home in Shanghai, God as her mother and grandfather had known Him had been banned. She had intended to start life anew here where Caucasians still ruled. The discovery of the pregnancy and the Hong Kong Chinese' disdain for "half-breeds" put her in this dilemma.

A few days after her discharge, my mother brought me here to the Fortune-Telling Alley. Then, as now, the pungency of salted fish and seasoned octopus permeated the atmosphere. Black snakes and white ginseng roots in sorghum liquor provided a visual association of male virility. Bowls of brown-colored medicinal tea brewed from turtle shells cooled on square kitchen block tables, which doubled as *mahjong* battlegrounds by night. Open stalls displayed air-dried deer penises and seahorses. South China Sea tropical mosquitoes and Pearl River Delta fruit flies buzzed around. Shirtless, toothless men in raw silk boxer shorts and open-toed rattan slippers called out to their male customers:

"Must have! Must have! Our secret recipe concoction will light your fire like nobody's business!"

Such a potion had no practical value to my mother. Her future as a budding pianist may have already been ruined by someone who had never had such a drink. She had come to the Fortune-Telling Alley for a dose of superstitious guidance that was no longer available in her native land.

"*Lai! Lai!* Come over here!" She heard the beckoning of a blind man in wire-rimmed dark glasses and turned to look at his brush-written sign: *Name Giving. Fate Analysis. Life Advice.*

His weather-beaten skin was just a shade lighter than his spectacles, his chin hanging like the wattle of a cock. My mother equated his age with wisdom.

One by one she handed him Hong Kong dollar coins. The sage clenched the embossed heads of Queen Elizabeth II with his thumb and finger. "Sit on the stool, sister. Let old blind man feel your baby for proper naming. Ah ... straight nose bridge and high cheekbones ... baby has beautiful white girl features. Daddy English gentleman?"

After a hesitance she answered, "The family name in Chinese is Mo, shortened from Molotov."

The man uttered an instant snicker. "Ahh -- Russian --"

Silence ensued.

My mother tugged his sleeve. He made no move. She rested me on her forearm and fumbled in her pocket. Coins rattled. She looked on as the master turned his head skywards in a circular motion and began to drone a litany of the Eight Characters System pairing the Heavenly Stems and the Earthly Branches. As he unleashed a long exhalation he reached forward, palms up. Taking the cue, my mother placed one shining head of Elizabeth II on either hand.

"She should be named Mo, the character for *Jasmine*, the kind with the fragrant white flowers and evergreen bushes."

"Mo Mo?" My mother repeated, her tone rising.

Noting her doubt, the master affirmed his choice. "A beautiful girl needs a feminine name to match and ..." he paused.

She produced a note bearing the Queen then repeated, "And ...?"

A faint smile. "And sister should flaunt what you have to get ahead."

"I know that and I've used my assets all along, but it's so hard for me to carry on here ... and with this burden ..."

"Sister must have heard of the saying 'Of the thirty-six stratagems, to leave is the best'?"

"Of course, but wouldn't that make me a cop out?"

"Come. Let me feel your beautiful face to confirm that you are not a cop out."

She flung her free arm at him and knocked his glasses off.

The sage fumbled on the ground for his eyewear and stood up. Then he laughed. Turning in the direction of a tea stand, he hollered, "Bring me a bowl here, now!"

I returned to the flat still in a trance. A red light on the phone was blinking. I pressed the button.

"It's me, darling. Please call as soon as you can. I've got something to tell you." The tone was a bit tense. Uncle Fly must have also heard the news.

I called.

"Hello, Mo Mo?"

The familiar mellifluous baritone opened the floodgate of bereavement in me. "Un-uncle Fly ..."

"Darling ... you heard?"

I continued to weep, struggling to resume talking. "Y-yes ... I think she's really dead ... How did you find out?"

"Your friend Wang Hong came here this morning and dropped off a letter for you. It was sent from a maximum security prison in Tokyo to your former address. She had just returned from Japan last week and told me about your mother and the man who sent the letter."

"Wang Hong's back, too? And what does the letter say?"

"It's sealed of course but she claims to know its contents. She said that your condemned friend has registered the Russian Orthodox Church under your name as a parting gift."

"What? That's not possible ... He jilted me years ago ... before you and I met ... and ... I can't believe this!"

There was no response from his end.

"But if this were true, then I would be the owner of the old church, wouldn't I? Why don't you open the letter for me?"

"It's addressed to you."

"But I'm anxious to verify. Wouldn't it be great if ... anyway, he's on death row and he means nothing to me anymore. Please open the letter for me, Uncle Fly."

"I can forward it to you in Hong Kong."

"Why do you do this to me? It'll be faster if I just return to Shanghai to read it."

After a moment of silence, he said, "The fellow means nothing to you anymore?"

"No."

"Even if turns out to be true that he'll give the place?"

"Oh, Uncle Fly, I'm all muddle-headed and I'm still in shock from it all! What do you want me to say? What do you want me to do? Just tell me!"

Another spell of quietness.

With a little catch in his voice, he asked, "Is there ... someone in Hong Kong that you cannot part with ... or in Japan that you would like to see?"

"No."

His exhalation was audible.

"Would you consider returning to Shanghai, then? This could be an opportunity for you to shine. Ah Fang can tidy up the spare room ..."

Hot, fresh tears sprang to my eyes.

"Sleep over it, darling." His tone was affectionate.

"Yes ... thanks ... I will. Besides, I need to give my notice."

"Only if you do make that decision, and be sure to tie up the loose ends and thank Mr. Hua for what he has done for you."

"I know. I won't burn my bridges."

I heard him chuckle. "There's my girl."

"Thanks again for everything, Uncle Fly."

"*A bientôt*, darling."

That was how he had left it: *A bientôt*.

He wished to see me soon.

20 And Quiet Flows the Huanpu

Hongqiao International Airport.

Evening hustle and bustle.

Travelers. Greeters. Farewell-bidders.

People lining up, pacing up and down, or rushing by.

Sounds of my mother tongue.

I was barely four years old the last time I came to Shanghai, on a train, with my mother, dreading eye contact with anyone.

I met for the only time the man who I would know years later was my father.

Now, *Mother*, dead.

Father, newly rehabilitated, yet long gone.

I, *Mo Mo*, returned to a city now full of cars, where my appearance no longer commanded intuitive head-turnings,

To acknowledge my heritage,

To validate my love,

To fulfill my dream.

A few days ago in Hong Kong, when I gave him my arrival information over the phone, there was no offer to pick me up. He had opted against seeing me off when I left Shanghai.

"Airports are sad places," he had said.

The Smirnoff and Kahlua Coffee Liqueur would be for him. As were the newly purchased albums of The Byrds' *Turn! Turn! Turn!* and *The Glory of Gershwin*. Bracing myself for finding no greeters, I nonetheless searched beyond the plate-glass partition, beyond the crowds pushing against the railing three or four deep, for the man with Byronic looks.

And there he stood, in all his Old World politesse, next to a row of attached seats, a dozen white roses in hand. I dashed forward and flung my arms around him. The edge of the cellophane, coupled with his day's worth of beard framing those sharply angled cheekbones, produced an electrifying sensation on my cheek.

"Welcome home," he said with a smoldering look, easing out of the embrace that was still a rare sight in public.

He handed me the bouquet.

"Thank you, Uncle Fly! They're *beau*-ti-ful. I wasn't exactly expecting this ... or your coming here."

In the taxi home, I held the bouquet upright like a baby. "What do white roses symbolize?" I asked *sotto voce*, tugging at his sleeve.

"Purity."

The spare room was waiting for me. The floor light was giving off a soft glow next to the twin bed. A vase was on the bedside table, water already in it. I glanced at Uncle Fly and he replied to my tacit question. "A nice touch for your boudoir, isn't it?"

"It sure is. Thanks for being so thoughtful," I said, arranging the roses in the vase. Still in my heeled sandals and the cream crêpe-de-chine dress, I turned to face him, holding out both arms.

He stood stationary and asked, "Wouldn't you like to read it first?"

I dropped my hands and nodded.

He produced the letter. "You've had a lot to deal with in a short time. Get some rest and think things over. I'll see you tomorrow. Good night, darling."

Dear Mo Mo,

> *By the time you read this I will already have been hanged in Tokyo. I will receive this punishment because I killed Mori Matoko who had murdered your mother. I thought I could get away with not being caught as I had done many times before but luck was not on my side this time. Please understand that I am not afraid of dying and I will die a hero's death.*

> *I avenged her for you to prove that I was a true hero so you would come to Japan now that your mother was gone. She had been so strongly against my sponsoring you that she threatened to report me to the authorities should I do so.*

> *With this last act of my life – well-intended but unfortunately not seamlessly carried out -- I ask that you forgive me for my abrupt departure years ago. I loved you, Mo Mo, but didn't know how to best*

express it. After you went to the Film Studio, I sensed our ever-widening gap and couldn't bear the thought of being eventually told to end our relationship. So I "took the initiative to gain the upper hand," as the saying goes.

Things didn't work out in Beijing and within a few months I was back in my hometown. It was there that I heard about the Japanese baseball superstar Sadaharu Oh, whose father was actually from my home county Qingtian. My competitive streak got the better of me and I got on a sampan alone and sailed across the Japan Sea just as Oh's father had done in the 1920's , convinced that Oh would help a fellow athlete from his ancestral home to get his foot in the door in Japan.

How naïve I was! The closest I got to Sadaharu Oh was the television screen. I got bumped around but kept my eyes on the prize. I set a goal for myself to make it big in ten years and contact you again as an accomplished man. I think I've made it pretty close. That was why I had your friend Wang Hong forward you the visa application to Japan as I was living under a fictitious identity. I retained my Chinese surname Long, which is also a Japanese surname of the same Chinese character for dragon, but spelled as Ryu and gave myself the first name Hideo, the same Chinese characters for hero, because you used to say I was your hero.

My dear Mo Mo, I have achieved what I set out to do a decade ago and have a sizable operation in Shinjuku and beyond. You must be aware of the renovation and conversion into a restaurant of the former Russian Orthodox Church in Shanghai. I had you in mind when we bid for the building and wanted to show you how different a man I am today from the Coach Long you knew. I have instructed my people in Shanghai to have the business registered under your name, so the Church is yours, Mo Mo. This is a present from me for which I do not expect

acknowledgement as I have already derived
satisfaction from having known you and leaving you
with something that is part of your heritage.
Goodbye, Mo Mo. You are forever my fairest
film starlet and my Little Kemaneiqi!

Ryu Hideo

In contrast to my reaction to Mick's letter which was not intended for me, I read through Coach Long's highly personal last words with composure, even emotional detachment. Although shocked at the speed of his execution, I was almost relieved that he was dead.

The immediate urge was to break the news to Uncle Fly so that he could be free of the concerns of a potential romantic rival. I also wanted to share my excitement of becoming the owner of the former church and my amazement that it was indeed being converted into a restaurant. How prescient of Uncle Fly that he should have already suggested the space to be a restaurant named after me -- Maison Jasmine.

I tiptoed down the corridor to the outside of his suite and listened for a moment -- all quietness within. Then I took the liquors, the CDs and the player and the copy of *The Mandarin Literati* upstairs to the pavilion room. On the rosewood desk he had written me the *Zeng Bie* scroll, I left the journal open to the page where my letter was printed.

Back in my room, I lay tossing about, eyes wide shut as if existing in an abyss. I tried to picture Coach Long as he would have looked as Ryu Hideo. Events real and imagined played in my head. Coach Long standing like a pagoda by the poolside holding out a rod attached to a plastic lasso. His defiant facial expression as the Japanese executioners pulled the noose. My maternal grandparents Kirill and Nga Bu cuddling at dawn on the double-spanned Garden Bridge. The resulting child that was my mother and the beginning of all of our troubles. The determined, risk-taking expressions on Mother's beautiful albeit conniving visage – in the end a severed head. The way Uncle Chief -- my father's stiffened body might have looked when discovered hanging from a rope in the piano room. And the

robust yet amateurish manner of Man Wah chopping aqua in the
Ladies Entertainment Club pool ...

Sleepless in Shanghai.

A distant chorus of shrill cries of roosters revived me from a semi-
slumbering state. I lifted the curtains and looked up to the eastern sky
above the garden. It was a hue of diffusing translucent white, like that
of my skin. Then, there were more melodic crows -- happy, hearty,
harbingering morning -- followed by Mother's faint voice humming
Kirill Molotov's love song to Nga Bu *Utro* (Morning):

"I love you!" (*"Ljublju tebja!"*)
Daybreak whispered to day
and, while enfolding the skies, blushed from that confession,
and a sunbeam, illuminating nature,
with a smile sent her a burning kiss.

Taking the present for Ah Fang with me, I went down to the
kitchen.

"Mo Mo, you really returned, and beautiful as ever. Why up so
early? Bed comfortable?"

"Oh, everything was perfect. Thanks so much, Ah Bu Fang, and
good morning."

"Yes, I was just going out to buy our breakfast. He'll have the
usual toast and marmalade with coffee but I thought you might have
missed genuine Shanghainese. Will rice congee with osmanthus
flowers and fried donut sticks be to your taste?"

"Sounds yummy. Thanks for being so considerate. Here, I've
got you something from Hong Kong, imported from Myanmar,
actually. See if it fits."

"Oh, you shouldn't have ..." she said as she opened the red and
golden bordered jewelry box. "Ahhh ... a bangle in Burmese jade ... so
precious ... must have been pricey."

I slid it on for her. "Don't worry about it. I'm just happy that
the size was right. When I was little in Hong Kong, a Shanghainese *ah
bu* as kind as you are took care of me. She used to wear a jade bangle
like this so I thought you might like this."

Examining the bangle in an appreciative fashion, Ah Fang
reached to hold my hand and said, "I'll treasure it forever. Ah Zheng
and the others would be so envious if they saw this."

"I'm glad. By the way, you know the girl who just returned from Tokyo, Wang Hong? What is she doing?"

"Yes, Ah Zheng said she is helping out at her boyfriend's place."

"Who's the boyfriend?"

"The one from the soy sauce shop. Looking at him now you'd never guess. He seems to be doing well with his friend, also returned from Japan. Young people nowadays, like the tide of the Huangpu River coming and going wave after wave."

"That's because there are more opportunities in Shanghai now. Even I returned, you see."

"Oh yes, of course. Don't get me wrong, Mo Mo, I'm happy you returned. It pains me so to see him missing you, you know. Now everything will be fine."

"Let's go out together but I'll get my own breakfast outside. Thanks just the same. Could you tell him that I should be back by late morning? Thanks."

Standing outside the house the Jewish-Hungarian architect Laszlo Hudec built over half a century ago, I experienced a familiar feeling of homecoming until I remembered I was calling on Wang Hong. Step by step I climbed the circular stairs to the second floor, my hand on the banister throughout. I sucked in a quick breath and knocked on the door to the two-room flat.

"Who is it?" asked a man's voice that didn't seem to belong to Old Wang.

"It's Wang Hong's friend Mo Mo. Is she in?"

Nobody replied but I could hear commotion inside. Then the door opened to an angle just enough to block the view to the toilet area and Wang Hong threw herself at me. "Mo Mo, you are back! The Renaissance Shanghainese contacted you, right? I'm so sorry about your loss."

"Thanks ... and thanks for delivering the letter, too. Let me wait outside here while you get ready and we'll catch up over breakfast somewhere."

Through the half-opened door I could see a Japanese futon mattress on the floor and a bed sheet tied to the column separating the area where my *ximengss* bed once was. Condiments must have moved in with her and Wang Hong has learned the concept of privacy in Japan, I thought. The door to the bedroom was closed and I found myself picturing the FOREVER padlock on it, on the suitcase Mother took with her to Tokyo, and then on the same suitcase containing her mutilated body ...

At the sight of the space Mother and I used to share, the bereavement that I had suppressed until now overcame me. Grief surged up my nose as though I had mistakenly downed rice vinegar for shots of *baijiu*. Closing the flat door from the outside, I began to sob against the wall, my body shuddering.

Moments later Wang Hong came out and, seeing me in this state, embraced me. "Cry your heart out if you want, Mo Mo ... you are with me now."

Towards the end of my cathartic release against her shoulder, Wang Hong fished out tissue after tissue from a packet advertising a female skin-whitening product.

"Thanks," I said, sniffing.

"Use up the whole packet. They distribute these for free on the streets of Tokyo. I brought tons of them back," she said as she blotted the area surrounding my eyes. "There, no more tears. Let's go and conquer Huaihai Road once again."

"For breakfast?"

"Sure, and our treat, too!"

"You and Condiments'?"

"Right. He and his business partner own this *Yoshoku* joint and their Western breakfast set is great. All Japanese standards maintained."

"And what's *Yoshoku*?"

"It's European foods with a Japanese flair, perfect for the East meets West former Avenue Joffre, don't you think? It was my idea and they stole it, ha!"

Suddenly I noticed a changed Wang Hong with her stylishly layered bob, natural looking makeup, nude gloss on her full lips and sleek form-fitting sheaths. "You look wonderful ... and so smartly put together."

"*Arigato*." A ready Thank You came from someone who had never used to say it. "When you work in the service industry you have to present yourself at your best for your customers' sake. It wasn't that hard, really. I mean I did learn a lot in Tokyo but the seeds of our sophistication were sown right here in the French Concession, weren't they, Mo Mo?"

"You're absolutely right."

"*Ikimasho!*" she said. *Let's go!*

Wang Hong was anxious to see Hideo's letter. "What do you mean you didn't bring it for me read?" she protested. "I tried so hard not to open it because I had to respect your privacy. I asked the Renaissance Shanghainese for your number in Hong Kong but he said he'd asked for your permission first. He must be in love with you to be so protective."

Blushing, I changed the subject. "Since when have you cared about other people's privacy?"

"Since Japan," she declared matter-of-factly. "The place has certainly taught me a thing or two. Anyway, what did Hideo say?"

I exhaled. "First of all, he's dead, and that was the letter he was allowed to send the day of his execution."

"Are you serious? Thank Buddha I listened to Condiment's appeal over the phone and returned – must have been just before they hanged Hideo. He said I should flee immediately rather than being a sitting duck waiting to be deported. He knew it was all over for Hideo as homicide was a big crime and he had already transferred funds around. Oh, by the way, he must have told you that the old church is in your name now, right? Guess what, Condiment and his partner are involved in the restaurant conversion so keep us all in mind when it comes to staffing, Boss!" She said the last sentence with a kind of bow that almost made me laugh.

"I'll rely on you all to make things happen. And please tell Condiments that I appreciate what he and his friends have done for the project and I hold no grudges. Let's work together in the future."

As I pushed the pavilion room door open, strains of *Turn! Turn! Turn!* greeted me. The sunlight, partly filtered through the slatted shutters, threw an expansive and dotted stream on the wax polished floor. Against the glare I could make out that his eyes were half closed, the stately wing chair offering a stately refuge, a glass in hand.

"I'm back, Uncle Fly."

Slowly, he rose and gazed at me with a wistful look on his face.

"They've already hanged him so everything is over. He did leave me the church and it is being converted into a restaurant."

"Ahh," he uttered, his facial muscles twitching. "Oh, by the way, thanks for the presents. I've already availed myself of them. Let me fix you a White Russian, too."

Uncle Fly turned the music volume down and walked toward the table. I could see his hands shaking when he poured the Kahlua.

"Congratulations and cheers," he said.

We touched glasses and he swallowed his drink in one gulp. "I won't ask any questions now that your benefactor is gone. It's your chance to interrogate me about Helen if you so wish."

I took the empty glass from him and placed it on the teapoy. "'Interrogate' would be the wrong word but I am dying to find out why you wouldn't let us meet. After all, she's also my benefactor -- to use your term, isn't she?"

"That's what she's tried to make you think. The truth is, she couldn't wait to see you leave Shanghai ... she went ballistic when she realized that my heart had long been ..." He stopped, his searing eyes darting towards mine.

My stomach lurched. "... been?" I prompted.

His eyes never leaving me, Uncle Fly took my hand and pressed his lips against it. I felt the warmth of his breath.

And his heart.

"I had been fighting back my feelings for you for so long. I thought – initially – that it would be selfish of me to prevent you from pursuing the life you wanted ... so I asked her to find you a sponsor in Hong Kong and she was only too happy to do so."

"You don't think that now," I said in a trembling voice.

"No, darling. The Lord has answered my prayers and you're back by my side," he whispered, drawing me close. "I have missed you so ... *Je t'aime, ma chérie.*"

I felt my eyes warming up.

"*Moi aussi, je t'aime.*"

......

There is a season - turn, turn, turn
And a time for every purpose under heaven

......

A time to build up, a time to break down
A time to dance, a time to mourn

......

A time of love, a time of hate
A time you may embrace

And a time you may kiss ...

The Chinese say that the success of a venture depends on three factors: *tianshi* (heavenly timing), *dili* (advantageous location), and *renhe* (harmonious people). I was lucky to have simultaneously possessed all three.

My return to Shanghai coincided with the early days of China's market economy. Maison Jasmine could not have found a better venue. And the team of people had already begun some of the work without me.

The weeks that followed were spent in a whirl of excitement in preparation for the grand opening.

The first floor would house the bar and the jazz piano salon. The second floor would feature The Europa and La Changhaï, the two restaurants each occupying half the space. Anchoring the Art Deco-style Dragon Room, named in memory of Coach Long, was the Long (*dragon*) Bar with its copper and dark pomelo woods that were salvaged from the Church's benches. Uncle Fly, however, insisted on interpreting the homonym *Long* as a throwback to the namesake longest bar in the world in the former British Men's Club in Shanghai. On display in the foreground was the WWII-era Harley motorcycle that was donated by Uncle Fly.

Salon Nadia was a tribute to Mother and the era during which her parents had met. Lining the walls were sepia toned photographs of the Bund, the Garden Bridge, the French Public Garden (today's Fuxing Park), the original Pushkin statue, and the Ziccawei Ward of the St. Ignatius Cathedral where Nadia Molotova was born. The lounge conjured up a world reminiscent of the kind of nightclubs that Coco & Molo performed in during Shanghai's glamorous "Paris of the East" days when guests could sway to the sounds of jazz and dance to a DJ's spins.

A lustrous birdcage-shaped chandelier was suspended from the soaring vault in the center of the 2,000 square meter space, giving off a romantic glow. The Europa served continental fusion amidst meticulously restored frescos in homage to Tsar Nicholas II, with the portrait of Madonna and Child smiling at diners from the alcove. Dishes ranged from Maison Rouge-inspired French to Russian to Xinjiang, all grounded in classical European techniques.

La Changhaï featured authentic Shanghainese *Benbangcai* cuisine epitomized by the use of the cooking wine and soy sauce. The signature "Hairy Peas with Preserved Vegetables" used Ah Bu's recipe. *Baijiu* was the default liquor of choice and *yanqishui*, the salty, carbonated Coca-Cola of Shanghai, the most welcomed soft drink.

Uncle Fly had been on site to give advice on everything from interior décor to furnishings to crockery. Looking at him from a corner of the room, Wang Hong whispered into my ear, "I wouldn't give him up for anything, Mo Mo. He's the perfect Shanghai gentleman for you."

"You and Condiments are well matched, too, not to mention that Condiments doesn't have a glint of gray hair at the temples."

"Not yet, but he's already using Japanese dye to touch up his hair. But no matter what he does, there'll only be one Renaissance Shanghainese, and he's yours."

Uncle Fly had decided to introduce me to his fellow Christian and best friend Peter. We would meet for dinner.

"So what have you told him about me?"

Uncle Fly didn't reply, only smiled.

Suddenly I felt as if I was being taken to meet the family. "That's unfair! What did you tell him about me?"

"Peter has known of you for a long time. He works for the Conservatoire, remember?"

"So he must have known my mother and her ...?"

"I would think so. They were colleagues. He was made a lyricist for proletariat marching songs during the Cultural Revolution, not his strongest suit apparently. He majored in English at St. John's and used to dabble in writing love verses in English to the McTyeire School girls."

"Peter the poet."

"He'll feel flattered if he hears you say that. Now don't worry, darling. You'll like him. He is a dear friend."

Peter said that he hadn't seen the Renaissance Shanghainese this happy for decades, thanks to me.

"What was he like at St. John's?" I asked.

The men exchanged a look.

"You can mention Helen," I said to Peter. "He's told me about her."

"There's no need to bring her up," said Uncle Fly.

"Except that Peter may be amused to hear what you told me she had said over the phone."

"Right. Helen Jen returned to California as you know, Peter, and called to scold me for having my soul snatched – if I ever had a soul to begin with -- her exact words."

"That's what I want to know," Peter said, laughing. "But seriously, little Mo Mo, he had made up his mind from the time you first rescued Daisy. He's been raving about you to me ever since."

I stared at Uncle Fly. His eyes smiled back at me.

"I have to confess ... and to apologize to you now that I met the wonderful girl in person that I did have my doubts at the outset, but he assured me that it was a case of Like mother, unlike daughter."

"What do you mean? My mother ...?"

Uncle Fly interrupted. "I just wanted to tell him how fantastically different you were. And Peter, why don't you show Mo Mo your hand and she'll understand what I meant."

Peter hesitated, then said, "First of all Mo Mo, please accept my condolences, and you carry yourself unbelievably well. The Renaissance Shanghainese always has impeccable taste. Now please don't take offence. What I'm going to tell you is in no way meant to tarnish the memory of Teacher Mo."

"Now, Mo Mo, I don't suppose you've ever seen a cast of Chopin's left hand as sculptured by Auguste Clésinger, but it is perhaps the most famous representation of the pianist's hand and ..." Uncle Fly urged Peter to continue with a look.

"... Teacher Mo used to have a replica cast on top of her piano. One day ... at the beginning of the Cultural Revolution, I was attending a criticism meeting organized by some Red Guard students, and my colleagues and I were all in her piano room. At one point Teacher Mo, to show how revolutionary she was, stood up to take the Chopin cast as if she wanted to smash it in front of everybody. I ... I ... this is difficult to say right now but ... I had been quite infatuated with her beauty and talent at that time and had been watching her every move. So I charged toward the cast and hugged it to my chest before she could reach it. The Red Guards were infuriated. They grabbed the cast from me, put it on the piano keyboard and positioned my own left hand on it. Then ... then they repeatedly slammed the piano shut. Instead of asking them to stop, she helped the Red Guards by pressing my hand down ..."

Peter showed me his hand: several finger joints appeared crooked.

I touched them. "I am so very sorry, Peter. I'm sorry my mother hurt you so cruelly. I wish I ..."

Peter smiled weakly. "It was that time of pervasive madness ... I wouldn't have brought it up had ..."

"... had I not insisted," said Uncle Fly.

"Thankfully, it's all in the past. '*Yesterday is History, 'Tis so far away.*'"

"Is that a quote?"

"Yes. Emily Dickinson," answered Uncle Fly.

After saying goodbye to Peter, Uncle Fly and I went to Salon Nadia. The bandstand was already set up and soft music was playing. The candlelight from the wall sconces reflected the mosaic window panels, giving off a sense of tranquility.

"Do you think Kirill Molotov fell for my Nga Bu because she was racially different or because she was an attractive girl who happened to be Shanghainese?" I asked after studying the sepia photo of the Garden Bridge where my grandparents had their first kiss.

He considered for a moment. "While I cannot speak for another man, I would not fall for a girl because ..." He stopped short as though he had an epiphany. "I see ... and all your rants published in *The Mandarin Literati* ... but no, do not doubt for one moment how I feel for you ..."

He drew me close, took my hand, put my head on his chest where I could sense his heartbeats, and we swayed to the rhythm of the slow tune.

"What do you say we host a literary salon here, darling? We can start with you and Peter with short pieces and grow into marathon readings of Pushkin's *Eugene Onegin.*"

"That's a great idea, my dear Renaissance Man."

For that night I had put on the black velvet *cheongsam* with silk charcoal gray piping custom-made by Uncle Fly's master tailor. Chinese love-knot frogs secured the dress at my neck, bosom, armpit, and down my side where the slits began just inches below. I also wore matching jade earrings, bangle and ring – all heirlooms from him.

A long-stemmed red rose in hand and chin held high, I strode to the center of Salon Nadia's bandstand wearing a smile. From the middle of the front row where Uncle Fly and Peter sat, people started clapping. Within seconds it turned into full applause.

I noticed Chinese as well as Western faces in the audience, with some couples bringing their biracial kids along. A toddler with curly locks, pacifier in the mouth, waved enthusiastically from the lap of her Chinese Mom as her Western father clapped. Holding the smile, I acknowledged the audience with brisk side-to-side nods, sensing the return of my Film Studio training.

In Mandarin, English, and Shanghainese, I welcomed everyone and thanked them for their presence. They would be vital to the making or breaking of Maison Jasmine. If I did the right thing, there might be people among this international crowd who would patronize a restaurant of mine in another city or another country.

New York.

St. Petersburg.

Man Wah had said that expanding into such a Westerner-dominated metropolis would be difficult from a marketing standpoint but therein would lie the challenges for me.

I began reciting the Emily Dickinson poem:

> *Yesterday is History,*
> *'Tis so far away*
> *Yesterday is Poetry*
> *'Tis Philosophy*
> *Yesterday is mystery*
> *Where it is Today*
> *While we shrewdly speculate*
> *Flutter both away.*

Beyond the confines of this room in this historic edifice, beyond the former "Neva Street" in the Western concessions of the Native City, Shanghai met the tide of its mother river Huangpu, ebbing and flowing out of the East China Sea into the other coast of the vast Pacific Ocean ...

I, the confessional raconteur, began my story with a quote from Anton Chekhov who said that what he believed to be reality was a dream, and vice versa. Let me end it with something from his theater director friend Konstantin Stanislavsky. "The ultimate goal of a thespian is to be believed rather than to be recognized or understood by the audience," *Si-tan-ni-si-la-fu-si-ji* had said.

You, my dear Western friend, have loaned me your attentive ears and your captivated eyes. What you now need to do for this life is to believe.

Appendix A:

A conversation with *Vivian Yang*, author of *Memoirs of a Eurasian* and *Shanghai Girl*

Q. MEMOIRS OF A EURASIAN and SHANGHAI GIRL both tell unusual stories set in Shanghai and cities outside China. What are they each about?

A. Both are about a strong heroine with roots in Shanghai's former French Concession overcoming extraordinary odds in pursuit of a dream. MEMOIRS OF A EURASIAN is set in Shanghai, Hong Kong, and Tokyo, with snippets of St. Petersburg and Warsaw. It is about the vicissitudes of three generations of a Eurasian family beginning with the Russian branch fleeing the Bolshevik Revolution to 1930s Shanghai, to the fate of its descendants during the radical Cultural Revolution and finally to the economic boom of more recent times. SHANGHAI GIRL is set in Shanghai and New York in the 1980s and early 1990s. It's a story of love, ambition, intrigue, interracial relations, and the American Dream that is narrated by a post-adolescent girl from Shanghai, a Shanghai-born American businessman, and a young American Asia-aficionado.

Q. The political nature of the Cultural Revolution features prominently especially in MEMOIRS OF A EURASIAN. Can the novel be seen as yet another book about that period in China?

A. I wouldn't say so. MEMOIRS OF A EURASIAN is a historical novel about the vicissitudes of three generations of a Eurasian family in the Far East. The Cultural Revolution is just an anchoring point and it certainly was a very political time. But the novel is really about unique individual experiences of the characters that are not familiar to a Western reader. And I want to evoke a sense of time, place, and culture – a kind of unique reading experience, if you will.

Q. Both novels have murders in them and involve the Chinese, Japanese, and Caucasians in some way. How did this come about?

A. Interracial relations is one of the multifaceted themes in both books. In a way, MEMOIRS OF A EURASIAN is an exploration of the Asian male psyche when it comes to the Caucasian female and SHANGHAI GIRL is the opposite – that of the Caucasian obsession with the Asian female. I wanted to examine the universality of humanity and the complexity of the world without sacrificing the novels' entertainment value.

Q. Are you suggesting that Asian ideas about eroticism differ from Western ones?

A. I'm suggesting nothing of that sort. Ideas about beauty, sensuality, romantic engagements, and sexuality can be highly personal and individualistic. A novelist is neither a moralist nor a social scientist. Her role as a literary artist is to create a world which the readers can be transported to and experience vicariously.

Q. MEMOIRS OF A EURASIAN describes racially motivated cannibalism in the contemporary developed world. Is it pure fiction?

A. Unfortunately, the incident that is fictionalized in the book was based on true crimes committed in Asia and Europe. Richard Lloyd Parry's book *People Who Eat Darkness* and Mick Jagger's song *Too Much Blood*, for instance, deal with this matter. While a novelist is subject to the same stringent requirements for accuracy as a historian, she has no business perpetuating falsehoods.

Q. Both protagonists in MEMOIRS OF A EURASIAN and SHANGHAI GIRL are young Shanghai girls who go to the West, at least for a sojourn – just as you did. Can they be seen as your alter-egos?

A. The writer James Baldwin said that all first novels are autobiographical to a certain extent. So SHANGHAI GIRL's Sha-fei Hong, who was named after the famous the French Concession's Avenue Joffre, shares some of my emotional growth experiences, as I was born in the former International Settlement and grew up in the French Concession. I am also the only child of parents who were university professors, and I later came to America for graduate school, just like Sha-fei. But the story proper is fictional. Mo Mo in MEMOIRS OF A EURASIAN, by contrast, bears little biographical resemblance to me.

Q. You have created original characters one seldom comes across in existing literature – including the principled and helplessly romantic "Renaissance Shanghainese" flâneur, the Eurasian orphan with pianist Van Cliburn as her unlikely hero who debases herself to survive the Communist regime in MEMOIRS OF A EURASIAN, and the pre-Communist mission-schooled Chinese-American businessman Gordon Lou in SHANGHAI GIRL. How did those unique fictional people come to you? Who is your favorite character in each?

A. My characters are composites of people I knew growing up in the 1970s and 80s in Shanghai's former European quarters. Many were disenfranchised former elites who had gone to Western mission schools, like the "Renaissance Shanghainese" and Gordon Lou. Others were working-class Christian converts who had to survive and adapt to the new Communist regime. Still others – the few but memorable ones I knew – were Eurasians who continued to live in Shanghai after the 1949 Liberation. Most Westerners, of course, had long been "shanghaied" out of China by the time I was born, and anything not regarded as proletariat was banned during that period - particularly English and Western culture. "Renaissance Shanghainese" is my personal favorite in MEMOIRS OF A EURASIAN, and Sha-fei Hong, the first-person female narrator of SHANGHAI GIRL, is the character I feel most attached to. The other two narrators of that novel are men, although Gordon Lou and Ed Cook are both distinctive and strong characters in their own right.

Q. Is the Shanghai you write about consistent with the West's image of this Chinese city?

A. While I don't believe that there exists one codified image of Shanghai even among the Chinese, I imagine that some Western readers may think of China as being culturally and ethnically homogeneous. By setting my novels partly in its former French Concession, Shanghai's unique position in China can be fleshed out, and its less-known but fascinating stories can be told in an entertaining way. I'll leave it to my readers to judge whether or not my Shanghai matches their own vision of it, but I certainly hope they'll enjoy the stories no matter what their notion of the city is, glamorous or otherwise.

Appendix B:

A Brief Timeline for *Memoirs of a Eurasian*

Actual Historical Events in the 20th Century	As depicted in the novel (chapters mentioned are in parentheses)
In 1917, The Russian Bolshevik (Communist) Revolution succeeded in overthrowing the Tsar and founded the Soviet Union. A sizable Russian Diaspora flourished in Shanghai's European quarters, notably the French Concession, a key setting of the novel. By 1937, an estimated 25,000 anti-Bolshevik Russians were living in Shanghai.	Kirill Molotov, the protagonist Mo Mo(lotova)'s maternal grandfather, is one of the Russians in the French Concession and presumed to have been involved in the erection of the Pushkin Statue in 1937, the centenary of the Russian poet's death. (3, 6, 15)
In 1922, French marshal Joseph Joffre unveiled the boulevard named after him in Shanghai's French Concession. Avenue Joffre had since developed into Shanghai's premier residential and retail district, with many establishments operated by the Russian and other European communities. Known today as Huaihai Road, it has retained its distinct European character.	Fuxing Park (formerly the French Public Garden), just off Huaihai Road, is the setting where the relationship between two main characters thrives. (12)
In 1949, the Chinese Communist Party takes control, founding the People's Republic. Almost all Westerners were expelled in the	Kirill Molotov leaves Shanghai for the Philippines, leaving behind his Russian-Chinese daughter Na-di Mo(lotova).

ensuing years. Most Russians went to the U.S. and Australia via the Philippines. Since 1956, the Chinese and the Soviet Communists had been diverging ideologically over the interpretation of Marxism-Leninism, leading to the Chinese denunciation of "The Revisionist Traitor Group of Soviet Leadership" in 1961.	She struggles to survive in light of being Eurasian and the political turmoil of the Sino-Soviet ideological split, becomes a pianist, and gives birth to Mo Mo in 1962 in British-ruled Hong Kong. The identity of her ethnic Chinese father is unknown to Mo Mo. (1, 6, 13)
From 1966 to 1976, the (Great Proletarian) Cultural Revolution brought major changes to China's political, economic and social landscape. It was launched by Chairman Mao, who believed that bourgeois elements were permeating the government and society at large and that they wanted to restore capitalism. China's youth responded by forming the Red Guard groups who often resorted to violent means. The 1976 death of Mao and the arrest of the Gang of Four headed by his wife Madame Mao marked the end of the Cultural Revolution.	Na-di Mo brings Mo Mo to Shanghai just before the beginning of the Cultural Revolution. Mo Mo grows up as a rare three-quarters Chinese and one-quarter Caucasian girl in China. (Much of the novel chronicles Mo Mo's experiences in various chapters)
In February 1972, U.S. President Richard Nixon visited China, and in September, Japan and China reestablished diplomatic ties. In 1979, reform-minded Chinese leader Deng Xiaoping visited the U.S. Deng introduced "socialism with Chinese characteristics" -- typically taken to mean Western-style market economy with heavy	Mo Mo comes of age during these tumultuous years and shares her life experiences with other characters of the novel, some of them eventually go to Japan during its "bubble years". Some return to Shanghai in the 1990s. (various chapters)

ideological restrictions. Westerners were allowed to visit China again, and selected Chinese citizens could now go abroad. Many Chinese went to neighboring Japan during the latter's "economic bubble" years of the late 1980s to early 1990s to study and to be part of the cheap overseas labor force.	
1984, The Sino-British Joint Declaration was signed, handing sovereignty over Hong Kong from the United Kingdom to China, effective July 1st 1997 (the Handover).	Mo Mo sojourns in Hong Kong during the time before the Handover, sees the world outside of China, and returns to Shanghai more mature and with higher aspirations. (16, 17, 18, 19)
From the late-1980s to the 1990s and beyond, China becomes a world economic power with double-digit annual growth. It has entered what has been dubbed as the "bamboo capitalism" stage, with its fast-growing economy fueled mainly by a multitude of vigorous, extremely private and enterprising entrepreneurs.	Mo Mo possesses all three factors the Chinese believe will ensure the success of any venture: *tianshi* (heavenly timing), *dili* (advantageous location), and *renhe* (harmonious people). She is on her way to becoming a success in business, love, and life. (20)

"Shanghai Girl is superb literature...one of the best of contemporary novels written by Chinese authors; we eagerly await Yang's next literary feat." -- EVE magazine

SHANGHAI GIRL

A Novel

VIVIAN YANG

Author of Memoirs of a Eurasian
Winner of the WNYC Leopard Lopate Essay Contest

WINNING ENTRY OF *The New Jersey Arts Council*
LITERATURE FELLOWSHIP

AN EXCERPT OF VIVIAN YANG'S NOVEL

Shanghai Girl

From the shadows of the Cultural Revolution-era Shanghai to the
streets of New York City, a compelling story of love, ambition,
intrigue, interracial relations and murder by the author of
Memoirs of a Eurasian

First published in 2001 to critical acclaim, this new and revised
edition of *Shanghai Girl* features a *South China Morning Post* Books
pages author interview. Read an awarding-winning chapter below.

Newly revised edition now in book form and on Kindle

Sha-Fei Hong: Exile from Avenue Joffre

Upon first hearing, my name sounds commonplace enough for a
Chinese girl: pretty and prosaic. Few have asked me why I am called
Sha-Fei. People assume that I must have been born at dawn when the
morning light, *Sha*, was glowing, and *Fei*, the rosy clouds, were
floating. But I know I was named after the trendiest street in
Shanghai's former French Concession, Avenue Joffre. The Chinese
translation for the onetime marshal of France was Sha-Fei.
  Sha-Fei.
  My life as a Shanghai girl began in the same gardened
Western-style house in the heart of the Concession where my father
had grown up in the 1930's. Father named me. In 1964, Shanghai had
already been liberated by the Party for fifteen years. Any sentimental
display towards her colonial past would have been severely punished.
Father used a pun in naming me and kept his genuine intent deep in
his heart.

My earliest recollection of was the ambiance surrounding our neighborhood, the part of town known to the locals as "The Upper Corner." Images of our house remain in my head like snapshots -- the red tiles on tapered roof, the gray steel window frames shipped in from Lyons when the house was built, 14-foot ceilings, French windows opening to the verandah, the fenced in garden with Chinese parasol trees and a rosebush. There was the sound of crying cicadas on humid summer nights, when the ceiling fans ran all night long and the smell of the mosquito-repellent incense permeated the house. For reasons unclear to me, I was not allowed to enter two places in the house: the Ancestor Worshipping Hall and the servant's quarters. My favorite indoor play area was the pantry adjacent to the kitchen where a giant GE refrigerator stood, its motor buzzing. The pantry had a small door opening from below the kitchen counter through which freshly prepared food was brought to the dining room. Just above the house's top floor solarium, between the stucco overhangs, were the words *1928 A.D.*, in relief.

A block away from our house was the entrance to Club Jingjiang, the former Cercle Sportif Francais on rue. Cardinal Mercier, now Maoming Road. Only occasionally would Father mention such facts to me at home, peppering our native Shanghai dialect with English and French words. He had, after all, been a student in New York City.

After the Cultural Revolution started, I never heard a foreign word from him again. Then one day, the changing tides of the Huangpu had flooded our home. The Red Guards from Shanghai's Pujiang University where Father taught decided to "sweep" us out "like dirt on the floor." Nine proletariat families moved in and partitioned the house. In an act of mercy on the part of the university, a dormitory unit was assigned to us three. Father died in 1979. Mother remarried and moved out. I have lived here since.

It is the summer I turn twenty. Love is no longer a banned word on university campuses. I am nebulously in love. I met Lu Long during our first semester together at Pujiang. The closest physical contact we've had is fleetingly holding hands when nobody is around. A month ago, he received a scholarship and went to study in New York. A vacuum has since filled my heart. I am now in love with a vision, perhaps more that of America than that of Lu Long. I am lovesick yet lovelorn.

One man who truly loved me was Father. I keep his photo by my bed and think of him as he was in that photo: glasses were his most prominent feature; lenses as thick as the bottom of a soy sauce bottle rested on a soiled plastic frame. The right pad was long gone, replaced by adhesive tape stuck as a cushion against his nose. He is wearing a gray Lenin suit with the bottom button missing. The expression in his eyes through the lenses is disturbingly disinterested. The man in this faded, over-exposed color photo is my father, shortly after he left prison.

Father went to jail not long after our family was swept out of the former Avenue Joffre, during the nationwide Campaign to Purify Class Ranks. Father was accused of having been a spy. Of course, he never was a spy. He was a returning student from America: M.S., Electrical Engineering, Columbia University, Class of 1951. During the Cultural Revolution, that was enough for him to be accused and incarcerated for five years.

During the week I first began to menstruate, he was released and came home. I was thirteen and he, forty-three. The year was 1977. Two years later, Father passed away. Colon cancer, advanced stage. Someone who had known him well remarked that Father actually died of an ulcer in the heart.

On his deathbed I held his limp hand, gazing into his half-closed eyes and hollowed sockets and listening to his waning breath. My teenage life was on hold. Outside, beyond the four walls of the terminally ill ward, a different Chinese world was in the making. The Cultural Revolution was over. Selected foreign films were beginning to be shown. My favorite one chronicled the life of Ciprian Porumbescu, the 19th-century Romanian composer. In it, Porumbescu and his girlfriend danced in what appeared to be endless swirls, culminating in a deep French kiss. "I love you," he told her through the dubbing actor's mesmerizing voice. *Wo Ai Ni*, the three words most Chinese are too embarrassed to utter.

At Father's side, I daydreamed of being told *Wo Ai Ni* by a handsome and smart high school classmate who did not wear glasses. But I'd heard he took another girl out for a date, during which he bought a bowl of wonton soup and shared it with her. My *qingdou chukai*, the dawning of puberty was like the virgin budding of a love flower. But nobody asked me for a wonton date despite my large almond eyes and deep dimples. It was because I was the daughter of a "counter-revolutionary spy."

Tears rolled down my face as I watched Father and fantasized about him opening his eyes wide, sitting up on his bed, kissing me on the cheeks, and saying the as yet never spoken, "*Wo Ai Ni!*"

Two days before his death, Father held my hand and told me a secret: He had had a girlfriend named Marlene Koo in New York. Like Father, Miss Koo had come from a wealthy, Westernized Shanghai family, which sent her to Barnard after graduating from the McTyeire Methodist School for Girls, where Madame Chiang Kai-shek and her sisters had gone. She was named after Marlene Dietrich, her parents' favorite Western actress. Father spoke of his heartbreak over losing Marlene, whom he had known as a family friend's daughter in Shanghai and dated while both of them were in New York. "Marlene was quite spoiled and was a bit headstrong like you, Sha-fei," Father said with a faint smile of helplessness. "Uncertain about the new regime back in China, she refused to return with me. Of course our communication became impossible over time. I was so determined to contribute the knowledge I had acquired abroad to our motherland that I sacrificed my personal happiness . . ."

Father gave me a most unusual look and said haltingly, "I know it's ridiculous of me to think so, but if you ever make it to America and see Marlene, tell her that she won our debate. She was right to stay on. I just wish I'd listened to her."

Not until then did I realize the truth behind the lurking tension that seemed to have existed between my parents. Father was eleven years older than Mother and had a life of his own before they met in a Shanghai factory workshop in 1961. He was the engineer in charge for a technological innovation project initiated by the University, and she was an innocent and attractive apprentice fresh out of middle school. She offered him daily drinks of green tea in an enamel mug. At the end of the project, he asked for her hand . . .

Father's last words to me were: "Remember, my child, life is hard. Be strong and resourceful. Don't be an idealistic intellectual like me. Survive first. Then, thrive in this world."

Before I insert the key to my apartment door, I always look around. Everyone in the neighborhood watches a young college student if she lives alone. Just to make sure she's respectable.

Something on the other side of my door makes me stop. It's the odor of cigarettes seeping through the keyhole. My heart starts to thump. I glue one ear to the door and stick a finger into my free ear to block out the neighborhood noise.

As the door flings open, I fall against the torso of my stepfather. Before I can scream, he pulls me in. "I heard your footsteps already, Sha-fei," he says, laughing, his two gold-capped front teeth glaring. "I opened the door for you so you wouldn't be startled."

"You just did. I didn't know anybody else had the key besides Mother. What wind has blown you here?" I throw out the familiar greeting in an effort to appear calm.

"I'm here on business," Stepfather announces in an official tone. After almost three decades as a cadre, he is used to talking as if lecturing. "It's the 80's now and China is opening up to the world. Even government functionaries like us are thinking of making money. That's why I'm in Shanghai for a few days."

I nod but don't know what to say. This is the first time we are together without Mother. Mother married him during my freshman year and went to live with him in Nanjing, where he was a ranking cadre. I had seen him three or four times during Mother's visits. I know little about the man except that he blames Mother for not bearing him a son. Instead, Mother had a baby girl last year. Stepfather's clout made it possible for him to bypass the "one child" policy. After obtaining the quota for another child, my 43-year-old mother is pregnant again. This one, the sonogram has confirmed, will be a boy to carry on Stepfather's family lineage.

Stepfather takes a deep draw on his "Panda" cigarette and sinks down on my bed like a big bag of rice, next to his lumpy army coat. Pieces of peeling plaster hang from the low ceiling like pages from an old newspaper. I move away from him to a corner of the room under my only window.

Stepfather clears his throat and takes a folded envelope from the breast pocket of his Mao-style tunic. "Since I'd be in town anyway, I told your mother I'd bring this to you. Saves her a trip to the post office, especially with that tummy the size of a land mine planted by the Eight Route Red Army to blow up the Japanese devils. Ha-ha-ha!"

"Thank you very much," I say. Stepfather provides my monthly living expenses. I don't have to pay university tuition. The government takes care of that.

Pointing at the chair next to my bed, he orders, "Don't stand there like a statue. Come sit here and we'll talk."

I sit down.

"See what I've brought for you from the market?" He dangles a bunch of bananas in front of me. "Come on. Take one," he urges.

I shake my hand and say, "Thanks, but no. You don't have to bring me anything. Why don't you take these with you to eat later?"

Stepfather's thick black eyebrows knot in displeasure. "Nonsense! I bought them especially for you. I want to see you eat one right now." He snaps one off from the bunch, peels off its top, and thrusts it into my hand.

Without a word, I begin to eat.

"You eat like your mother, pouting your little cherry mouth," he says, gazing at me.

My mouth ceases moving. I stare back at him.

"Keep eating. Don't stop," he urges. In a gentler tone, he asks, "So how's school?"

"Fine."

"Graduating soon, eh?"

"Yes, in the summer."

"You have to write a paper to graduate?"

"Yes."

There are also the Comprehensive Examinations to pass. But what does he know? As for the paper, I cannot be more frustrated. The topic I chose, a preliminary study of the father of political science Machiavelli, was turned down by the teacher.

"Sha-fei Hong, I'm disappointed you chose such a despicable person who advocated the notion that 'The ends justify the means.' Remember, we should always put revolutionary politics first, as Chairman Mao taught us. We should stick to the principles of Marxist-Leninist and Mao Zedong thought."

I glance at Stepfather. The teacher's words sounded like something he might have said to me.

Stepfather extinguishes his butt on a section of the banana skin and hits the front of his leg with excitement. "You're mother-fucking lucky. You'll be graduating from the Political Science Department at just the right time. Trade with the West is booming. Our motherland needs young people like you who know how to build up our socialist economy with Chinese characteristics. Chairman Mao said that we should critically assimilate foreign practices to serve China." He pats me heavily on the shoulder as he speaks, our first physical contact ever. I stiffen but do not move.

"How's my old subordinate doing?" Stepfather continues, referring to Mr. Chen, the number one man at the University. To Stepfather, Chen is just a small potato.

"I haven't seen him on campus for a while. I imagine he's fine."

"Good, Sha-fei. Now you study hard. Come graduation time, I'll give that dog a call, get you a decent job assignment, and make your mother happy. How's that?"

"Thank you very much. I'd certainly appreciate it."

My objection to Mother's marrying Stepfather notwithstanding, I'm fully aware of the benefits he's brought me. He supports me financially, since Father left almost nothing. One reason I believe Mother agreed to marry Stepfather is that she was sick and tired of living on a meager income and with ample fear. She hated being powerless. In a different way, I hate being powerless, too.

I knew I would not be staying in this dormitory had it not been for Stepfather's intervention. The property belongs to the University, which assigned the unit to Father as a professor. When he died and Mother moved away, the apartment technically should have been returned to the school, since I was beyond the legal age of eighteen. Our neighbor the Chengs had been coveting our unit for years. Their family of four -- the couple and a grown son and a daughter -- only has one room, so the son sleeps on the floor of the narrow corridor. The daughter has registered for marriage for over a year now but still lives at home because her husband's home is equally small and they are on the waiting list for their work unit to assign them a room. Mrs. Cheng, whom I respectfully address as Aunt Cheng, has the benefit of being a secretary at Mr. Chen's office. She begged Mr. Chen to assign our apartment to her family. It was only after Stepfather mentioned the case to his old comrade-in-arms, Mr. Chen, that the apartment was salvaged for me.

In a rare instance when Mother mentioned Father and Stepfather in the same sentence, she said, "He is a very different man from your father. Your father was an honest man who didn't know how to play the game of life, a pampered son of the wealthy who was naïve and vulnerable. But your stepfather has been a revolutionary all his life. He is a success despite the fact that he remains a rough and ready type of man, a *Da Lao Cu,*" (literally: Big Old Thick.) Mother added, "With all our sufferings brought on by your father, you should really be grateful to your stepfather for who he is."

Stepfather rises from my bed and stands in front of me. He puts his hands on his belt and searches around as if looking for the bathroom. I'm glad he's finally ready to leave.

"The men's room is outside the apartment, down the hallway," I tell him. Our building only has two communal bathrooms, one for each gender.

Stepfather laughs in a way that betrays his peasant origins, his gleaming teeth reflecting the rays from the setting wintry sun. Suddenly, he drops his navy khaki pants before my eyes. "No!" I cringe and turn my head away -- he has no underwear on! His appendage hangs out like the neck of a Peking duck on display in a deli window. A pile of flesh shaped like two used green tea bags sag under the duck neck, dangling.

A falcon snatching a chick, he grabs me and thrusts me down on my knees. Towering over me, his voice turns uncharacteristically soft. "Show me how much you appreciate, Sha-fei."

"No! Let go of me or I'll scream!"

"No, you won't. You don't want to disturb the neighbors, do you?"

No, I don't. Only a thin board separates our apartment from our neighbors, all of whom, like my late Father, have family members associated with the university. Growing up here, I've learned to ignore the sounds of the neighbors' kids screaming, spouses and in-laws fighting, neighbors quarreling, and pans and jars clanging together. I've learned to survive and study in an atmosphere of symphonic chaos. But no, I certainly don't want to let them hear *this*.

"Come," Stepfather coaxes, leading my left hand onto him. The covering skin is moved up and I see the tip of the meat, as red as the leanest part of pork Mother would have loved back in the days when meats were rationed. I shut my eyes and continue to struggle. The next thing I know, the "Big Old Thick" gags me.

He moves my head back and forth like someone doing *tai chi* holding an imaginary ball. For a split second, Father's photo enters my blurring vision before fading out, resembling the ripple-like circles on Father's lenses. Ethereal blindness.

Stepfather is slow and rhythmic, making my cheeks suck in and out like a toilet plunger. Then he becomes sporadic and jerky, sending my ponytail bouncing. Abruptly, his palms squeeze my head like a nutcracker. I cough. I choke. Stepfather lets go and cries out. I smell rotten fish, slimy and raw.

I now sit at the edge of my bed, head bent, tears streaking my cheeks. Stepfather moves closer to me and picks up his army coat. From its inside pocket he takes out forty *yuan* and stuffs the bills into my hand.

I look up at him and shake my head. The band on my ponytail falls off and my black hair, down. Stepfather lifts my chin and sweeps away the hair covering my eyes. "Take it, Sha-fei. As long as you're obedient, everything's going to be okay for you, understand?"

I take the money and look down again.

Stepfather lights another "Panda" and inhales deeply. He puts one foot on the edge of my bed and says, "Let me tell you, Sha-fei Hong. If you're a smart girl like I hope you are, you won't breathe a word to anyone, understand?"

I look up at him, sobbing, "Mother will kill me if she finds out."

"How can she find out if you shut the fuck up? Besides, she won't dare kill you if you're good to me."

He puts on his coat. "So be good, Sha-fei. Don't let your mother . . . and me worry. Next time we see you, you'll have a baby brother. By the way, don't forget to send my greetings to Old Chen."

Stepfather closes my apartment door, leaving behind a trail of smoke, a bunch of bananas with one missing, and me.

In the days following Stepfather's visit, I develop an urge to spit. I rinse my mouth all day long. Then I spit. I spit until my throat hurts.

There is no sink within the apartment. Running water is only available from the two taps in our building's communal kitchen. One pail at a time, I go to fetch water and bring it into my apartment, where I rinse my mouth and spit into a spittoon. The spittoon is usually for the night soil, which I dump each morning in the female communal bathroom.

The Sunday after, I drag my feet to the tiny kitchen shared by six families, empty pail in hand. Aunt Cheng and Teacher Gao are already there preparing lunch, but I am relieved to find that Mrs. Wu is not among them. Her husband, Master Worker Wu, is neither a faculty member nor a school administrator. He is the Party branch secretary of all the janitors. Because of his proletarian background, he has been appointed the Building Representative, with his homemaker wife serving on the Neighborhood Revolutionary Committee. When we first moved here, the Wus were put in charge of supervising us as a family "to be reformed under surveillance."

The shared kitchen has only one window directly above a large, cold-water-only communal sink for washing produce, clothes, dishes, human body parts, anything and everything. It is not uncommon for people to wait their turn for the sink, which is flanked by three gas stoves on each adjacent wall. Over each stove hangs a 15-watt bulb, which has to be turned on even during the day due to the dimness of the kitchen. Right below the yellow, grease-coated ceiling hangs a cobweb of electrical wires, as each family uses its own power meters extended from the various apartments.

I try to avoid eye contact with the two ladies, but Aunt Cheng calls out to me. "Sha-fei, you seem to be getting an awful lot of water in the past week. You shouldn't cheat us all on your share of the water bill come month's end!"

I lower my head and say nothing. Teacher Gao comes to my rescue. "Say, Sister Cheng, how much water can she use? She doesn't have sink after sink of diapers to wash, like some people. She always pays her own share."

Aunt Cheng gives Teacher Gao a sideways glance and says, "That's exactly my point, Teacher Gao. She pays one person's share, but she is using more water than usual. That's taking advantage of all of us neighbors."

"If you think I use too much, I'll pay one and a half persons this month, then. Okay?" I say, turning on the tap to make the water splash, drowning her voice.

Pointing a frostbitten index finger in my direction, Aunt Cheng says gleefully, "One and a half persons this month, Sha-fei. I have your word for it. Teacher Gao can be my witness."

"Okay, okay," says Teacher Gao.

When I turn off the tap, I hear someone outside yelling, "Tao Hong! Comrade Tao Hong! Bring down your chop for special delivery!"

The three pairs of eyes in the kitchen stare at each other. Tao Hong was my late father. Without thinking further, I answer the postman, "Coming! Coming!" I run back to my apartment to fetch Father's seal, an individual's essential identification.

Dashing down to our building's entrance, I see Aunt Cheng and Teacher Gao chatting with the green-uniformed postman leaning against his matching mail bicycle. "There she is," Aunt Cheng shouts. "That's Tao Hong's daughter."

"What is it?" I ask the postman.

"Give me Tao Hong's seal and you'll know in a minute."

He checks Father's name on the chop before stamping it on an aerogramme that looks tattered. It was forwarded from our old French Concession address and has American-flag stamps on it.

"*Meiguo! Meiguo!* Letter from the U.S. for your father!" Aunt Cheng announces, her voice's pitch an octave higher. "Open it right away, Sha-fei!"

My hands start to tremble. I see Father's face in front of me. For a split second, I think the letter could be from Marlene Koo.

"No," I resist. "I can't open Father's mail."

"What a silly girl you are. Your father's dead and your mother has remarried. You're the only Hong here. Open it, Sha-fei. See what America has to say to you," urges Aunt Cheng.

"That's right. That's right. You're the only legitimate Hong here, Sha-fei," says, Teacher Gao, smiling. Her bespectacled head hovers over the mail in my hands.

"Sorry, I have to go. I may have forgotten to lock my apartment door when I got the chop."

I run to the apartment and lock the door behind me. Holding my breath, I tear the aerogramme open.

Dear old pal Tao,

Yes, this is your good old Gordon Lou from Columbia -- long time no see. Three decades have passed in the blink of an eye. Believe it or not, I have a last-minute arrangement to visit Shanghai the 2nd week of January '85 for some business. Will stay at the Shanghai Plaza. I'd be happy to see you during my one-week's stay.

Hope all is well.

Gordon

"Gordon," I repeat the name under my breath, not Marlene. Mr. Gordon Lou apparently doesn't know that Father has died five years ago. His scheduled arrival is just is a week from now, at the beginning of my winter break. Father's old friend from America is coming to visit Shanghai! What should I do? Contact Mother? But her stomach is like a watermelon right now. A male watermelon Stepfather's likeness, an orangutan in the flesh, suddenly appears before my eyes. I choke on the thought, my throat again a drought-devastated land. I am hit by the urge to get the pail of water still in the kitchen.

Ignoring my neighbors in the kitchen as I carry the pail out proves difficult. Aunt Cheng puts down her cooking spatula and blocks my way. "What does the American letter say, Sha-fei?"

I want to say I didn't read it, but the words come out differently. "Nothing. Someone's looking for Father, but you all know it's impossible now," I say coldly, trying to leave.

Aunt Cheng snatches the pail in my hand and drops it on the concrete floor near our feet, sending cold water spattering. "Who is he? An American?" she demands.

"No. I don't know who he is. Someone who knew Father."

Aunt Cheng's eyes become two surprised ping-pong balls. "Wonderful, Sha-fei! Your rich relative from America is here. Now you can finally go abroad. Don't forget us poor folks here, Sha-fei girl!"

"What are you talking about?"

Aunt Cheng puts her arm around my neck and presses my shoulder. "Just think, Sha-fei, your father suffered so much since you people moved here from the Upper Corner. It's all because of his overseas connections. At least now you can benefit from his past."

Father's past. A past once considered disgraceful and suddenly so desirable in the eyes of these same neighbors. They were eyewitnesses to his arrest on that autumn day. I was barely seven.

Father was preparing lessons at his desk while I folded origami dolls on the floor by his feet. An approaching siren pierced my ears. I clasped my hands on the windowsill and looked down. Struck by the rare sight of an army-green jeep parking in front of our building's common entrance, I called out, "Father, look! There's a jeep downstairs."

Rising, Father frowned, his face turning grim. I sensed something wrong. Before I could ask, our door was kicked open. Three ferocious-looking men in navy-blue uniforms stormed in. The man in the lead shouted, "Is Tao Hong home?"

Father came forward, "I'm Tao Hong. What do you-?"

Two men grabbed his arms and pinned them behind his back. The third man pulled out a dirty white towel and shoved it into Father's mouth. He then took out a rope and tied Father's hands.

"We're from the Public Security Bureau," the man in the lead announced. "You are under arrest, Tao Hong!"

The men pushed Father against his desk, where his class notes lay. Trailing them silently into my parents' bedroom that also served as Father's study, I was too frightened to know what to do. Mother was at work in the factory. We didn't have a telephone.

As the men searched and ransacked our place, one of them threw an English engineering textbook on the floor as if smashing a rice bowl, shouting, "Imperialist trash!"

"Careful! These materials in stinking foreign languages are evidence of his crimes against the people," the older man warned.

After the men bundled up Father's books and handwritten notes with my parents' bed sheets, they shoved Father toward our apartment door. "Father! Father! No! No!" I screamed. He could not speak, but his eyes looked painfully wronged.

As if a circus had arrived, the entire neighborhood rushed out to watch my father being whisked away in the unmarked jeep. Out of the crowd of agitated and gossiping onlookers, a deep voice yelled, "Everybody go home. Let's all go home, comrades. What's there to see? It's a good thing that our community is cleared of a class enemy!" It was Master Worker Wu.

With stiff faces, the neighbors stopped talking and dispersed. There were a few minutes of frightening silence before life in our building resumed its usual chaos. I was left scrunched up under the building's staircase, where I sobbed uncontrollably for a couple of hours. With the Wus in proximity, nobody dared to come near me. It was as if I had suddenly contracted leprosy . . .

Some of the same people are so interested in today's letter to Father from abroad. How things have changed since the days of the Cultural Revolution. Stepfather's words resound in my ears: "It's the 80's now. China is opening up to the world." If Father were alive today, he would never be accused of being a spy for the U.S. but instead be eagerly courted. A connection with America is seen as a godsend to most people now.

"The past is history, Aunt Cheng," I say. "What's there to benefit from?"

"What kind of attitude is that, Sha-fei girl?" Aunt Cheng exclaims. "We saw you moving in here, a chit of a girl in that lacy pink fairy dress. We remember how you had to be stripped down and change into those split-crotch pants to look more like the kids who lived in this area. We all shared your family's happiness and sorrow. Now that you have some good news, you think you can hide it from us?" She swallows with effort and comes up with a little saliva, which she promptly spits into the sink. "Pooh!"

Teacher Gao puts on a mediating smile. "Come on, Comrade Cheng. We're all happy for Sha-fei. Let Sha-fei tell us the details of the news from America." She motions to Aunt Cheng, and then grins at me.

"You both seem to know more than I do. All I know is that Father's long-lost friend might be visiting Shanghai. I don't even know what to do yet."

Aunt Cheng's face lights up, revealing her tea-stained teeth with years of lack of toothpaste. "Ai-ya!" she shrieks with delight. "Our Sha-fei will go to America and become Mrs. Americana. Once you're there, you mustn't forget all of us here, Sha-fei girl!"

I reply with a forced smile. "Aunt Cheng, what you've said is all in your imagination. I don't have any idea what's going to happen. And I don't know where this notion about a rich American husband comes from."

With the chopsticks she used for cooking hanging out of her mouth like two long cigarettes, Aunt Cheng retorts, "Come, come, Sha-fei. Nowadays, who doesn't want to marry an American? Look at my husband's cousin twice removed. To go abroad, the girl even married a Chinese-American in his late sixties with grown children older than herself. But her letter home says that *Meiguo* is paradise, just as the written characters themselves promise – 'Beautiful Country.' Everyone drives a car. Nobody uses bicycles. Their garages are larger than our apartments!"

"I'm not surprised," says Teacher Gao. "Some of my former students write to me from America saying the same thing. Over there, warm water flows from the tap. American women don't have needles pinching their fingers while doing dishes and laundry in bone-chilling water, as we do here." She emphasizes her point by wiggling her freezing, carrot-like fingers in front of me.

I am glad the conversation seems to have shifted its focus from the aerogramme from America to the United States in general. The U.S. is one of my favorite topics, too. I associate America not only with material comfort, but also with individual freedom. I've heard that in the United States, teenagers are allowed to date, not to mention university students like me. American gentlemen look like the actor Gregory Peck in the black-and-white film, *The Million Pound Note,* the only American film I've ever had the privilege to see. American men always open doors for women and let them have the first choice of everything. It's called "Ladies first." I would definitely have a boyfriend who loves me if I lived in America.

The bulb over the Wu family stove is suddenly lit, indicating that Mrs. Wu will be in the kitchen momentarily. Teacher Gao and Aunt Cheng look at each other and stop talking. I pick up my pail and rush back to my apartment.

Mid-afternoon, the same day, I am alerted by repeated knocks on my apartment door, followed by a throaty voice. "Sha-fei Hong, Sha-fei Hong, are you in?"

Terrified that Stepfather may be here again, I brace myself, tiptoe to the door, and look out through the keyhole. Two familiar but unwelcome people stand outside -- Mrs. Wu and Master Worker Wu. I open the door. Master Worker Wu's barrel-like body rolls in, trailed by Mrs. Wu's hopping gait, her rotund figure bouncing like a wound-up toy.

"Good news, Sha-fei." she squeals as she holds out both hands to shake my ill-prepared right hand. "It's wonderful news for our community," she giggles, her eyes becoming two glistening slits of joy.

Master Worker Wu silences her with a hard look and says, "According to Marxist materialist dialectics, everything has two sides to it. It can be good and it can be bad. That's why we're seeking your cooperation to achieve the best result."

"My cooperation?"

"We'll sit down and talk," he says, resting himself on the same spot where Stepfather was a few days ago and lights a cigarette. I hand him a soy sauce dish for an ashtray. Mrs. Wu stands beside him like a maid waiting to be given an order. I sit on the chair by the bed and stare at Master Worker Wu's crooked front teeth, waiting for him to drop the bomb, my heart racing. Does the Neighborhood Revolutionary Committee want me to "cooperate" when it comes to what happened between Stepfather and me? But "good news" – does that mean the authorities are happy about Gordon Lou's visit? What sort of cooperation does Master Worker Wu want from me? My thoughts swing like a pendulum as he sucks on his cigarette, puffing circles of smoke into the room.

"So we've all heard the news, Sha-fei," he begins. "As you must know from going to the university, the Party's policy currently is to encourage cultural and business exchanges with the Americans. American friends and business partners are welcome."

I am more than relieved. This is not about Stepfather and me. "What am I supposed to do, then, Uncle Wu?"

"You may go and meet with the Chinese-American on your father's behalf. Just bear in mind that you should report anything suspicious about our overseas compatriots to the grassroots authorities."

In other words, to him. After promising with a straight face that I'll do as he says, I sit passively through his droning lecture. As Master Worker Wu rises to leave, Mrs. Wu slaps me on the shoulder and says, "Do let me know what your American friend looks like after you see him, Sha-fei."

What does Gordon Lou look like? I wonder myself. When Father mentioned Marlene Koo to me, I had asked if he had a picture of her. "No. The Red Guards burned all my photos in our house on Joffre and confiscated many old belongings." I have no reference point as to what a Chinese from America would look like.

I lounge in bed, staring at the wall, trying to picture Gordon Lou. He must be around Father's age, mid-fifties. Maybe he wears glasses, just like Father did. But his glasses would come with a chic, "MADE IN USA" frame, unlike Father's old, broken pair he had worn throughout the decade of the Cultural Revolution. But what would a pair of American eyeglasses look like? Suddenly I remember the American who visited China when I was a teenager -- Henry Kissinger. He wore thick-rimmed glasses that made him look like a curly-haired panda. Is it possible that Gordon Lou looks like Henry Kissinger, only with a Chinese face? I chuckle at the absurdity of my thoughts. No matter what Father's old schoolmate looks like, something in my life is going to change. I hope for the better.